MW00909521

SHADOW HUNTERS

SHADOW
HUNTERS

BRIAN NOWAK

Sense of Wonder Press
JAMES A. ROCK & COMPANY, PUBLISHERS
ROCKVILLE • MARYLAND

Shadow Hunters by Brian Nowak

SENSE OF WONDER PRESS
is an imprint of JAMES A. ROCK & CO., PUBLISHERS

Shadow Hunters copyright ©2007 by Brian Nowak

Special contents of this edition copyright ©2007
by James A. Rock & Co., Publishers

Address comments and inquiries to:
SENSE OF WONDER PRESS
James A. Rock & Company, Publishers
9710 Traville Gateway Drive, #305
Rockville, MD 20850
E-mail:
jrock@rockpublishing.com   lrock@rockpublishing.com
Internet URL: www.rockpublishing.com

ISBN: 978-1-59663-538-8

Library of Congress Control Number: 2007923186

Printed in the United States of America

First Edition: 2007

To my two Marys …

One for giving me life,

The other for sharing in it …

ACKNOWLEDGMENTS

I would like to thank the following people, for without their help, I couldn't have done this.

My grandmother and my father for their financial support ... and a special thanks to my father, for being nothing like the father in this novel. I could always count on you.

My brother, Steve, for his technical support. I can't thank you enough for bailing me and my computer out...more than once.

And to Nick. You did more for this book's substance than anyone else. Your criticism, although harsh at times, was needed.

To anyone I didn't mention (but around me a lot) thanks for putting up with me ...

PART I

And the Sky Darkened . . .

Chapter One

The floor was cold and damp. The young boy felt his way from one end of the room to the other. He had no idea where he was, knew only that fear consumed him. He had to do his best to be quiet, so the people chasing him wouldn't find him. But the grit on the floor gave his position away every time he moved.

From somewhere in the building, the boy could hear two people arguing. One voice was a man's, loud, and almost thundering. The other voice could barely be heard. Tommy listened as closely as he could, but the words were difficult to make out. There was one sentence the boy could hear however. "Find that little shit so I can kill him … slowly!"

Tommy was shaking. All he wanted was to go home. But he didn't know where he was. Home could be next door or a world away for all he knew. He stopped moving now and sat with his knees bent up to his chin, his head buried. He sobbed, and he thought back to how he got here. It was blurry at best. He was in the backyard, throwing the baseball around, when from out of nowhere he was tackled to the ground. That was it. That's the last of his memory. He had a gash on his arm now crusted with day-old blood. He knew how he got that wound. Dad gave him that. Tommy always hated it when Daddy drank.

But drunk or not, Tommy wished his dad would barge in and take him out of this place. It was musty and dirty. There were windows in the room, some of them broken, allowing the warm,

August breeze into the room. Tommy wiped the tears from his face, and he scanned the room. He couldn't see much, at least nothing that would be of any use to him.

Just then he saw a soft, orange glow on the wall outside the room. He couldn't hear anybody coming, but he knew someone was there. Tommy got up and made his way as quietly as he could to a desk in the middle of the room. He curled up beneath it and held his breath. A sliver of light appeared under the front of the desk. Tommy closed his eyes and prayed.

A few moments had passed and Tommy was still alive. The light was gone and he decided to come out from under the desk. He slowly got to his knees and peered around the desk, towards the door. He could still see a faint trace of light on the wall outside the room, but it was coming from the other direction. Whoever was carrying the light had passed him by. It was time to leave the room and search for a way out.

Tommy got to his feet and tip-toed to the doorway. He poked his head out, the light was gone. He stepped outside the room and decided to make a left. The building itself was a maze-like structure. He had no clue where he was going but he wasn't going in the direction of the light, that's for sure. He was out in the open and exposed to the kidnappers, his only aid the darkness surrounding him. His breathing got heavier, and before he knew it he was nearly panting. When he turned around to make sure the person with the light wasn't there, he tripped over something metal. A loud 'Clang' echoed throughout the halls of the old building.

Tommy got to his knees and waited for the sounds to stop. His hands were covered with a layer of slime. His shin was throbbing. He began to cry when he heard the man's voice coming from down the hallway. "You can't escape! We know you're there! We will find you!"

Tommy got up and began running down the hallway. He didn't look behind him but just ran as fast as he could. He got to the end of the hallway and ran to the right. There at the far end of the hallway was a speck of yellow coming right at him. He stopped, not realizing at first that it was the other man with a flashlight headed right for him.

"I see you, little boy! You can't hide!"

Tommy went back around the corner and darted into the first room he saw. He went in and shut the door. He took a peek out of the glass window, but saw nothing, not even light.

The room was pitch black. The windows were no help, as they were few and were as black as night. He began to move across the room when he kicked something. He caught his balance, and once he was standing up again, he heard a moaning sound. He stood perfectly still. The room was still, nothing but the sound of Tommy breathing.

He was about to move when he heard the moan again. This time, however, something grabbed Tommy's leg. Tommy looked down and saw a hand wrapped around his puny leg. He then saw a pair of yellow eyes come at him out of the darkness. Tommy froze, unable to move or scream, until he saw the person's face. His skin was pale. There was blood around his mouth. Tommy screamed when he saw that the person's lips were sewn together with a thin wire.

He didn't care if he got caught at this point. The person let go of his leg as he screamed as loud as he ever had. Tommy backed up towards the door and felt another hand, this time on his shoulder.

"I told you you couldn't hide. It's time to meet your master."

Tommy blacked out. The man dragged Tommy out of the room and set him down, propping him against the wall. The man then went back into the room and knelt down beside the person lying on the floor. "Thank you. Thank you for finding the boy. The master will not forget this." The man got to his feet and left the room laughing.

✳✳✳

Summers in Alden, in Western New York, brought hot afternoons, followed by cool, refreshing evenings. The old factory was a sauna during the day, as the hot air had nowhere to escape. There were a few broken windows and cracks in the foundation that allowed a breeze to enter, but no cool zephyrs passed through the boiler room.

As he woke, Tommy saw the last few rays of sunlight fade. The windows went from orange to blue to purple. With the disappearance of light, Tommy noticed a fire burning in the boiler. The fire sent shadows dancing about the walls, which were covered with mold and fungus. His eyes began to well with tears, and he would have wiped them away if his hands hadn't been tied behind his back. If he could have seen his arm, he would have cried even more. An infection was growing in the open wound. Thin ropes kept his legs fastened securely to the chair. The gag in his mouth tasted awful. All he could do was pray that someone would come for him.

Perhaps because he was sobbing, he did not hear the person come up from behind him. Tommy jumped at the hand put on his shoulders. But fear quickly turned to confusion when the person began massaging Tommy's neck. Tommy stopped crying. He tried to see who it was, but he could not turn around quite enough. A voice soothed him. "Relax. We want to help you. We want to give you the family you never had."

The man's voice was effeminate. This was not the man he heard yelling the night before. Tommy relaxed his arms and did not think about escaping. But as quickly as the man came in, he was gone. Tommy tried to turn and see where he went, but he couldn't.

He could feel the end of the rope in his hands. He began examining it, praying that he could loosen the knot enough to get free. It had worked the night before. But tonight, the rope gave no slack.

Just as he gave up trying to untie the rope, he heard people talking behind him. He couldn't hear what they were saying. But at least they weren't fighting. A moment later, the same man who left the room a minute earlier entered again pushing a cart. He ignored Tommy and left the cart nearby. The man exited a second time and Tommy began checking out the objects on the cart. He noticed a cup, a book, and a knife. It had a long handle and the blade was glistening in the fire light.

The butterflies were back in his stomach again. He tried to look away from the knife but could not. Tommy began to squirm in the chair, but for the third time, was approached from behind. "Sit still. This won't hurt a bit," said the voice from before.

This time, however, a second person entered the room. The man was tall, with dark, long hair that hid most of his face. He was dressed all in black, the back of his long coat trailing him around like a cape.

The tall man walked over to the cart and opened the book. The book had a black binding and a very large gold star on the cover. Not a star like he drew at home; it was upside down. The man thumbed through the pages, stopping every few seconds to study the words. Finally, after a minute or two of reading, the man shut the book and stared at Tommy, who wasn't scared by the man but rather comforted by his smile. The man pulled up a chair and sat down, facing Tommy.

"You were a bad little boy last night. You know you shouldn't have done that, right?"

Tommy nodded absently. His eyes were locked on the man's smile.

"I know you're scared, but you are safe. We are not going to hurt you. In fact, we are going to be your new family." The man got up and from the cart picked up the cup. He walked back over to Tommy and held the cup by his mouth. "We will never hurt you."

The man removed the gag from Tommy's mouth and placed the cup at his lips. The other man grabbed Tommy's hair, pulling his head back. The liquid in the cup was cold. It tasted terrible, but Tommy drank it down. As he did, he could feel one of the men untying his hands. Tommy wiped his mouth with his hand and despite being free, he had no impulse to run. Instead, he sat perfectly still, and he noticed the shadows on the wall going in and out of focus.

The man behind him whispered in his ear. Tommy turned his head. As he did, the other man moved in and kissed Tommy on the side of his neck. The man's breath was hot and sticky, but Tommy did not move. Just before Tommy blacked out for the second straight night, he felt the man's kiss, a kiss long, and painful ...

✳✳✳

That night Tommy became seriously ill. He vomited every few minutes. He crapped in his pants. He tossed and turned for hours. The pain in his stomach was unbearable. He cried out, but no one came to help. He could not sleep. Finally, he noticed the two men standing over him. Tommy cried out to them for help, but they just stood there, watching him.

The smaller man finally spoke up, talking to the other man. "He's in rough shape."

"Well, fix him up."

"I don't think it's going to be that easy," the small man said, kneeling down to Tommy's side.

"What do you mean? He's just ill, right?"

"Look here at his arm." The man held Tommy's arm up. The wound was now deep purple and black. As the man squeezed at the wound, puss rolled down Tommy's arm. "It's infected. I'm no doctor. I can't fix that."

The tall man stood there with a confused look on his face, deep in thought. He finally put his hands on his hips and dropped his shoulders as though defeated. He shook his head and looked at the other man. "So, there's nothing you can do for him?"

The smaller man shook his head and put Tommy's arm back by his side.

"Fine. Fine. We'll put him out of his misery tomorrow night. Put the gag back in his mouth." The tall man walked out of the room, but the gag was not put in Tommy's mouth. The other man rubbed Tommy's head and walked out.

✳✳✳

Tommy watched the sun come up that morning. The stench coming from his clothes was wretched, but he didn't care. He was alive and felt better than he had during the night. There was no sign of the two men. He felt relieved that the man didn't cut him. He had been cut enough times by his father. He didn't know why his father always brought the knife out, but Tommy figured his father must have had a reason, for it worked. Whenever Tommy was bad, he got cut and soon straightened out his act.

As the midday sun passed over the building, Tommy sat up, his back against the wall. He looked at his arm, which was throbbing. The pain shot all the way up to his shoulder, which caused his eyes to water. The colors were odd. The cut was black now, with white fluid oozing.

Every so often, Tommy could hear a car horn in the distance. He figured there must be a road nearby. However the windows were up near the ceiling and Tommy had no way of seeing out of them. He tried to open the door to the boiler room, but it was locked. There was no way of getting out of the room, and he quickly gave up trying to find a way. He was tired and weak. He found a clean spot on the floor and curled up. It would be nighttime before he would wake up again.

***

When Tommy finally awoke he could barely open his eyes. He just lay there, motionless, waiting for someone to rescue him. Tommy could see the moon through the windows. Its rays outlined the weeds and shrubs alongside the windows and it had a yellowish tinge to it, perhaps from storm clouds. He stared at it for several minutes.

The old factory had many rooms, all of them filthy. It had been neglected for more than twenty years and its newest tenants were not in the business of cleaning it up. The foundation was crumbling, the vents were crawling with rats and mice, and the steel doors were rusting. Tommy was not the only child to be held captive within these aging walls. The two men had been busy the past few months, finding as many children as they could to further their cause.

Tommy was lost in thought when the two men finally came back to get him. The small man picked him up and sat him back in the chair. The tall man had the knife in his hand and was pacing back and forth in front of Tommy. He finally looked the boy in the eye.

"I tried to save you and let you down. Your body was not ready for the burden. I will release you into death, but your blood will be the very food of our family. Your death will serve as a form of life for our people. Your life will not be wasted."

With one flick of his wrist, the tall man cut Tommy's throat from ear to ear. Tommy gurgled a bit before his eyes rolled back into his head. His blood flowed onto his clothes, but not before the smaller man tried to stop the bleeding.

"Don't let too much go to waste," the tall man said.

They laid the boy on his back, doing their best to stop the blood from flowing. The tall man stepped back and looked at his partner. "We will have to find a replacement for him. Who do you have in mind?"

"I've had my eye on one boy in particular. He's older, and stronger. He will help our cause."

The tall man walked over to the window and stared out at the moon. He could hear the sound of cars going by on Route 33, just outside the building. He knew people would eventually catch on to them.

"What are you thinking?" asked the other man.

"This is a dark night for us," he said still staring out at the night sky. "There will be many obstacles along the way. The war we wage is biblical. It will be good versus evil in its truest sense. We are engaging the world in a battle it isn't prepared to fight. Our army is growing, but not quickly enough. You and your brother must get more recruits if we are to win the war."

"We must be careful though, master. Some may catch wind of our plan."

"Yes. The day will come when a hero will come along and try to save the day, bring us to justice, win his glory. He may not know it yet, but he is taking on an ancient evil. His love of his god will be his only weapon and his faith will be put to the test." The tall man looked at the other man. "We must be wary of the hero. He will be driven. And we must know his face before he knows ours. We must not leave the shadows …"

Chapter TWO

Will hated nothing more than the ringing of the phone first thing in the morning, especially when he had to get up early for work. He got more and more aggravated with every ring and would usually ignore it. However, it was unusual for him to receive a call at 4 a.m on a Monday. Something must be wrong at home.

As Will got out of bed and went into the kitchen, the answering machine picked up. Once the message finished playing, Will was startled at the voice being recorded. It was that of Mark Thornton, Will's best friend from his hometown of Alden, NY, and deputy of the town's police force.

"Will, this is Mark. I know it's early, but—"

Will picked up the phone. "Mark, hey, sorry the machine picked up. What's going on?"

There was a hesitation, before Mark continued. "Will, I'm not really sure how to tell you this, so I'm going to do my best. Your brother was found dead this morning."

Will, still rubbing his eyes, stopped and thought for a second. "Mark, if this is a joke …"

"This is no joke. Eric never came home last night. I found him about two miles from your house, dead," said Mark.

There was silence at Will's end of the line.

"Will, I really don't want to talk about this over the phone. I've already spoken with your mother, so don't worry about her. Just get home as soon as possible. I'll pick you up," Mark said.

With that, Will hung up and sat down at the kitchen table. He put his head in his hands and tried to process what his best friend just told him. He stared at the table, thoughts coursing through his mind: How did he die? Was he murdered? How was his mother going to take this? He could drive himself crazy thinking about all of this, so he set about booking a flight, and the earlier, the better.

Will thought it was fitting that the plane land in the dead of night. This was probably the darkest time in Will's life, seeing as he was going home to bury his younger brother, possibly murdered in the same small town of Alden that prided itself on being one of the safest towns in America.

William Sandwith, had left Alden to attend Boston College and rarely came home. He met the girl of his dreams at college. He came home for the holidays, but he was never sad to return to Boston. Will was an up-and-coming reporter with the *Boston Globe*. Life was good in Boston, but anything but good back home.

The plane touched down on the runway at Buffalo/Niagara International Airport Tuesday night. As Will stepped off the plane, the humid, August air hit him hard. Despite having been away from the area for the better part of five years, the smell and feel of the air always let him know he was home.

He reached the terminal where he was greeted by Mark, Will's closest friend growing up. "Hey, man, it's good to see you," Mark said as he hugged Will. "How was your flight?"

"It was all right. No problems," Will said in a monotone.

"C'mon, I've got the squad car parked right out front."

Will always knew Mark would be on the Alden police force, even back in high school. Mark was a class clown of sorts, but was so intelligent he could have a good time and still get his schoolwork done. He often got knocked for being shorter than most of the other guys on the football team, but he was solid and still in fine shape.

The two stepped out into the midnight air. On a typical Tuesday night back in Boston, Will would be settled in in front of the television with his girlfriend. He wanted nothing more to be back with her. At least there, it wouldn't be as awkward as this moment was. His life would be normal and boring.

* * *

There were too many questions for Will to ask. He didn't even know where to begin. Mark, then, began things as he drove. "I was the one who went over and gave your mother the news. I mean, you were the second person to be contacted, because you guys were so close," he said barely above a whisper. "Your mother took it real hard, so I made sure you found out right away."

"I can imagine what my mother was like. I'm actually glad you were the one to tell me. She would have painted an awful horror story of a murder," Will said staring out the window at a yellow moon. He then looked over at Mark. "Was it a murder?"

Mark hesitated. "Yeah. He was killed."

Will looked back out the window, perfectly silent.

Mark knew he had to get off of the killing, if he could. "As I told you over the phone, your mother's at home, obviously distressed. A lot of the ladies in town have been consoling her, but she keeps asking when you're getting home."

"What a fucking mess. She's a scared worry-wart as it is, and now this happens. Please tell me that you guys have some leads, some clue as to what happened."

"Right now, we're doing a lot of tests. Fibers, blood samples, hair. You name it, we're looking into it. All that was at the scene of the crime was some of Eric's blood and a few footprints. Whoever killed him had it planned perfectly. We have very little to work with," said Mark.

"What exactly happened?"

"Around eleven at night, I got a call at the station from your mother. She was worried about Eric. She said he was usually home by ten, so she was concerned. She said he was at Lindsay's. So I drove out to the Adams' place and went home the way I think Eric would have gone. As I went down Route 33 getting closer and closer to your house, I saw a car parked on the side of the road. The driver door was open and when I pulled up behind the car, I realized it was Eric's. I walked up to the car and it was still running. I walked out in front of the car and I saw a body about ten yards from the car face down," Mark said. "It was Eric."

"Well, how did he die?"

"He was struck on the back of the head with a blunt object. We're guessing it was a baseball bat or a piece of wood. We're not really sure yet. There were a few lacerations on his body, scratches and bruises. We figure this is where the blood was lost. Somebody jumped him from behind. All it took was one hit."

Signs for Alden became more and more common along the roadside now. Will wasn't sure he wanted to know any more than what Mark told him. His brother was dead. What could Will possibly do about it now?

Will wished Mark could just take him back to the Boston. For all of the tragedies he reported on in Boston, nothing could possibly have prepared him for the whirlwind of emotions that were wreaking havoc on his mind. Above all, though, guilt was the one emotion Will couldn't shake.

Just outside of Alden, Mark stopped for gas. Will got out of the car as well and stared up at the sky. It was clear, perfectly clear. The moon was now full and bright. The stars could easily be counted and the outline of the trees and hills in the distance were etched into the bottom of the blackness that surrounded them.

Mark was about to get into the car when Will started talking about the night.

"You know, for as long as I've been in Boston, I don't think I've ever once ever just stopped and looked at the sky at night. I mean, I usually get out of work after dark and not once have I noticed the stars. I tell you what, if there is any good that can come from this whole experience, it's that I am going to give Mira all of my attention. I can't protect Eric anymore, but I can help her," Will said without looking away from the moon.

Mark said nothing, simply nodded and waited for Will to get into the car. But he didn't.

"I remember being about nine, which made Eric around four, lying out in the field by the church with our cousins when they still lived around here. We just stared out into space. We saw these red, flashing dots that my cousin kept saying was a Russian satellite. We'd see falling stars and constellations. Eric was so naïve, so trusting, that he believed every word they said. But he was bright. So the next time we saw our cousins, he told them how wrong they were and how stupid they were." Will smirked.

Will stopped talking and looked down at the ground. He sniffled a little bit, but did not shed a tear. He leaned against the white police car and crossed his arms.

"He was really going to make something of himself, Mark. He was going to be something great. He was so smart, so gifted."

Mark cut in. "As great as he was, he owed most of it to you. Sure, your mom gets most of the credit when it comes to you and Eric, but Eric idolized you. I swear he wanted to be you. You do know that he wore your old football number this past season, right?"

"Yeah, I heard that," Will said with a laugh.

"You did all you could have for him."

"Did I?" Will asked looking right at Mark. "Honestly, do you think that if I had never left, if I had stayed here, that he would still be alive?"

"Honestly? No. He was coming home from his girlfriend's house. Do you think you really would have been there to stop him from going there?"

"No," Will said as though he were disappointed with his answer.

"You're damn right you wouldn't have stopped him. You did all you could for him. Now let's get in the car and get you home."

"Alright," Will said. "And," he added, "Thanks for everything you've done for me and for my mother."

"It's my job. But I do still have to get you home."

The two drove down Route 33, into Alden, where the closer they got, the fewer stars they saw.

Chapter Three

Alden held every adolescent memory Will had. Returning home was like opening a mental photo album that spanned the better part of his life. Unfortunately, Will was about to make another memory.

Alden started out as a small farming community in the early 1800s. While Buffalo grew into one the nation's largest cities and a major steel producers, Alden remained in quaint contrast to the hustle and bustle of Buffalo. The ground was perfect for farming, particularly corn and cabbage. It wasn't until the latter half of the 20th century that Alden saw big businesses move in, grocery stores and restaurant chains. But it didn't diminish the small, private community feel Alden always had.

The town was still quiet. There were only about 3,000 people. Will was one of the few to escape the boredom that seemed to grow out of the town's soil like fruits and vegetables.

Most of Will's family was gone. Some had died, like his grandparents. Some moved, like his cousins, who went with their families to accept better jobs down south. And then there were some who ran out of Alden and abandoned the town … in particular, Will's father, Joseph.

If Will had only one reason to get out of Alden, it was because of his father. Will remembered his father as a hard-working, blue-collar man, who always smelled of smoke from the only steel factory Alden ever had. Will always thought his parents had the perfect marriage. He thought his father would never lie to him, and he believed his father would come back someday. Ten years passed and Will still had not heard from his father. He imagined the worst and sometimes wished for it, but he always corrected himself when he did that. He was not going to end up like his father. He was going to do better than that.

The town did have a few shining moments throughout its history. There was the state championship high school football team back in 1953, and in the 1980s, Alden was among the top 25 safest towns in America. But substantial success and prosperity rarely found Alden. The annual corn parade down the middle of town was nothing to brag about, and now that Will had a taste for the big city life in Boston, Alden almost seemed, in a word, immature.

Mark slowed down once he passed the sign on the edge of town that read:

WELCOME TO
ALDEN
ONE OF THE SAFEST PLACES IN AMERICA

Will started laughing to himself when he read that faded sign. It was painted blue and yellow, on old oak.

Will was able to find a few reasons to go home, however. Most of his friends from school were still there, his favorite drinking establishment was still thriving in the heart of the town. The most important reason to go home was to be with his mother, the parent who was always there for Will and Eric.

The car rode along the winding and empty road that led right in the center of Alden. Will saw many things that brought back a flood of memories.

Off to one side was the old Janzforth Factory, the same factory that Will's father was employed at before he blew out of town. It closed about twenty years earlier, though, after the owner, George Janzforth, died suddenly in his office. No one bought the building.

"They haven't gotten rid of that place yet?" Will asked.

"The town won't put up the money to have it torn down. It's kind of a landmark anyways," Mark said.

A little farther up the road Will saw Mrs. Timmerman's house on the corner of Main Street and Wolcott Avenue. It had been almost twenty years since she taught at Alden High, but she kept up on her gossip and knew pretty much everything about everyone, even people who left the area.

Mark and Will continued along and passed Augusta Road. Mark made nothing of it because he passed it every day on patrol. Will however made a majority of his fondest memories on this road. This was where Shannon, his first love, lived. Will's first kiss, his first moonlight walk, his first time all took place at 53 Augusta.

"Whatever happened to Shannon?" Will said with a wry smile.

"Well, she went to school down south and then her folks moved down to Florida. I don't think she's been around here for over five or six years now."

The two continued down Main Street, past the police station and through the middle of town.

Just beyond town hall, where Will's mother worked, Will realized that Alden was not, inevitably, the same town that he left almost five years earlier.

"Harrison Road, this is your stop," Mark said as he pulled into the driveway.

Mark stopped the car, keeping the lights shining on the house. It looked exactly the same way it did when Will was a boy. The porch was still the same shade of faded white, the shutters were not as red as they were when Will was a boy, but there was no mistaking this was the house. The chain on the porch swing was rusted and one of the garage windows was broken.

Will was not completely out of the car when the front door opened, pouring a heavy yellow light over the porch floor. A shadowy figure stood in the doorway and pushed open the screen door. It was Will's mother.

She looked surprisingly young for her age. She had shoulder-length, dirty blonde hair. She was plump, but not heavy. She had green eyes that Will used to think were x-ray eyes because they saw through all of his lies. She stood there in a flower-pattern dress, daisies scattered all over it.

She did have a few more lines around her eyes this time. The lines were actually the first thing Will noticed as he looked at her. His mother had gone through more than most of Alden's mothers, but she always managed to stay tough.

Mark followed Will up the stairs of the porch, but he did not look at Mrs. Sandwith. He couldn't bring himself to do it. The last time he walked up these stairs, he gave her the worst news of her life.

"Oh, thank God you're here," Morgan Sandwith said. She embraced Will and began to sob.

"Mom, it's after one in the morning. You should be asleep."

"I couldn't sleep. I haven't slept since I heard about your brother. And then I thought something might have happened to you—"

"Mom, nothing is going to happen to me," Will said. "I'm here now. It's alright. You're going to be okay."

"C'mon, let's go inside." Will put his arm around her and walked her into the house.

Chapter *Four*

Alden had a solid reputation as one the safest towns in America, but that did not mean it didn't have some small time criminal activity going on. There were the usual crimes you would find in any small town: vandalism, burglary, drunken driving.

One crime in Alden that barely made the radar screen was drug use. Perhaps the most popular spot for drug users to beg, deal and inhale was the Janzforth factory. Its location was prime. There were no houses near it for miles, there was plenty of cover from passing cop cars by trees and overgrown shrubs and there was nothing but moonlight to give passing cars a chance to see anyone in or around the plant.

There weren't a lot of burnouts in Alden, but there were two youths in particular who had earned the reputation as Alden's most regular "street pharmacists," Darren Banyan and Steve Murphy. These two could normally be found roaming the streets of Alden but rarely caused trouble; they just polluted the minds of innocent teens in the area.

It was a quiet night for the two, no customers and very few passing cars. They saw Mark's car go by as they sat on the lawn in front of the factory. They called the factory their "office," but lately their office seemed to liven up a bit. Strange noises, flashes of light, foul odors were just some of problems the two noticed.

"Dude, do you think we need to look for a new place to make camp?" Murphy asked.

"No, this is our spot. People know they can find us here," Banyon said, taking another drag of a half-burned cigarette.

Murphy shook his head as if to agree with Darren, when he saw one of the basement windows light up for just a second.

"Did you see that?" Steve said.

"See what?"

"That window just lit up."

"What in the hell are you talking about? It couldn't just light up. And there were no cars or anything," said Banyon, starting to get irritated.

"I know what I saw and I saw a light in there." Murphy got up and approached the building. "There's got to be somebody in there."

"Fuck that, man. I ain't goin' in there," Darren said.

Murphy went over and picked up a rock. He flung his arm back and rocketed the stone at the window, hitting it dead on. The glass shattered.

"What the fuck, man?" Darren said. "Are you trying to blow our—"

Darren stopped mid sentence. A moan came from inside the factory. Darren rose from the ground slowly.

"What the hell was that?" Darren said, not taking his eyes off the window.

"Do you think I killed something in there?"

"Rats don't moan, dipshit," said Darren walking towards the building.

Darren and Steve moved closer and closer to the building, then stopped. There was no moan but rather a faint scream. The two didn't so much as take a breath as they stared at the building. Then the light that Steve originally saw flashed once again and got brighter and brighter.

"Let's get the fuck out of here," Darren said. They did not look back as they ran down the road to where Steve had parked his car. Neither said a word while they raced down Route 33. Finally, Darren broke the silence.

"That was no rat screaming in there."

"Yeah, no shit. What was it then?" Steve said.

"I don't know, man. Maybe there was a squeaky door or a rat killed a mouse or a cat or something."

"That was no animal. Animals don't moan like that. Anyways, how do you explain the light that came out of that room?"

Again, there was silence. They called it an early night. They both agreed, though, that they were not to mention a word of it to anyone else. They wouldn't want business to drop.

Chapter *Five*

The story behind the Janzforth factory and its closing is a simple one, but it was a secret within the town of Alden's inner circle. It was taboo to talk about it and it was never discussed above a whisper. Alden's reputation was sacred to natives of the town.

When George Janzforth opened the Janzforth Steel factory in the 1950s, he brought a small piece of the city of Buffalo to Alden, a taste of big-city life. It was a huge success, creating many new jobs, bringing business and money to a struggling town. Janzforth himself became one of the most influential people in the town.

George and his family, a wife and three sons, fit in perfectly with the town's simple way of life. The factory was thriving and it seemed that George's grandkids would live in Alden living a peaceful life with George as the mayor.

In the 1970s, the steel industry took a terrible turn for the worse in the western New York area. Buffalo took serious hits to its economy and its job market, which of course had a ripple effect into the suburbs, including Alden. George Janzforth began losing both money and his approval within the town's elite. He began sleeping in his office, trying desperately to come up with ways to keep his factory afloat. He lost countless hours of sleep wondering not only how his family would survive, but also how the workers that he would have to let go should the plant go under ever get by.

At home, George's life was not much better. His sons began drifting away from him. The oldest went off to college, the second got involved with drug users and the youngest was arrested several times. George's wife was understanding at first, standing by her husband during their struggles.

Inevitably, Mrs. Janzforth left her husband, taking her sons with her. George lost his business, Alden's economy hit an all time low, the unemployment number went sky high and Alden had its first recorded suicide: George Janzforth used a shotgun to solve his problems. He was found by Joseph Sandwith just moments after George's life ended, the blood was still running down the wall behind George's body that lay slumped over in his chair.

Over the next two decades, various people and groups tried to convince the town's hierarchy to have the factory destroyed, but with no luck. Year after year, the factory remained and other than the occasional youth who lost a bet, few ventured into the building.

Yet, when Darren and Steve broke the window, they were not the only ones present at the factory.

Darren and Steve were in far too much of a hurry to notice the figure standing near the entrance to the factory, hidden in the darkness. The figure watched the two run to their car, just to make sure they left, before heading into the factory.

The man picked the padlock keeping the front entrance chained up and made his way into the main corridor. He lit the torch hanging on the wall and slowly made his way down the hall. The whole building had a musty smell to it, with mold and fungus growing on the walls, floors and ceiling. As he made his way down the hall, he came to the end and veered off to the right. There was another torch on the wall, lighting the way as the man continued on.

Finally, he went down the stairs and entered what was at one time the break room for the factory workers. There was another person, this one with a muscular build and stringy hair. He stood next to a table, leaned on it and took a deep breath. He then pointed an axe at the man who was now in the doorway.

"What happened out there last night? He was not supposed to die," he said. His voice was deep and without emotion.

"I don't know," replied the shorter man. "I guess I hit him in just the right spot. Everything was going along just as planned until—"

"Until you messed up," the tall man yelled. "If we are going to be successful, if we are going to follow through on our plan, we cannot have these types of screw ups."

The shorter man stood there, taking in everything the other man said.

He continued, "What happened outside tonight?"

"It was just a couple of losers hanging out on the lawn. Apparently they saw a flicker of light and got suspicious. That damn kid screaming didn't help either."

"I'll take care of the ones in here. You worry about the people outside. This is our sanctuary. This is where we will carry out our plan. This where our world begins and theirs ends. Make sure we are not interrupted." He wiped the blood off his axe.

"Yes. I'll go keep watch outside."

As the short man made his way out of the cafeteria and back outside, the other man swung the axe up over his head and took a powerful chop that hit the table he was working on.

Chapter Six

When Will awoke the next morning he felt refreshed, as if maybe things weren't as bad as they seemed the night before. He looked around his old room and found it was exactly as he had left it before leaving for college. The sunlight spread out across the floor and reached the bed and Will felt a warmth. He realized that he really didn't mind having grown up in Alden.

The shelves above his desk were still the same as when he left, except for a coating of dust on his trophies and awards. The bookshelf in the corner was just as dusty, but a few streaks were embedded into the dust sheet, probably from Eric taking a few books.

Will got out of bed, went into the bathroom and stared directly into the mirror. His light-brown hair covered most of his forehead. His hazel eyes were surrounded by red this morning. Despite sleeping soundly, he did not get as much sleep as he was used to in Boston. His complexion always got dark in the summer months, even when a majority of the daylight hours were spent in front of a computer.

Will rinsed his face, took a deep breath and again stared at his reflection. It was remarkable how much he resembled his brother. He always got a kick out of how people would often mistake the two when they saw the brothers.

Will wiped his face with the washcloth his mother had set aside for him and headed downstairs.

He turned the corner, and entered the kitchen to see a plate of food ready for him. He sat down just as Will's mother came in from the den and began to sob.

"Every time I see you, I see your brother," Morgan said, beginning to break down into a stream of tears.

Will got up and hugged his mother. He guided his mother to a chair next to the window overlooking the backyard. She wiped the tears away from her eyes and took a few deep breaths.

"I couldn't believe it when Mark first told me. I had called him and asked him if he could keep an eye out for your brother. I was almost asleep when I heard a knock on the door. It's the knock a parent dreads more than anything," Morgan said, staring out the window. "I nearly collapsed when he told me."

"Mark said you did collapse."

"Okay, I did. But not for very long."

"I don't get it. Did he stay out longer than usual?"

"No. I mean, he didn't come home when he usually did, but the Adams said he left Lauren's about the same time he always did," Will's mother said looking at Will closely. "Do they suspect anyone?"

"No, not right now. They figure it was someone here in town who knew Eric's usual route home."

"I can't talk about this anymore right now," said Morgan. "How's Mira? You two are still together, right? Or is there something you want to tell me?"

This was probably the first time Will smiled since arriving back home.

"Yes, mom. She's fine, we're fine. That's one area of my life that is going just fine."

"Any plans for a wedding?"

"I should have known this question was coming. Not yet, but the topic has come up you'll be happy to know."

"Are you planning on moving back here?"

"No. And on that note, I'm gonna go get ready," Will said with a grin.

"Where are you off to today?"

"Actually, it's 'Where are *we* off to today'," Will said as he put his plate in the sink. "You're off to the Adams to help them prepare dinner tonight. I'm off to the police station to meet with Mark and Chief McGillis. We're gonna go over some of the evidence and try to get a list of suspects."

It was at this point that Will's mother got that all-too-familiar tone of anger in her voice. Will had heard it a thousand times growing up.

"Why are you getting involved in that? That really can't wait until after the funeral."

"Mom, the funeral arrangements are all made, I can't cook for shit and I am more concerned right now with finding the bastard who did this."

"Don't use that tone of voice with me. Just wait until Friday." Morgan began to sob. "Whoever did it is probably three states away by now."

"Maybe so, but all I can think about right now is the person who did this thinking they got away with it. I'll be at the Adams by six o'clock and I will not mention anything about Eric or his funeral at all tonight."

Will headed up the stairs and into his room. He sat down on the bed and dropped his head into his hands. With all his mother had been through over the past few days, Will still managed to piss her off, make her cry and make her life even more miserable than it was before he got home.

Will looked out the window, and he thought about all of the arguments he and his mother had after his father walked out. Will hated fighting with her, but at times his mother needed someone to argue with. Why did Will have to do it now? Some things in Alden never changed.

Chapter Seven

Mark was originally going to go to the Sandwiths to pick Will up and go to the police station, but Will decided he would rather walk. It was a gorgeous day, not a cloud in the sky, high eighties and plenty of green all around. The police station was on Main Street about six or seven blocks from Will's street.

The walk, though, seemed to take ages. With each house and store Will passed, another face from the past came to his mind. There were very few people in Alden he did not know.

Will came to Fairview Market next to the police station, still musing, and bumped into Hilda Timmerman.

"I'm sorry Mrs. Timmerman. I've got a lot on my mind right now."

"And you should. This is a tough time for everyone."

Hilda Timmerman was a heavy set woman who always had her reading glasses hanging around her neck and her silver hair up in a bun. She was the grandmother Will never knew.

"Well, hopefully we'll catch the killer before he strikes again," Will said looking up at the sun, which wasn't quite overhead yet.

"You know, Chief McGillis has already started questioning some of the local kids about it. The first ones he questioned were Darren Banyan and Steve Murphy."

"Do you think they did it?"

"It wouldn't surprise me if they did it. Some say there would be no drug problem in this town if they were gone."

"We may find out soon."

"I hope so. Are you going to the Adams tonight for dinner?"

"Yeah, I'll be there. My mother would hunt me down if I didn't show."

"It'll be good for you, help take your mind off things," Hilda said as she grabbed Will's arm and squeezed it.

When Will approached the police station, he wondered why Mrs. Timmerman didn't work as an investigator for the police. She probably knew more about the case than anyone.

"Hey, there you are," Mark said as he patted Will on the back. "We were waiting for you so we could go out to the scene one more time."

"Thanks for waiting. I've been wanting to go there, to see exactly where it happened."

"The chief's gonna go with us, but it shouldn't take too long. There's no evidence or anything to collect."

"Just between you and me, how is the chief treating this? I mean, are the state police involved?"

"The state police have been notified and they'll be sending some people in from Buffalo up here in a few days. They're a little tied up right now."

Mark was interrupted by Chief Nick McGillis, who walked out of his office and into the main hallway where Mark and Will were talking.

Nick McGillis was a tall man, but solid, an imposing figure. He was in his forties and his hair was now getting some gray in it. He always seemed to have a cigarette burning. Will always found himself looking at the chief's yellowish teeth, which were one of Nick's few distinguishing features. Will, though, looked up to Nick and respected him and his authority.

"Will Sandwith. I'd ask how you're doin', but I think I already know."

"I'm sure you do, although murder is pretty unheard of in this part of the world."

"There's procedure for everything, even murder, even in Alden," McGillis said. "Let's get rollin'. I've still got a shitload of paperwork to fill out."

The three went down Route 33, driving down about three or four miles from the police station, until they came across a stretch of road marked off with yellow police tape tied to some of the trees lining the shoulder of the road.

The car was gone, towed away to the police station. A tarp had been put up above a five-foot section of the shoulder so that any rain would not wash away any blood, hair or fibers.

"I can tell you with the utmost confidence, Will, that we have combed every inch of this shoulder ten times over and have come up with nothing more than a few blood spots," McGillis said.

"And the blood is all Eric's?" asked Will.

"We don't have the test results back yet, but we are led to believe that it is all from Eric."

"Come here, Will, take a look at this," said Mark near the edge of the road where the shoulder met the woods lining Route 33.

As Will got closer to where Mark was standing, Mark pointed to the ground. There was a footprint heading out of the woods.

"Based on this footprint, the attacker probably came out of the woods and waited for Eric to come down the road, same time he always did."

"Obviously there were no signs of a struggle," Will asked.

"No," said Chief McGillis. "That's what has us baffled. There is one set of prints coming from the woods. Yet your brother got hit in the back of the head. We're wondering how someone got behind him."

"Do you think two people were involved?"

"That's a definite possibility," said Mark. "The only thing missing is another set of tracks."

"What was he hit with?"

"Forensic tests will tell us that, but right now, we believe it to be either a baseball bat or a two-by-four. It only took one swing," McGillis said.

"So, what we know for sure is that Eric pulled off to the side of the road, got out of the car, walked out front of the car and got struck in the back of the head by a wooden object," Will said. "And more than likely, there were two people involved."

Will thought, if this was all they had to go on, this case would never get solved. He stared at the footprints in the grass. "You guys realize that unless we find a miracle piece of evidence or the killer turns himself in, we're never going to know exactly what happened."

Mark thought for a second, then said, "C'mon, Will, let's go. I'll give you a lift back to the station. We'll go over a few small detail items and some pictures there."

Will sat in the back seat and stared out the window, but wasn't paying attention to anyone or anything. Mark and Chief McGillis were talking but Will didn't hear a thing they were saying.

They were about three blocks away from the station when they passed the funeral home where Will's brother was being laid out. That caught Will's attention immediately.

"Pull over! Pull over to the funeral home!"

Mark and the chief glanced at each other and pulled into the empty parking lot without argument. The sign of the home simply read: Neumann's Funeral Home, est. 1971. Nothing fancy about it, just plain and simple, the way a funeral parlor should be.

The three men made their way into the building slowly. Will wanted to run in, but managed to calm himself down. Geoff Neumann, owner of the home, met the three in the hallway.

"Chief. What can I do for you? Is anything wrong?"

"No, no. We were driving by, and, well, do you remember Will Sandwith, Eric's brother?"

"I think I've seen you around before, quite a few years ago, though," Neumann said.

"Yeah, I've been out of town for about five years now."

"I'm assuming you're here to see your brother." Neumann paused and Will nodded. "He's in the first room on your right."

"I'll only be a minute," Will said.

He made his way down the hallway. When he got to the doorway, he abruptly stopped. He could see Eric's coffin and he felt as though it were staring back at him. He slowly made his way across the floor, then stood over his brother.

Will had no idea what to say. He was hoping his little brother would open his eyes and laugh at Will, as though it were all a part of an elaborate joke. But Eric's body did not move. Will stretched out his hand and grabbed Eric's hands, which were crossed holding a rosary. They were ice cold and perhaps it was just through the touch of Eric's hands, but Will now knew exactly what to say.

"Oh, man. Eric, Eric, I am so sorry I wasn't there for you. I should have been there for you. Instead I took off and hardly returned for five years." Will laughed to himself and was talking to Eric as though he could actually hear him. "I'll never forget the last time I came home and you farted right in the middle of grace. I thought Mom was gonna kill you."

Will then choked up. "I don't know what happened to you, but I promise I'm gonna find the bastards that did this to you. And when I do, they're gonna pay for what they did with their own blood."

Will leaned over and kissed Eric's head. He turned around and walked out of the room.

The three got back into the car and drove back to the police station. They went inside and sat down in the chief's office. It was there that Will got his first look at the pictures from the crime scene taken just an hour after the murder.

"This one shows the head wound up close. Whoever did it had one powerful swing," Mark said.

"So blood went everywhere, right?"

"Pretty much. We found blood spatters nearly ten feet away and some on the gravel and leaves," said Mark.

"How much blood did he lose?"

"Well, he lost a lot, it would have been more, but he landed face down, so the wound didn't spill out on the ground. We'll know exactly how much he lost when the tests come back," said Mark.

Mark was skimming through some of the other pictures, when Will came across one that caught his attention.

"Mark, take a look at this."

"What do you got there?"

"I'm not sure, really. Maybe nothing, but it looks like a single drop of blood on the front of Eric's shirt, there, on the collar."

"Yeah, you're right. What do you think of it?"

"Well, you're the cop. What do make of it?"

"It's possible that one of the blood droplets went straight up in the air on contact and landed on the collar. Perhaps he got hit so hard a drop of blood came from his mouth and fell from his mouth onto the collar. I'd have to think about it."

"I suppose one of those scenarios is possible, but if he got hit in the back of the head and fell forward, how could only a single drop of blood land on the front?"

Chief McGillis, who was taking a call in another room, came into the office. He scanned over the table of pictures and sighed. "Come up with anything?"

"Will found something in this picture here, Chief," said Mark and handed over the picture. "There is a single drop of blood on the collar. We're trying to figure out how it could have gotten there."

Chief McGillis took a look at the picture and examined it for a few moments. "It was a pretty hard hit to the skull. Anything is possible. We can check with the town medical examiner tomorrow if you'd like, Will."

"Yeah, maybe he's got an idea. I'm just lobbing pitches out there, hoping for a homerun."

"Sure, we'll check it out. But for now, go on home and get ready for tomorrow. You've got an emotional day ahead of you."

"Chief? Just curious, but were the state police or the sheriff's department coming in to do an investigation?"

Mark and the chief looked at each other for a brief second before the chief responded.

"The state police came in the day of the murder and did an investigation. But it's our jurisdiction, so they are only available if we need or ask for assistance."

Then Mark said, "C'mon, Will. We better get going so you can meet up with your mother."

"It's been a long day," said the chief. "I'm gonna head for home and sleep on it. I'll see you tomorrow, Mark."

As the two drove off, Will couldn't help but think about the picture and what might have caused that one drop of blood to land on the front of Eric's shirt. He mulled over countless possibilities. A hit to the head could do it, and most likely did in this case, but how? The two approached the Sandwith residence and Mark told Will he'd see him later.

"I'm gonna go back to the station and try to figure something out by taking another look at those pictures. I'll swing by later, though."

"Cool, man. Thanks for the ride back. I'll talk to you later."

Will stood in his mother's driveway and stared out into the sky. The sun wouldn't set for a few hours yet, but Will was exhausted and really wanted nothing more than to go home and go to bed. He then looked at the house and wondered if anyone was watching him. Was the killer out there right now looking at Will? Was the killer in Will's mother's home right now? Will shook his head and laughed. I've got to stop doing this to myself, he thought. How could Will possibly survive if he was looking over his shoulder every two minutes and checking every dark corner, even in his home, for a killer who probably wasn't even there? He walked into the house and got ready for dinner at the Adams place.

Mr. And Mrs. Henry Adams were having a big dinner at their home to try and take people's minds off of the tragic events of just a few short days ago. Will thought maybe the Adams were having a dinner because they felt guilty. After all, Eric was leaving their home the night he was murdered. He never mentioned this to his mother, though.

Henry Adams was a tall man, lanky, with a thick brown mustache and a comb over. Sylvia Adams was also quite tall compared with other women in Alden. She had short blonde hair and a small gap between her two front teeth.

Mr. Adams was the owner of Fairview Market. He inherited the business from his father, who took over for his father, and so on and so on.

They had two children, Henry Jr., who attended school with Will and was better known as Hank, and Lindsay, the last person other than the killer to see Eric alive. Hank was working alongside his father at the store, but he was looking for any reason at all to get out of Alden.

Lindsay, however, was leaving Alden to go to college in North Carolina. She was beautiful, with blonde hair and deep brown eyes. Will's mother called her the typical "product of Alden soil." She wasn't tall like her parents, wasn't short, but right in the middle of the pack. She was going to college on a partial scholarship and took great pride in her academics, at least that's what Eric told Will when they talked. She had a politeness that made anyone who just met her become either totally taken with her charm or completely jealous.

After Will changed his clothes, he headed over to the Adams place on foot. His mother had gone over earlier in the day to help prepare dinner.

The house was typical Alden living. It was yellow with light-blue shutters around each window. The flower garden's rows ran perfectly, almost mathematically, in line.

At six o'clock the sun began to set. Will wanted nothing more than for the sun to stay out all night today. Tomorrow was approaching too fast, the last time Will would see Eric. Out of the corner of his eye, Will saw a rat run out the tall grass along the road and run across the street into the grass on the other side. In all his memories as a child and a teenager, Will never saw a rat outside of the industrial zone of Alden.

As Will approached the house, he thought about all the times in high school when the guys would go into the Adams' basement to get hammered on a Friday night. The only time Will got high was in Hank's garage his junior year of high school. Will didn't talk to Hank much anymore, but the memories were still lingering in the summer air.

Will walked up the driveway and to the backyard. Most of the guests were seated at tables spread out all over the lawn. The grass was freshly cut.

Will nodded to some of the guests while walking to the table where his mother sat. He put his hands on her shoulders, leaned over and kissed her cheek.

"I made it."

"Oh, good. Did you eat anything yet?"

"No, I just got here."

"Did you say hello to the Adams?"

"No, I just got here," Will said in his most sarcastic tone.

"Smartass. Go and be social. Everyone has been asking about you."

Will walked into the kitchen where Mr. And Mrs. Adams were still cooking, doing their best to accommodate the ever-growing number guests.

"Well, hello, William," Mr. Adams said extending his hand to Will, shaking his hand with a firm grip. Will could tell his being there made them uneasy.

"Mr. Adams, Mrs. Adams. How are you both doing?"

"It is so good to see you. Where is this girl your mother has been telling us about?" Mrs. Adams asked as she washed her hands.

"She's back in Boston. She works for one of the television stations back there and wasn't able to get the time off."

"How is your work going?" asked Mr. Adams.

"Good. I'm moving up the ladder at the paper, so things are going pretty good right now."

"No plans to come back here, eh?" asked Mr. Adams.

"No, not right now. How is Hank doing?"

"He's working late, closing up the store. He may be joining you in Boston, though. He's looking to Boston University for business," replied Mrs. Adams. "Have you seen Lindsay yet?"

"No, is she around?"

"She just went out front a second ago. Take a look there," said Mrs. Adams.

"Sounds good. It was good seeing you again."

Will had watched Lindsay grow up, seeing as he spent so many useless hours at the Adams house. He hadn't seen her in almost three years, but from what Eric had told him she was as beautiful as ever and the complete opposite of her brother. Not that Will didn't like Hank, he just wasn't the best influence on people.

Will walked to the front of the house. He saw Lindsay sitting by herself on the porch swing that faced the street. She was wearing a pair of jean shorts and a black tee-shirt, Eric's shirt actually. Her blonde hair was pulled back into a ponytail and she was staring off into the night sky. The sun had now fallen behind the trees lining the street.

She turned and saw Will walking up the walkway towards the porch. She got off the swing and jumped up to give Will a hug before he even stepped onto the porch.

"Oh my God, it is so good to see you," Lindsay said and began to sob.

"Likewise. You're looking good." Lindsay returned to the swing. Will propped himself on the banister overlooking the garden. "How are you holding up?" he asked

"Not so good. Every time I think of Eric, I think about how he died coming from my house. If he weren't here, it wouldn't have happened."

"I wouldn't say that. The police think that whoever murdered Eric had the whole thing planned. He walked right into it." Will couldn't believe how much he was starting to sound like Mark.

"Do you think that?"

"Yeah, I do. It's too clean, too perfect. The crime scene that is. Whoever did it knew how to cover their tracks. So, no more talk about you being the one to blame. The only person to blame is the killer."

Lindsay wiped a tear away from her eye and smiled.

"What are you smiling about?" Will asked.

"I was just thinking about how happy I was when I was with your brother. He made me very happy."

"Take it from me, you made him pretty happy too. The last time I talked to him, he spent most of the conversation bragging about you. I was glad he had someone like you." Will got off the banister and started heading down the steps to the walkway. "But don't get too high on yourself. He always liked me better."

Lindsay smiled again. "Eleven o'clock tomorrow, right?"

"Yeah. Time to say goodbye," Will said, glancing at the setting sun. It was now below the trees, giving the sky a crimson tinge. "See ya there."

Will walked to the back of the house. He had not even been at the Adams house for twenty minutes and was ready to go home. He knew that no matter how many familiar faces he saw and voices from the past he heard, he would not be able to get his mind off what tomorrow held for him.

Across town, Nick McGillis was at home in front of the TV with the remote in one hand, a beer in the other. He had been Chief of the Alden Police force for about four years now and had an impeccable record. There was little crime and he was respected.

McGillis had waited a long time to become police chief, almost twenty years. The previous chief, Ben Watson, was a shining example of excellence in police work and left the town as he had upon being named chief of police: in great shape. It was now McGillis' job to keep the town that way.

He had not told anybody, but Eric's murder was eating him up inside. He couldn't have possibly prevented the murder, but was now starting to think the townspeople were talking about him behind his back. His biggest fear was letting down the people of Alden. And he felt it was starting to happen.

Chapter Eight

Darren Banyan and Steve Murphy figured there had to be a reasonable explanation for the noises they heard coming from inside the factory. The Janzforth factory was home to many rats and there were sure to be more than a few cats in there as well. So when customers came calling the next day, they told the customers to go back to their office.

It was about nine o'clock at night and two more of Alden's most notable miscreants were out front of the Janzforth factory. Adam Connolly and Matt Burton were smoking on the lawn watching the cars go by on Route 33, waiting for Darren and Steve to show up with the goods.

"Where the fuck are those two? They're already fifteen minutes late," Connolly said, flicking his cigarette butt in the bushes.

"Who knows. Those two assholes are always late," said Burton as he threw a stone at one of the factory windows. "So are you goin' to Sandwith's funeral tomorrow?"

"I don't know. I might go late, you know, the girls that go will be depressed and lonely. It's the perfect opportunity to get some sympathy sex," said Connolly.

"Now you're talkin'. Lauren's available now."

"Yeah, but, I feel weird even talking to her. She's gonna be a wreck for a little while."

The two heard a rustling in the bushes where Adam threw his cigarette. They stood in silence waiting for another sound.

"What's in there?" Burton said.

A rat shot out of the brush and towards the road. Both boys caught their breath.

Connolly said, "Holy shit, man. Those two better get here soon or they're gonna lose a fuckin' sale."

Matt glanced at the factory for a second. He looked back at Adam and stared in horror. Someone had run Adam through from behind with a stake. Blood was all over the front of Adam's shirt on the end of the shaft and dripping from his mouth and down his chin.

Matt could see the person standing behind Adam, but could not make out any features. Then the figure drew the stake back through Adam who slumped to the ground. The man wore a black trench coat and a winter hat. The man's face was concealed by the darkness. He took a step towards Matt.

Matt took a few backward steps. The killer moved slowly, and Matt couldn't help but move at the same pace. He wanted to turn and run screaming at the top of his lungs but all he could do was piss in his pants.

Finally, Matt turned and ran towards the factory. As he busted through the doors, he knew he should have run away from the building into the woods, but he figured he could lose the murderer in the mazelike building. He ran as fast as he could, checking over his shoulder.

When he neared the end of the main hallway, he saw the person in the doorway of the building. He stopped for a split second and made a right. He knew the man saw him, but there were plenty of rooms in which to hide. He got about ten steps down the hallway and picked a door. It was open. He went in, and he closed the door behind him.

The room had a terrible odor to it, like rotted milk left on the kitchen counter for days. He spied the room for a place to hide. He hid behind a table in the back of the room. But, just his luck, he found a room with no windows. He would have to leave through the door he came in. Despite the need to hide, he had to make sure the door was in sight.

Matt wished at that moment he had never smoked a cigarette in his life. He was out of breath to the point that he couldn't breathe through his nose. He was sure the killer would hear him huffing and puffing away. A million thoughts raced through his brain as he sat there crouched and ready to lunge out from behind that table.

Finally Matt saw a shadow by the door. The window in the door was filthy and difficult to see through, but someone was definitely there. Matt held his breath as best he could. He ducked back quickly behind the table and waited a few seconds before taking another look.

He peeked his head out slowly and did not see anyone there. The door was open slightly more than when he checked it last.

Matt sat there in his urine soaked jeans for what seemed to be an hour. He finally decided to make a run for it. 'Okay. Go!' he said to himself. As he sprang to his feet he slipped on something and fell. Matt slowly made his way to his feet and put his hand on the floor to see what he slipped on.

Matt felt something cold and wet on the floor and brought his hand close to his face. It was blood. Matt let out a scream but caught himself. He bolted to the door, almost losing his step. Matt dove out of the doorway. When he hit the wall he felt something soft cushion the blow. He stared at the corpse of a young girl. Her lifeless eyes stared back at Matt.

Matt turned the other way towards the door and saw the man standing there. Before he could scream, Matt was hit in the head. The man stood over him, watching the blood trickle down his forehead as he lay senseless. He turned slowly and made his way outside. He picked up Adam's corpse and carried it into the building. Adam and Matt would not be attending Eric's funeral after all.

Chapter *Nine*

Will was waiting in his mother's car in the Adams' driveway, waiting for his mother to say her goodbyes so he could drive her home and get a good night's sleep. As Will sat behind the wheel, he thought about what might go on at Eric's funeral the next morning. Who would show? Would Will break down and cry or would his anger be his focus?

It was almost ten o'clock and Will was exhausted. He had spent much of the evening reliving the past, reminiscing about his brother, wondering about his own life. Will shook his head and hit the horn on the steering wheel. A few moments later his mother appeared through the front door and made her way down the driveway to the car.

"What's the matter with you? You'll wake the whole neighborhood," Will's mother said doing her best to sound angry.

"I've been sitting here waiting for you for over ten minutes. We've got an early morning, you know."

It was a quiet ride home. Neither one really knew what to say. Will was preoccupied with the picture he saw earlier, trying to figure out how the blood drop got on Eric's collar. Will's mother was concerned with what she was going to wear to the funeral. They were alone on the road, nothing but streetlights to keep them company.

As they approached the house, Will noticed a car in the driveway.

"Mom, whose car is that?"

"I don't know. I wasn't expecting anyone."

Will's first thought was that Mira came into town from Boston and it was her rental car. But as he pulled in the driveway, he noticed the car had Florida license plates on it.

"Holy shit," Will said.

"What? Who is it?"

"It's Shannon."

The first love of Will's life stepped out of the car and stood waving. She was still as beautiful as ever, although her hair was curled now. She was thinner than he remembered, but still had the same radiant smile.

"Hey, Will. How are ya?" Shannon said as she gave Will a hug.

"I'm doin' all right. What are you doing here?"

"Hello, Mrs. Sandwith. I'm sorry to hear about Eric," said Shannon, holding Will's mother's hands.

"Thank you, honey. You look great. It's great of you to come." Will's mother began to sob.

"Shannon, wait here for a second. I'm gonna take her inside."

Will grabbed his mother's purse from the car along with some baked goods she brought home from the dinner. Shannon smiled at Will. Will hadn't seen her in almost five years, but the same butterflies he had the first time he asked her out came back as strong as ever. Will loved Mira very much, but at this moment, she was in Boston … thankfully.

Will got his mother situated and ready for bed. He went outside and found Shannon sitting on the front steps. Will sat down next to her and smiled.

"I can't believe you're here. I didn't know if I'd ever see you again," Will said.

"Would you rather I wasn't here?"

"No, no. It's good to see you again. I just wish it were under happier circumstances. No offense, I'd rather be sitting here with my brother than you."

"No offense taken. I'd rather he were here too."

"It appears we both have a crush on Eric."

Shannon laughed and took a deep breath. "Hey, I had a long drive in from Jacksonville. I'm starved. What do ya say we head over to Denny's for something to eat. You know, just like the old days."

Will wished it was old times; not so much to have Shannon back, but to have his brother back. And he couldn't believe she drove all that way for the funeral. How could he turn her down?

"Sounds good. But I'll drive. I have not forgotten how bad of a driver you were. I don't think my mother could handle losing Eric and me in the same week."

Shannon glared at Will with a half smile. The two got in the car. Will thought about all the times he and Shannon had been in this situation before: Will behind the wheel, Shannon riding shotgun. In all of the excitement, Will forgot to check the time.

Chapter Ten

"Well what do you expect, asshole? We were supposed to meet them here an hour ago. I'm sure they took off by now. Just another lost fucking sale," Darren said.

"If they wanted the goods, they would have waited. Where else are they gonna get shit this good?" Steve said.

Steve and Darren began walking around the building, hoping to find their missing customers. They made sure to be extra quiet to avoid a repeat performance of a night earlier. They walked next to each other making sure nothing got by them. There was the occasional owl hooting, a passing car on Route 33, and a rat sighting every so often.

The old factory seemed especially quiet this evening. Steve and Darren tried their best not to even look in the direction of the building. Yet they seemed drawn to it, checking the windows every few seconds to make sure there were no flashes of light or animals trying to get out.

Steve said, "I don't get it, man. Their car's parked next to the motel where we told them to leave it. Where are they?"

"How the hell would I know?" Darren said. "This place spooks the shit out of me though. Let's get out of here."

As the two made their way to the road, Steve lost his balance. He regained his balance, but was pissed off that he just about fell on his ass.

"What the hell's the matter with you, shithead?" Darren said.

"I don't know. There's some fuckin' mud or something."

"Mud? You dick, it hasn't rained for two days. There's no mud."

Steve thought it over and decided that Darren had a good point. It's not like it was a damp time of year in Alden. Steve turned and examined the ground where he almost fell. He could see something on the grass, but it was thicker than water. He put his hand down, touched the wet grass and rubbed his fingers together. He put his fingers to his nose and smelled.

"Dude, it's blood."

"What? Blood? Like from a rat?" Darren said.

"That's a pretty big fucking rat if that's true," Steve said, pointing. The area was a few feet in diameter and the ground was soaked.

"Holy shit. Dude, what the fuck happened here?"

The two began to look around in every direction, staring off into the blackness. They both found themselves staring at the factory. Darren finally broke the silence.

"Should we go in and check it out?"

"Are you out of your fuckin' mind? I ain't goin' in there."

As they stood in the blood puddle debating whether or not to go inside, they heard a sound resembling a scream. It was very quiet and easily could have been a rat or a bat. They didn't move from their spot and continued to go over their options. The lights from a passing car caught their attention and they both turned to see. They never imagined they would want the police to come to their office, but it would be just fine with them at this point. While they watched the road, a gust of wind swept by the two boys, swinging the doors of the factory open. The screech of the metal on the floor scared both boys half to death.

Without any argument, they ran as fast as they could to Darren's car, just as they did the previous night.

"C'mon! C'mon! C'mon!" Darren yelled as he floored the gas pedal. He turned the ignition until finally it caught. Darren slammed the car into drive and peeled off down Route 33.

There in the trees, not far from where the car had been parked,

stood the man who killed Adam, wielding a switchblade. Another
minute longer and there would have been two more missing souls
from Alden's already diminishing population.

Chapter Eleven

When Will and Shannon broke up almost five years ago, it was an amicable separation. They had dated for three years in high school. And although they had their disagreements and fought from time to time, they both wondered if they would end up together. They didn't break up because they fell out of love, but rather, they grew up and further apart.

She was the one who suggested they go their separate ways before heading off to college. Will was going to Boston, she was headed off to Jacksonville. Trying to keep that type of long-distance relationship alive and healthy would be almost impossible, and Will agreed. It was difficult for both of them at first, especially Will. He wanted to try the long-distance relationship, so leaving her behind was tough. He didn't date much his first two years at college, until Mira came along. She introduced him to his heart-felt emotions for the second time.

As they drove to the restaurant, they both sat quietly, neither of them knowing exactly what to say. Will had moved on and so did Shannon. And although Will had the perfect girl waiting for him, he always wanted to hear that Shannon was having problems finding Mr. Right.

They arrived at the restaurant and pulled into the parking lot. They got to the door and Will got there first and held the door open for Shannon. As he stepped through the door, a gentleman bumped into Will sending him back a step. The two looked at each other with menacing glares, but both continued on their respective ways. Will didn't recognize him, but was a step away from following him out the door.

"Who was that?" Shannon asked.

"I don't know. I've been away too long, I guess."

The two sat down in a booth and ordered their meals. Again, their was an awkward silence, so Will decided he would start the conversation.

"So how did you hear about Eric?"

"Well, my aunt still lives on Lake Avenue, so she called me as soon as she heard."

"And you just got in your car and drove twenty-some-odd hours to get here for a funeral, hang out for a few hours and drive back?"

"I had some personal days coming, so I used 'em. As for why I came back, I can't imagine not being here. I grew up for three years in your house, practically. He was like my little brother, too. Plus, I love both you and your mom. I came back to show my support to the both of you."

"Well, thank you very much for coming back. It means a lot to both me and my mother to see you here. It lets us know there are people out there who haven't forgotten us." Will looked down at the table.

Shannon paused before speaking. "So, have you heard from your father since Eric's death?"

"No, I haven't. I'm assuming my Uncle Chris told him about it, but then again, I haven't even heard from Uncle Chris. I'm hoping he stays away because I don't know if I can handle seeing him right now."

Will leaned back in the booth and rubbed his eyes. He desperately needed to change the subject.

"So how are your parents doing?" he asked.

"They're good. My dad's retiring next year and my mother is spending a lot of time at church. My sister is getting married in a few months, so, we're very busy."

"So, any marriage plans in the near future for you?"

"No, not really. I'm kind of seeing someone right now, but I don't think he's the one I'm looking for. I guess we'll see how things progress," she said. "What about you, I hear you're seeing someone?"

They continued on with small talk for about two hours, reminiscing and laughing, before finally heading off for home. Will didn't want the evening to end, but he knew it had to. He had to be up early to prepare himself for the long day ahead and the hours were slipping away. Shannon left the car running as Will got out.

"After the funeral tomorrow, do you want to get together for lunch or something?" Shannon asked.

"Yeah, that sounds good. I'll see you tomorrow morning and we'll make plans then."

"Okay. Good luck tomorrow."

Shannon gave Will a long hug. Will walked slowly into the house and waited for Shannon to drive out of sight. As the tail lights faded, Will thought about what might have happened if Mira was not in the picture. It was then that Will realized he had forgotten to call Mira. It would take a lot of explaining to calm her down.

Chapter *Twelve*

Back at the Janzforth factory, things were finally quiet. In the past few nights, the old building saw more activity than it had since it shut down.

It was now in the early morning hours, and there weren't many cars on the road. In the factory there was just a single torch lit. There were now three people in the building, the long-haired man, the shorter man and Matt.

The two men were deep in the basement of the building where the long-haired man was sitting in an old rocking chair. He was staring at a map of the town that was tacked up to the wall. The other man was seated next to the man.

"How many were there tonight," the man asked.

"There were two at first, the one I killed and the one we've got. The other two who showed up were the two burnouts that were here the day before. I scared them off, though."

The man leaned forward and rubbed his face. He thought for a moment before finally speaking. "Those two are becoming a problem. Not to mention, they might have seen the blood out front of the building."

"Don't worry. The next time they come back will be the last."

"And what if they come back during the day? What then? If they come while the sun's up, I'm dead. Did you padlock the doors?"

"Yes. And don't worry, I'll be here during the day to make sure no one gets to you. You had better hide your coffin, though."

52

"You just make sure no one gets in and I'll take care of those two bastards myself."

On the first floor, Matt came to in a room nearly pitch black. His head was pounding, his hair damp with his own blood. His hands and feet were tied to the chair and his mouth had been covered with tape. Matt's heart began to pound. He tried to wriggle free of the rope binding him to the chair.

He stopped suddenly when he saw a light coming from down the hall. As the light got brighter, he started to hear footsteps getting closer. Matt's heart started pounding faster, his breaths getting shorter and shorter. He wondered if this would be the end.

Finally, the dark figure that killed Adam was now standing in the doorway holding a lantern. He made his way towards Matt stopping to get a chair. He pulled the chair over by Matt and sat down facing Matt, about two feet away from him. The figure proceeded to speak to Matt.

"You and your friends need to find a new place to hang out. Two more of your friends showed up after you and had they stayed around for a few more minutes, they would be down here with you. You see, the next time they decide to come around here, they will join you as one of the undead."

Matt's eyes got large.

"Oh, you probably, don't realize why you're here. Don't worry, we're not holding you for ransom or anything like that. No, no. You're here for a greater purpose than even you can imagine. An uprising has begun. The undead are no longer sleeping. You are about to join the world's newest army. And you will meet your maker tomorrow. Enjoy the sun. It will be the last time you see it."

The man rose from the chair and left the room. Matt watched as the light got dimmer and dimmer and he lost the sound of the footsteps. As much as his head hurt, as much as his stomach was churning, he could not fall back asleep. He did not want to see the sunlight, for it would mean he was one day closer to the end of his life.

Chapter Thirteen

Will had gotten home later than he planned the night before the funeral, and then had to call Mira and spend an hour apologizing and telling her how much he loved her. Did he tell her where he was the night before? No. He would tell her the next time he saw her. He knew he couldn't tell her over the phone. There's no way he could explain himself to her. So, he told her he was out with the guys and lost track of time. Did she buy it? Not really, but she didn't give him any grief for it … not yet.

Will's alarm clock went off, and he rolled over and hit the snooze. He knew he had to get up and get ready for the funeral, but he was exhausted. This would be without a doubt in his mind one of the toughest days of his life. He couldn't wait for the funeral to be over and for his brother to be laid to rest for the final time.

Will finally convinced himself to get out of bed and start his day. He leaned over and shut the alarm off and sat on the end of the bed rubbing his eyes. Unlike the morning the day before, there were no breakfast smells floating up into his room. There was no clatter of pans and skillets. His mother was not listening to the oldies station on the radio. Even the weather was different; there was no sun, just rain hitting the window. Perfect, Will thought. Let's stand out in the elements while Eric's final rites are said. As if the day wasn't going to be tough enough.

After Will showered, shaved and got dressed, he went to go downstairs to grab a bite to eat. On his way down the upstairs hallway, Will stopped and took a stroll around Eric's room. He looked at the pictures on the wall, checked out the books on the desk, and even checked for the porno mags Will gave to him that Eric had hidden in the floorboards under the bed. Still there.

Will thought about all the times he and Eric stayed up in his room talking about life, girls, the divorce. He sat down on the bed and noticed a yearbook on the floor just a foot away. He leaned over and thumbed through it. He found Eric's picture, Lindsay's picture and even read some of the notes some of the guys wrote in the book. Most of them were guys on the football team talking about how great the upcoming season was going to be. There was a message from Lindsay that Will did not read out of courtesy to his brother that took up half the page. And on the back page of the yearbook, there was a note in a girls handwriting that caught Will's eye. It was like she had a crush on him. Will was proud of Eric. He had taught his younger brother well.

Will shut the book and got off the bed. He left the room and made his way downstairs. He went into the front room and sat down in the recliner. It was about twenty after nine and Will and his mother were already running late. Will turned on the TV and checked the baseball scores. He was a wannabe sportswriter after all and he had to keep up on what was going on. After a minute or two, Will yelled through the house to his mother.

"Mom, c'mon, let's go! We're already late!"

"I'm almost ready."

After sitting through a few commercials, Will's mother came into the room dressed and ready to go. She was wearing a black suit with her sunglasses on. Her nose was red, and Will knew she had been up all night sobbing. He figured if nothing else, this would all be behind them in a matter of hours.

As the two drove to the funeral home, neither spoke. No one really knew what to say. Will was still a bit worried about Mira and what he would say when he saw her, and Will's mother was preoccupied with how she was going to handle the day.

They arrived at the funeral home and pulled up to the door. Mr. Neumann helped Will's mother out of the car and after Will got out, Neumann pulled the car around back. Will walked his mother into the room where Eric was being laid out and the two went directly to the coffin. Will's mother knelt down and prayed while Will stood next to the coffin and said a few words of his own to God. After a minute's worth of silence, Will's mother got up and stood with Will, looking at Eric.

"I picked out his suit. It always did fit him perfectly," Will's mother said.

"Mom, it's the only suit he owned."

"Well I coordinated his outfit for today. I'm stylish, you know."

Will was pleasantly surprised to see his mother was able to crack a joke at a time like this.

"What time is the prayer service?" Will asked.

"Ten-thirty. People should be getting here any minute now."

Sure enough, Will and his mother waited in the middle of the room, greeting and talking to people, thanking them for showing their support. Will knew most of the people who came through the door, but anyone he didn't know, his mother identified. And when Lindsay showed up, she told Will who all of the students were. Some of Will's old high school buddies came in and Will told them all the same thing: "See you later at the bar." Will thought how great it was to see so many familiar faces and how overwhelming it was to see so many people in the town showing their support to Will's family.

The room filled. It was approaching ten-thirty. Will finished making his rounds with all of the people there when he noticed an older man enter the room. The man was clean-shaven and his skin was wrinkled around his eyes. He wore a blue suit and glasses. It took a second for Will to realize who it was, but when he did, he made a direct line for the door. As Will got closer to the man, he could almost taste the nicotine. He grabbed the man by the arm and pulled him outside the room.

"What in the hell are you doing here?"

"Well it's good to see you too, Will."

"I think it'd be a good idea if you got the hell out of here."

"You listen to me, buddy. That's my son lying there and I have every right to be here. So why don't you loosen up."

"You have no right to be here. You gave up that right the moment you walked out of our lives."

Will took a look around and realized that his voice was rising and everyone in the room was looking at him, including his mother. She had a look of horror on her face. Will took his father outside.

"Why did you come here, really? I mean, you wanted nothing to do with us while you were alive. Why do you care now?"

"He's my son. And I'd do the same for you. I should be here."

"Bullshit! You walked out and didn't come back."

"I didn't think you'd want me around."

"What in the fuck are you talking about? Why would we not want you around? We both looked up to you. We needed you."

Will's dad stood in silence. Will could tell he caught his father off guard with that one. After a brief pause, he finally figured out what to say.

"I wanted to come back and see you guys. I mean, I thought about it all the time. But I felt I needed to change my life ... my whole life. I'm sorry."

"Well congratulations, you succeeded. You changed your life to the point your sons didn't have a father anymore."

Will's dad just stared at Will.

"Just, just get the hell out here. You're not welcome here," Will said as he started to choke up.

"Fine, fine. I'll go. But I do still want to talk to you. I'm not leaving this town without talking you first."

Will stared him down. He watched as his father got into his truck and drove off, back down Route 33. Will wasn't sad anymore; he was furious. All he wanted to do was hit his father, but now was not the time or the place.

Mark came outside. "Hey, you gonna be all right?" Mark said.

"That was the one thing I did not need today. I mean, what in the hell was he thinking showing his face here now?"

"He was Eric's father, Will."

Will turned and glared at Mark. "Oh, really, Mark. In what way was he a father to us? Was he a father when he walked out on us not to be heard from again for almost ten years?"

"I'm sorry, man. I'm just trying to help."

"I know. I know you didn't mean anything by that."

Will and Mark went back inside. Everyone was talking again, including Will's mother. She was with her sister, Janet, looking like she had just seen a ghost. Will went over to her first.

"Was that your father?" she said

"Yeah, but don't worry. He's not coming back here."

"What do you mean?"

"Don't worry about it. I told him he's not welcome here and that he should get out of town. He's not coming back here," Will said with just a hint of anger.

The priest started the service, but Will wasn't paying attention. He had too much on his mind now. Before he knew it, the service was over and it was off to the cemetery. Will and his mother didn't say a word to each other on their way to St. Stanislaus Cemetery, just five minutes from home.

The repetitive swing of the windshield wipers nearly put Will into a trance. It seemed fitting that it was a rainy, dreary day. Will's mother sat in the passenger seat motionless, totally zapped of emotion and energy. They pulled into the drive at the cemetery, and it seemed as though each was waiting for the other to get out of the car first. Will got out first and opened the door for his mother.

The people filed into the cemetery one car after another, until cars were parked out in the street. The circle surrounding the casket was at least six to seven people deep. Will's mother, her sister and Will himself were seated directly across from the priest. While Will's mother and sister were hiding from the rain under an umbrella, Will let the rain hit him.

Among those in attendance were all of Will's mother's church buddies, Will's high school friends, Eric's classmates, and, partially hidden behind a tree, Will's father.

Will did his best to pay attention to the prayers being said and to the ones he was spouting off in his mind, but there was too much going on. And to top it off, it seemed as though everyone there was looking directly at him. Will didn't really care to be the center of attention. Will looked around; he noticed that a lot of people weren't staring at him but instead were tearing up, wiping their eyes, glancing at the wet ground.

Shannon was there, crying. Mark was there, fumbling with his hat doing his best to figure out what to make of Eric's case. It started raining a little harder now and the priest was praying a bit faster. Will was still checking out the crowd when something caught his eye: one of Eric's classmates was smirking, as though she were laughing. Will had no clue who she was. He then looked at his mother, who was sobbing uncontrollably at this point.

The service ended. People left the cemetery as quickly as they arrived. There was to be a funeral breakfast at the fire hall in town, but Will was in no hurry to go. He was soaking wet, and in any event, his mother's car was the first car in line (other than the hearse, of course). Will's mother and her sister said their last goodbyes which left Will as the last man standing at the grave site.

The rain had subsided a little bit, but it was still enough to hide Will's tears. He didn't throw a rose on the coffin like his mother did, but he did place his hand on the lid. Will thought for a moment and then said the first thing that came to mind. "You were the best brother a guy could ask for. I'm gonna miss you, man. Hell, I missed you before all this happened. When I get my revenge I'll stand over his grave and smile. And you'll be there with me."

Will took his hand off the coffin and made his way to his mother's car. They drove to Alden Vol. Fire Hall No. 2 for the breakfast, Will thinking about the young girl laughing at the cemetery. He couldn't get her face out of his mind. The more he tried to forget about it, the more he saw her face, that smile. His mother was talking, but Will had no idea about what. He didn't even know who she was talking to.

"Mom, I think I'm gonna drop you guys off at the hall and go home. I wanna get out of these clothes and then I'll meet you there," Will said.

"All right. But hurry up. Not everybody wants to wait for you."

"Okay, I'll only be a few minutes," Will said as he parked the car in front of the building. He kissed her on the cheek and headed for home.

Will sped home, pulled in the driveway and ran into the house. He closed and locked the door, but didn't even take his coat off as he ran upstairs to Eric's room. Once inside, he made a bee-line for the bookcase with all of Eric's yearbooks on it.

He found Eric's most recent yearbook and began to thumb through it. He scanned each page of student portraits trying to find a match for the girl with the smile at the cemetery. Freshman class, no luck. Sophomores, nothing there. Juniors, nothing there either. Seniors, no matches found.

Will was about to close the book when he remembered that one of the girls at Eric's school seemed to have a crush on him. He found the note and read the name: Angela. Will again went through the book, class by class, girl by girl. There were only two Angelas in the entire school and neither one even closely resembled the girl at the cemetery.

Will headed to his room and changed into a more comfortable outfit. He headed outside and ran to the car. He drove to the fire hall and made his way inside. Shannon was standing outside the gymnasium and approached Will as soon as she saw him.

"Hey, Will. I hope you don't mind but I'm gonna head over to my aunt's house for a little while. I haven't had a chance to visit with her yet," she said.

"Yeah. That's cool. I'll be here for a while. I'll call you later after I get out of here."

"Yeah, we'll get a coffee or something before I head back."

"See ya later."

Will walked in and met up with Mark. He was standing by himself next to the door as though acting as the bouncer.

"Hey, there you are. How are you holding up?" Mark asked

"I'm all right. Mark, did you notice the one girl at the funeral? She had a black coat on with a white shirt on under it, strawberry blonde hair, no makeup on. Do you know her? I think she was a student."

"Yeah. She and her family are new in town. Her name's Angela Raines. Her father is a military man, so the family's on the go a lot," Mark said. "Why do you ask?"

"To be honest, I saw her laughing at the funeral."

"You saw her laughing?"

"Well, she wasn't laughing hysterically, but she was definitely giggling a little bit. I mean, maybe someone told her a joke, but you don't giggle at a good joke, do you?"

"Well I wouldn't," Mark said. "Dude, there could be a million reasons why she was smiling. If you're thinking she's a suspect, I'd have to tell you you're crazy. Her family's a bit different, but she's a sweet girl."

"I think she had a thing for Eric though."

"What makes you say that?" Mark asked.

"I found Eric's yearbook from this past school year and, well, I found a note from a girl named Angela that sounded like she had a crush on him."

"I suppose we could talk to her, but she's not the answer."

"You're probably right."

Mark hesitated for asking his next question, enough so that he put a warning label on the question.

"Will, don't get pissed at what I'm about to ask you, but, do you think it's possible that your father is a suspect?"

"It's not a bad idea, but I don't think he cared enough about either Eric or myself to come back here and kill us."

"Do you want me to question him?"

"No. No, don't bother. He'd just lie to you."

"All right, man."

For the remainder of the afternoon, Will stayed at the breakfast and chatted with old high school buddies, old family friends and did his best to forget about all the evil that had happened to him and his mother in the past four days.

Chapter Fourteen

Matt awoke for the second time in the factory, still tied up in the chair, but with the sunlight he was able to make out some of the objects in the room. Matt tried to get out of the chair but the more he struggled to get free of the knots, the tighter they got. He figured that he might as well save his strength for the time when he might be untied from the chair.

As he scanned the room, there were still some things he couldn't quite make out, for the light in the room was coming through only two sets of windows. In the far corner of the room, it looked like there was a desk, with one of the legs missing. And about ten feet to Matt's left it looked like there was another chair, but again, another leg was gone.

Almost right in front of Matt was what looked like a wallet. He did his best to jump and lunge the chair forward a few feet. As got closer, the chair tipped and Matt found himself eating dirt. The wallet was now right in front of his face. He sat perfectly still for a second and listened to hear if anyone was coming down the hallway. There was that same eerie silence. Matt nudged the wallet open with his nose and looked at the driver's license. It belonged to a boy from Ohio who had just turned sixteen.

Why was there a license from a kid in Ohio in the Janzforth factory? Matt's mind was working so hard that he didn't hear the footsteps coming from down the hall. He closed his eyes and acted as though he were sleeping.

Someone was now in the room. Matt's breathing got heavier and heavier. He sat still as a statue.

The man from the night before was there again and this time didn't say a word. The man kicked Matt in the arm and told him to wake up. "Wake up, asshole! And how did you get on the floor?"

Matt said nothing, just lay there.

The man got more abusive. He grabbed Matt violently by the arms and set the chair up straight.

"You know, it's a shame the chair didn't fall back the other way," the man said.

The man grabbed the chair by each arm and spun it around. Matt's cry was all the man needed to hear.

Matt could do nothing but gasp in horror. What he saw scared him more than seeing Adam get run through the night before. There, hung from the wall by rope and nails, was Adam's body. It was stretched out as if it was hung on a cross. His body had been mutilated. There were gashes on the wrists and neck. His face was a pale blue with his eyes still open gazing right at Matt.

The man stood behind Matt as though proud of his work, and he leaned in slowly right over Matt's right shoulder.

"If I come in here and find you on the floor again, you will look exactly like your friend. Just stay put and you'll never feel pain again."

The man left the room, leaving Matt all alone facing his best friend's body. Matt wasn't sobbing, but rather, breathing short breaths, doing his best to calm down. He couldn't figure out what was worse: ending up like Adam or meeting the fate promised to him by the man …

Chapter Fifteen

It was a little after five when Shannon arrived at Will's house to pick him up. The previous four hours drained him; fake smiles for people he didn't know, more handshakes than he'd given in three or four years and another quiet ride home with Mom. The two knew they had gotten through the worst of it and perhaps that's why they kept quiet. They had finally laid Eric to rest and could now move on with their lives. There was no need to dredge up the past, in particular, the murder.

Seeing Shannon made Will happy for some reason. He had Mira back in Boston and Shannon had a guy down in Florida. And yet, five years later, it was like they were dating again. As she pulled in the driveway, Will was outside sitting on the front porch. The rain had stopped and the sun was breaking through the last few remaining rain clouds.

"How was the breakfast?" Shannon asked.

"Oh, it was great," Will said rolling his eyes. "I can't figure out what was worse, sitting through a funeral or sitting in a room with people I don't want to see pretending to like them for a few hours."

"C'mon, it couldn't have been that bad."

"Please. I shouldn't even be talking to you after that crap you pulled. 'I gotta go. I gotta hang out with my aunt.' Thanks for leaving me there with all of the old people."

"I'll make it up to you right now. Let's go."

"Where are we going?"

"Get in the damn car," she said, doing her best to sound tough.

Will got into the car and sat patiently, waiting to see where she was going to take him. While he sat, a thousand thoughts ran through his head. He thought about the first time they met, the first kiss, the first breakup, and, more with the times, what might happen over the course of the next few hours. What if she went in to kiss him? What if she spilled her heart out to him? What if he spilled his heart out to her? Thankfully, she broke the silence.

"So is your girlfriend still talking to you?"

"I don't know," Will said, making Shannon laugh. "She was pretty pissed at me last night, but she at least told me to call her today. That's gotta be a good sign."

"Close your eyes. I don't want you to see where we're going."

After a few minutes and a few twists and turns, Shannon parked the car and got out. She told him to keep his eyes shut. She then opened his car door and helped him out. Still his eyes were shut. Finally, after about thirty paces, they stopped.

"Okay. Open 'em."

Will opened his eyes and was surprised to see he was standing on the high school football field. He hadn't been here since graduation. It hadn't changed a bit.

"Um, why are we here? I could be wrong, but, I don't think we're gonna get a meal with service and a smile here."

"God, stop thinking with your stomach. Please tell me you haven't forgotten the significance of this spot?"

"Don't worry, I remember why we're here. This is where I made the game-saving tackle against Lancaster."

Shannon hit his arm. "Try again."

"This is where we first kissed the night after that game."

"Very good. I'm surprised you remembered. You probably don't remember our anniversary date, though."

"September fourteenth," Will said without missing a beat.

"Where on earth did you pull that from, your ass?"

"Despite the fact that I wasn't exactly thrilled with you dumping me without a reason, I still remember everything we went through. I mean, how could I forget. You were the first."

"Yeah, I am. I just figured you went off to college and left our memories behind."

"That was the plan. I went off to school and instead of leaving you here in my past, I took you with me to Boston. It took a full year for me to get over you."

Will looked off towards the sun. He had never talked about the breakup before, not even with Eric.

Shannon was speechless after his last statement.

"I'm sorry. I don't hate you for what happened. I just never really got over the fact that we weren't going to be together. And seeing you and being here, I don't know. I just thought I was over you forever, and now, I see you and the feelings all come rushing back."

Shannon again said nothing. The two stood at the twenty-yard line staring at each other, neither knowing what to say. Shannon took a step towards Will.

As their lips were about lock, Will stopped and looked down. As long as he waited for this moment, he couldn't go through with it.

"Um, I'm sorry, Shannon. I can't. We both shouldn't be doing this."

"I know. You're right. I guess I wanted to see if the spark was still there."

"Don't get me wrong. If there was anyone I would love to be with other than Mira, it's you. But I can't hurt her like this."

Shannon looked off at the car and then looked back at Will. "She's lucky. Most guys I know would have gone for it."

Will said nothing and the two walked back to the car.

"We're still going to dinner, right?" Will asked.

Shannon looked at him with a grin. "Yes, we're still going."

Chapter Sixteen

Matt was exhausted. He spent several hours of the daylight trying in vain to get out of the ropes that kept him in the chair. The other hours that were left were spent trying to figure out what was going to happen to him when the sun went down. Having to look at Adam's body wasn't helping to put Matt's mind at ease.

The dimmer the light got in the room, the more settled Matt's stomach got. He had convinced himself that he couldn't wait to meet his fate, for at the very least, it would get him out of the chair. He had it down to two options: a) He would die and it would all be over, or b) he would get his chance to escape.

The sunlight was almost gone, or as best as Matt could tell. Darkness had just about filled the room and Matt wondered how long it would be before he met his "new master." Matt wondered what in the hell that could possibly mean. Was he going to have his identity erased and become a slave? Were they going to kidnap him and take him to Ohio?

Matt also wondered if he would get the chance to see the man's face. He wanted just one good look at the guy who killed his friend.

Down in the other end of the building, the man was back in the old cafeteria, standing over what looked like a coffin. He reached out his arm and opened the box. The long-haired man was in the box and opened his eyes.

"The sun has set. It's time for the army to grow," said the short man.

"Take me to him," the man said. "Has everything been prepared?"

"Everything has been arranged."

"Perfect. I'll be there in a moment. I have to get ready to meet our guest."

The short man left the room and headed down the hall. He took a left and went directly towards the room Matt was in.

Matt didn't see a light coming, but he heard the footsteps. For the first time since his capture, he wasn't scared. He was looking forward to the opportunity to confront the man.

The short man appeared in the doorway and flipped a switch on the wall. The lights flickered and hummed with an electronic buzz. The lights gave off a smell as though they were burning. Who knew what had died on top of those bulbs?

Matt was all set to give the man a verbal beating, when something in the doorway caught his attention. He had been pushing a small cart with some objects on it. There was a cup on one end, a knife on the other.

"Good evening," said the man.

"Shut up, asshole," Matt said.

The man stood in the doorway, apparently shocked by Matt's response. Matt couldn't tell because his had the mask on again.

"What, you didn't think I'd give you any shit? Why don't you take that fucking mask off and face me man to man?"

Matt heard a voice come from where the man was standing, but it wasn't his. It was a deeper voice, one that was totally unfamiliar to Matt.

"Because I'm the one you're gonna face man to man."

The long-haired man walked out from behind the other man and made his way across the room to where Matt was sitting. All of the confidence that Matt had built up had disappeared in no time flat.

The long-hired man looked at Matt for a moment before striking him with a backhand slap across the face. It bloodied Matt's lip. He then looked at Matt with concern.

"I apologize for striking you," he said. He turned around and waved the other man into the room. "I heard the way you talked to my family here and I got upset. But in a matter of minutes you too will be part of our family and I will never, never have to hit you again."

Matt stared at the man with a glassy look in his eyes, trying to figure out why he was being so polite.

"You see, we're starting a revolution here. It's been a few years in the making, but we're ready to take off. In mere moments, you will become one of the undead. I am going to give you everlasting life, killing those who get in your way, bringing others to me to help our army grow. Your town is going to be the first of many to succumb to my powers. And you're one of my first recruits."

The short man moved the cart right next to Matt and stood behind him. The long-haired man bowed his head and said something to himself that resembled a prayer over the cup. He then took the cup and put it to Matt's lips. The short man grabbed Matt's head and tilted it back. He lifted the cup and poured the liquid over Matt's lips. The fluid looked and tasted like blood, but there was definitely something strange in it.

The short man let go of Matt's head. The long-haired man stood by the cart for a few minutes as Matt became sleepy. It was getting harder and harder for Matt to keep his eyes open. He had no idea what was in the blood, but it went straight to his brain. He started seeing things, hallucinations, and then had to do his best to make out what the long-haired man was saying to him.

"You're ready now. You've been prepared for the end of your mortal life and the beginning of a new, fuller, better life."

He took a few steps towards Matt until he was standing directly over him. Matt saw it now. Two of the man's front teeth were very long and very sharp. That was the last thing Matt saw before the man bent down and plunged those long, sharp teeth into his neck …

Chapter Seventeen

Shannon pulled the car into the driveway at Will's mother's house and put it into park.

"Do you want to come in for a few minutes?" Will asked.

"I would, but I've got a long drive ahead of me."

"Yeah, I understand. Thank you so much for coming in. If nothing else, you helped take my mind off Eric and the murder. I can't thank you enough."

"Will, I wouldn't have missed it. He was like my brother, too."

"Well, drive home safe. And don't be a stranger. If you're ever in Beantown, gimme a call. I can show you around."

"You can come down to Florida, too, ya know."

"Get out of here," Will said.

The two didn't hug or kiss. They simply looked at each other. Will then got out of the car and stood at the end of the driveway until she left. He stared at the car until it was out of sight, wondering if letting her go again was the best thing to do.

Will went up to the house and was about to go inside, but decided to sit out on the front steps and take in the night air. He thought about their moment on the football field and wondered if he should have kissed her. What if Mira wasn't the one? Then he'd have lost both girls without a kiss goodbye.

He was knocked out of his brainstorm by a set of headlights pulling into the driveway. It was Mark in his black pick-up truck. He got out and walked over towards Will.

"Hey, man. Ready to go? The guys are already down there."

"Yeah. You're timing couldn't have been more perfect. Shannon just left."

"She's going back to Florida already?"

"Yeah. She could only get so many days off," Will said.

"How did you leave it with her?"

"We're both going to go on with our lives without the other in it for now. Who knows, maybe we'll get back together someday. But it'll be awhile."

The two got into the truck and drove off to Neighbors' Bar. It was probably the classiest tavern in Alden, but that really wasn't saying much. Will was used to the bars and pubs in Boston, but a trip back to the old bar sounded like a great way to spend time with his old high school buddies.

Mark and Will walked into the bar and were flagged down immediately by three men sitting at a table in the back corner. Will noticed Hank first. He looked the same as when Will last saw him almost three years earlier. His hair was a dirty blonde, his face cleanly shaven. He was about the same height as Will and his blue eyes were what people almost always noticed first. Next to Hank was Jack Watson. Will hadn't seen him since graduation and the only real difference was a little less hair and a goatee. Will never cared much for Jack, but he was tolerable, especially if only for a few hours. And sitting to the far right of the table was Rod Jankowski. He was one of Will's closest friends in high school, but the two lost touch once Will left for school. He was short, with light-brown hair and glasses. He was married now and a teacher at Alden High School.

Will got to the table and shook hands with all of them. They all had attended the funeral, but Will did not get an opportunity to talk with them at all. As the first couple hours flew by, the five touched on a bevy of topics, ranging from what they were up to now, to their high school mischief, to their love lives.

"I'm telling you guys, married life is the best life," Rod said as he leaned back on his chair and put his hands behind his head. "I don't have to worry about dating and break ups, and I can get some whenever I want some."

"Or whenever she lets you," Jack said.

"Hey, fuck you, dickhead. Your girlfriend doesn't even like you," Rod said with a smile.

"What about you, Will? Getting hitched any time soon?" asked Hank.

"I don't know. I've got a girlfriend back in Boston, but I'm not sure …"

"Why not?" Rod asked.

Mark jumped in before Will could answer. "Because Shannon was in town and it totally fucked with his head."

Will glared at Mark for a moment and then gave his answer. "You know, seeing Shannon did bring back some memories, but I think it gave me more of a longing for Mira. It sounds weird, but I have a greater appreciation for her now that I haven't seen her for a few days."

"Well if you love her, you better marry her before she gets away," Rod said.

"Shut up, Hoss. What if she did leave? It would only prove that she wasn't the one and that Will was right in waiting," said Jack. "There are other fish in the sea."

That simple statement hit Will like a bolt of lightning. There are other fish in the sea, Will thought. He got out of his chair and gave each of the guys a handshake. "Gotta run guys. I forgot that I have to pick up my mother from my aunt's."

Will and Mark got outside the bar and before Will could get into the truck, Mark stopped him. "What the hell was that about?"

"Dude, I'll explain it on the way. But we gotta get to Lindsay's house, pronto."

"Lindsay's house? Why are we going over there?"

As the two drove to the Adams' house Will did his best to explain his theory to Mark. "What Jack said got me to thinking. 'Other fish in the sea.' What if there was someone who figured with Eric out of the picture, Lindsay would look for another fish in the sea? We have to talk to her and find out if there was anyone who had a thing for her."

"Will, what if she doesn't know if anyone had a thing for her?"

"Then we haven't lost anything. But if she does know, well, we're on to something."

It was after one in the morning when Mark and Will finally got to Lindsay's. The house was totally dark. Will got out and rang the doorbell. No one answered at first. After a minute or two, the front porch light finally came on. Lindsay answered the door.

"Will? What are you doing here? Hank is out at the bar," she said, half asleep.

"I know. I'm not looking for Hank. I'm here to talk to you."

"Lindsay, do you mind if we ask you a few questions, you know, about the murder?" Mark asked.

Lindsay stepped out of the house and sat on the porch swing. "No, no. Go ahead, if you think it will help."

"Lindsay, was there anyone at school or anywhere else here in town that liked you? I mean, really liked you?" asked Will.

"I'm not sure I know what you mean?"

"Is there anybody who wanted to date you or wanted Eric and you to breakup so they could be with you?" Will asked.

"Wait, wait, wait. Are you saying that someone killed Eric to be with me? That's completely stupid."

Mark glanced at Will. "Yes, it is."

"Listen. I'm supposed to be leaving tomorrow. We have absolutely no leads. Yes, it sounds ridiculous. But we have nothing else to go on. And I don't care how crazy it sounds. People have been killed for lesser things," Will said.

"Well, there were guys who were friends who maybe wanted to be more than that, but no one who came right out and said it."

"Did Eric have any enemies who might want to get him out of the picture?" Will asked.

"Not that I can think of. He was pretty popular. Most of the students liked him."

"What do you know about Angela Raines?"

"Oh, God, that bitch. Okay, I forgot about her. She's one person I really didn't get along with. When she first came to our school, she had the biggest crush on Eric, tried to go out with him and everything. Finally, I confronted her and told her to leave him alone."

"Did it work?" asked Mark.

"Yeah, she pretty much kept away from Eric after that. She's pretty harmless, though. I mean, I got in her face and she backed right down. I thought she was gonna cry."

Will and Mark looked at each other with the same look: the look of frustration. Will thought for sure he had found something to go on, but instead found nothing.

"Alright. Thanks for your help. Go on and go back to bed," Will said.

Will and Mark made their way down the steps and were headed back to the truck when Lindsay came back out of the house again.

"Guys wait!" she yelled. "There's something I forgot to tell you."

"What's that?" Mark asked.

"There was one person that tried to ask me out once. He was a total stoner, I'm sure you know him, Mark. Darren Banyon."

"That loser?" Mark said in disbelief.

"Who's that?" asked Will.

"He's a regular offender in this town. Pretty much a burnout. Gets into all kinds off smalltime trouble: drugs, drinking. He's a real suspect," Mark said.

"Lindsay, thank you very much," Will said.

The two got back into the truck and sat for a minute in silence. Just the way they moved let the other know they may have a case after all. There was a sense of excitement in the air, a sense of purpose now.

"I can't question him until tomorrow, but I'll go over to his place and talk to him," Mark said.

"I'm gonna call the paper back in Boston tomorrow and let them know that I'm staying here indefinitely," said Will. "I've got a good feeling about this."

Chapter Eighteen

The following morning, Will made his phone call to the paper in Boston to let them know he was taking an extended leave of absence. He told his editor that he was in the middle of a homicide investigation and that he was needed to help the police catch his brother's killer. He asked for another two weeks.

Will grabbed a quick bite to eat and was on his way out the door when his mother came into the kitchen.

"I heard you come in pretty late last night. Have a good time with the boys?"

"Yeah, it was good seeing those guys again. We had a lot of catching up to do."

"Mira called last night. She said that she wasn't supposed to talk to you yesterday, but that she had some important news to tell you."

"Did she say what it was?"

"No. She just said she'll talk to you later."

Will did not respond and began putting his coat on.

"Who were you on the phone with?"

"My boss at the paper. I'm gonna be staying for another couple weeks."

"What for? Don't you have to make some kind of money?"

"Yes, Mother. Mark and I, though, we want to put a little more work into this before closing the door. We're exploring some potential leads."

Will's mother always got the same look on her face when she

got upset. She would tilt her head a little bit, roll her eyes and the pitch in her voice would get a little higher. "Why are you going to go messing around in that? Let the police handle it."

"Mom, I will let them handle it in two weeks. I can't go running off to Boston without looking into every possible angle."

"And what does Mira think about this? Did you happen to tell her about how much time you and Shannon spent together?"

"Mira will find out tonight about my staying here another two weeks. And, no, she doesn't know about Shannon because she doesn't have to know about Shannon. What she doesn't know can't hurt her, so keep your mouth shut about that."

"Hey, don't tell me what to do. You're going to hurt that girl, and when you do, you're going to lose her. Be honest with her."

"Bye, Mother. I'll be back later on tonight." Will slammed the front door. He hated it when his mother got confrontational with him. They both had the same stubborn personality, so they knocked heads when they got upset. Will knew the best thing to do was just to get out of the house. That way, she could cool off and he could get on with more important things.

Will took his mother's car and drove down to the station. Along the way, he passed the man he bumped shoulders with at the restaurant a few nights earlier when with Shannon. He was walking along the side of the road. The two exchanged glances.

As Will arrived at the station, Mark was already sitting out in his patrol car waiting for Will.

"C'mon, get in," Mark said.

Will got in the car and put his seatbelt on. "Are we going to Darren's house."

"Yeah. I already talked to the chief and he gave us the green light to go over to his house and question him."

The two left the station and drove down Route 33 for a few miles. They then took a right and went down a long, winding dirt road for about five minutes. There, on the right hand side of the road, was what looked like a shack. It hadn't been painted in years, the shutters were hanging off the house, and the yard hadn't been mowed in quite some time.

Mark pulled the car into the driveway, nothing more than a few stones and gravel and parked it next to the house. The two got out and knocked on the side door. A woman came to the door in her robe with a cigarette in her hand. "What do you boys want?"

"Sorry to bother you, ma'am. Is Darren around?" Mark asked.

"Is he in some kinda trouble?"

"We hope not. We just want to ask him a few questions."

She turned around and screamed for Darren. "Darren! Darren! Get your ass out here! The police are here to take your sorry ass out of here!"

Will and Mark just looked at each other.

Darren's mother went back into the house without saying anything to Mark and Will. A minute or two later, Darren, half-asleep, came to the door.

"Yes, officer? Can I help you with something?"

"Darren, I'm Officer Thornton. And this here is Will Sandwith, Eric's brother."

"Hey, man, I'm sorry to hear about your brother. He was a good dude," Darren said.

Will nodded.

"Darren, why don't you step outside," Mark said. The three stood out by the car, Darren leaning on the hood. "Darren, where were you the night Eric Sandwith was murdered?" Mark asked.

"I don't know? Here?"

"You were at home the entire night?"

"I think so. Why, am I a suspect?"

"Everyone's a suspect right now. And we'll ask the questions," Mark said. "What were you doing here that night."

"Playing with myself. I don't remember exactly who I was thinking about while I was doing it, but—"

"Listen, smartass," said Mark. "All we want to know is what you were doing that night. But if you want to be a tough guy, we'll just take you to the station and keep you there all day."

"You can't book me for being at home the night of a murder."

"You're right we can't," Mark said. He thought for a second and then looked at Will. "Will, do you smell that?"

"I definitely smell something," Will said.

"It smells like marijuana. Darren? Have you been hitting the hippie lettuce?"

"No, man, I'm clean," Darren said.

"So, I could go in the house there and take a look around and not find anything?" Mark asked.

"C'mon, man, I'll cooperate," Darren pleaded.

"Too late, dipshit. Get dressed. You're going to the station."

Darren went back into the house and came out a few minutes later dressed in the nicest clothes he owned. He was silent for the whole car ride back to the station, sitting in the back of the car with his arms crossed.

Once at the station, Mark put Darren in a small room and left him in there by himself. There was nothing in the room but a table and a chair. The light coming through the window was the only light in the room.

Mark passed the time in the chief's office. "Mark? What are we going to do with him? We can't just leave him in there all day," Chief McGillis said.

"Well, Chief, I think we should bring in his good buddy, Steve Murphy. There were two people at the crime scene, Murphy would have to have been the one to work with Darren, if he did it. Those two are inseparable," Mark said.

"Go bring in Murphy. We'll leave Darren in there, but don't tell him about Murphy."

"Sure thing, chief," Mark said.

Will went with Mark to go and get Steve Murphy, while the chief stayed at the station with Darren. Darren waited in the interrogation room for over two hours before Mark finally entered the room by himself. He walked in casually and sat down at the table across from Darren.

"Darren. Sorry to keep you waiting, but I had some stuff I had to take care of first. Are you feeling all right?" Mark asked.

"I'm okay," Darren replied.

"Darren, I know you weren't at home the night of the murder," Mark said, staring right at Darren. He hesitated before going on. "That means you lied to us, which leads me to believe you're trying to cover something up. What aren't you telling me?"

Darren stared blankly at the table. "How do you know I wasn't home? How could you know that?"

"Darren, after I left you here, I went and questioned Steve Murphy. You know, your partner in crime. Yeah, he told me everything you guys did that night. So I suggest you start talking if you want me to get your story straight."

"All right, I'll talk. I'll tell you anything you want to know."

"Where were you the night of the murder?"

"At the old Janzforth factory."

"What? You were in the old factory? That's private property, buddy. You just keep on racking up the violations."

"No, no. We weren't in the factory, just hanging out outside the factory."

"What were you doing outside the factory?"

"We were waiting for some guys to show up."

"What were you guys going to do there?"

"We were gonna—" Darren started to say without finishing.

"You were gonna what?"

"We were gonna … buy some drugs. We were gonna purchase some dope, okay?"

"Is that where you were around eleven o' clock?"

"Yeah. The guys finally showed up about ten-thirty and then we just stayed there for an hour or two. We didn't see or here anything regarding Eric."

Chief McGillis opened the door and asked Mark to step outside.

"So? What did you get out of him so far?"

"He claims he and Murphy bought some dope and hung out in front of the Janzforth factory all night. They don't know anything about the murder," Mark said.

"Did you tell him we haven't even talked to Murphy yet?"

"No, I told him Steve spilled his guts."

"Good. While you were in there, I got a phone call from Mrs. Burton. Apparently Matt Burton and Adam Connolly haven't been seen or heard from in two days now. Let's see if Darren knows anything about that."

Chief McGillis and Mark went into the room and sat down again with Darren.

"Darren, do you know where Matt Burton and Adam Connolly are?" McGillis asked.

You could almost hear the gears turning in Darren's head, trying to come up with the most appropriate answer. "All I know is that those two guys were supposed to hang out with Steve and me the night before the funeral and never showed up. I have no idea where they are. Really."

The chief and Mark excused themselves from the room and stood outside the door.

"You question Steve about the past few nights and I'll go over to the Burton's and the Connolly's and see if they know anything," McGillis said.

Mark went into the room where Steve was waiting to be questioned. He was sitting at Mark's desk tapping his fingers on the desktop.

"Steve, I just got done talking to Darren. He told us everything he knew. Now it's your turn. What were you guys doing the night Eric was killed?"

"We were at the Janzforth factory, just hanging out."

"Just hanging out? Why would anyone just hang out there?"

"Well, we were waiting for some friends to show up."

"Who?"

"Friends of Darren's cousin in Buffalo."

"Why were you meeting them there? Why not at Darren's house or your house?"

"Well, they were bringing us some booze, so we couldn't be around our parents."

Mark looked at Steve. "That's not what Darren told us. Would you care to tell me the real reason you were meeting those guys at the factory, or would you like to stay here for a couple of days?"

"Fine. They were selling us some drugs."

"That's better. How well do you know these guys?"

"Well, like I said, they're friends of Darren's cousin. I hardly know the guys."

"Did they kill Eric?"

"No, no!" Steve yelled. "They were late in arriving. By the time they finally showed up, it was almost ten-thirty. We hung out there for an hour or so, and they took off."

"How do you know they didn't kill Eric on their way home."

"They're not the type. They're all business."

"What do you know about Matt Burton and Adam Connolly? They're missing, you know?"

"I have no idea. We were supposed to catch up with them the night before the funeral, but they never showed up."

"You're sure you have no idea where they are?"

"Positive."

"Darren told us everything. Have you?"

"I swear to you I have told you all I know."

Mark left the room and found Will, who was waiting in the chief's office.

"This is going nowhere. Both of them have the same story and it doesn't involve murder," Mark said.

"Well, what now?"

"Well, I guess we could find the guys Steve and Darren met up with. They seem like pretty solid suspects."

"Yeah. I wonder what happened to the other two guys."

"Let's hope they didn't suffer the same fate as Eric."

Mark and Will went to the interrogation room to get Darren and take him home. Mark was going to question Darren about his cousin's buddies on the way to Darren's home. Darren however, broke down with some news he had kept from Mark during the questioning.

"Sir, there is something that I think you should know."

"What's that?" Mark asked.

"The night we were supposed to meet up with Matt and Adam, we got to the factory late and figured they were already there. However, they weren't."

"Go on," Mark said.

"We took a look around the outside of the factory and found …"

"What? What did you find?"

"Blood. A puddle of blood. It was huge, like five feet wide."

"Are you sure?"

"Yes, no doubt it was blood."

"Human blood?"

"I think so. I mean, it looked like it, but I didn't get a real good look at it. After we looked around the factory, we were chased out of there by a man."

"A man? What did he look like?"

"I have no clue. I didn't even get a good look. We bolted out of there."

"Well, how do you know it was a person chasing you?"

"Dude, there was a man there, I swear to you."

"Can you show us exactly where you saw the puddle?"

"Yeah. I'll never forget where I was that night."

Mark and Will stepped out of the room and gave each other the same wide-eyed stare.

"Is it possible the killer is in the factory?" Will asked.

"Not likely. The windows are barred on the inside and the doors are locked from the inside. The only person with a key to undo the dead bolts is the property owner, and he's a couple of state's away. Unless he's here, there's no one in there."

"We're gonna check it out, right?"

"Yeah. We'll get the two of them and go to the factory."

Mark, Will, Steve and Darren piled into the squad car. Mark looked in the rear view mirror at one point, and it seemed as though the two boys were frightened. It was almost five o'clock now, and the sun was beginning to set. The ride didn't take long. They passed the murder scene and soon came to the factory. Mark pulled the car onto the tall grass and got as close to the factory as he could.

As they all got out of the car, Mark and Will went first. They walked towards the factory and were almost exactly where the blood puddle was when Darren stopped them.

"Guys, that's where the blood was."

"Pretty much right where you're standing," Steve said.

"Right here?" Mark asked.

"Yeah, right about there. We were about ten feet from the front door when we almost slipped in it."

Mark knelt down and touched the ground. It had rained the day of the funeral. Mark rubbed the dirt with his fingers and found no trace of blood. "Guys. I don't know what to tell you. There's no blood here."

"We're telling you the truth, man! There was a huge puddle of blood there the other day. You have to believe us."

Mark felt that the two boys were just pulling his chain. "I don't believe you actually. I don't see any blood, and, in fact, don't even see any footprints."

"That guy was here!" Steve yelled.

"Yeah, he's in the factory," Darren said.

"Oh really? How did he get in there? He can't get in through the windows. And the doors are practically welded shut," Mark replied.

"He's got to be in there. We heard noises coming out of there the other night."

"The sounds you heard were probably just rats and mice, assuming you even heard anything at all."

"We did hear something coming out of there the other night and it wasn't a rat."

"You know what, guys? I've just about had it with your bullshit. I suggest you get the hell out of here and start walking home before I take you back to the station and arrest you both for lying to me."

The two boys looked at each other and started to leave.

"Don't think of skipping town guys. You're still suspects," Mark said.

"What if they're telling us the truth? I mean, I'm sure someone could get in the factory if they really tried," Will said.

"Those two are always bullshitting the police to get out of trouble. There's no one in the factory. There's no man chasing anyone. There's no blood puddle. It's all crap to get themselves out of trouble."

Mark and Will then went back to the car and got in. A few seconds later, the chief's voice came over the radio. "Mark? Mark, are you there?"

"Yeah, chief. I'm here."

"Hey, I went over to the Burtons and the Connollys. There's no sign of the boys and no one's seen them since the night before the funeral. We've got two missing persons to file reports on."

"All right, chief. I'm gonna drop Will off at home and go back to the station."

"See ya back there, Mark."

Mark and Will headed back to town and got back to Will's house. Will unbuckled his seatbelt and paused for a second. "Mark, who do you think did it?"

"I don't now, Will. I don't know. My gut tells me Steve, Darren and the two guys form the city had something to do with it, but I can't prove it. I want to bring those two guys in tomorrow."

"Well, keep me up to speed. I'll probably have dinner with my mother and call it an early night. I want to get up early tomorrow."

"I'll call you later."

Chapter Nineteen

It was after nine o'clock and Will was sitting in the living room watching TV. He and his mother had dinner together, and, much to Will's surprise, they didn't argue once. They talked a little about the investigation, about how long Will would be in town, about his plans with Mira, etc., etc.

The sun had set about a half an hour ago and Will's mother was asleep in her bedroom. Will could not sleep; he was waiting for a phone call from Mark in case anything new came up. As he flipped through the channels, there was nothing on that grabbed his interest. He turned the television off and walked over to the front window. He looked out at the street lights and watched as a car drove by.

Will thought about Shannon and their meetings. He thought about Mira and how much he wished she was here. He thought about how when he and Mira first met, they would walk the streets of Boston for hours, just talking.

Will opened the front door and stood on the front porch. He smelled the air; it was a warm night, just right for a walk.

Will locked the front door and stepped down the porch steps. He walked to the end of the driveway and looked up and down the street. There were no cars in sight and the only lights he could see were the street lights and the moon. As he was about to step out into the street, his stomach did a flip. Will stumbled a bit as he took his first step onto the street.

At the end of his street was a vacant lot, and, as Will passed it, he once again got a strange feeling in his stomach. His heart was beating a mile a minute. His mouth was dry. Was the killer watching him? Was the killer behind him, like he was behind Eric? Was Will about to meet his brother's killer?

He stared into the darkness behind the vacant lot. He turned and took a look behind him, all around him. There was no one in sight, but Will wanted there to be. He wanted to see the man who murdered his brother.

Will got to the end of his street and headed towards Route 33, to where his younger brother met his death. He had tunnel vision as he walked down the road. He was walking faster and faster with each mile. His breaths were long and going through him like fire.

Will saw the crime scene tape fluttering on the breeze in the distance. Will stopped and watched it.

Will's steps were softer now. His breathing was slow and quiet. The light was dim. The moon was hidden behind the clouds.

Will stopped exactly where his brother was killed. He looked around. Nothing. Darkness surrounded him and there was only the sound of crickets. Will found himself trying to summon up all of his courage, as he was about to scream out into the night for the killer to show himself once and for all. The words were on the tip of his tongue. " … C'mon you s—" was all Will got out.

Despite all of the confidence Will had mustered on his walk, he was caught completely off guard by the man who stepped out of the woods and stared at Will. Will never actually thought the killer would be there.

"Will Sandwith? Are you Will Sandwith?" said the stranger.

"Yes! Who the hell are you?" he replied.

As Will took a close look at the killer's face, he recognized him: it was the man Will had bumped shoulders with at the restaurant a few days earlier. "You shouldn't be here."

The man's face was clean-shaven. He had deep wrinkles around his eyes and mouth. His eyes were dark and his hair was neatly trimmed. He looked nothing like the killer Will imagined. Will had no idea what to say, so the man spoke instead. "What are you doing here? Trying to get yourself killed, because you almost succeeded?"

"Well, what are you doing here? Better yet, who are you?" Will asked.

As Will finished his question, someone else came out of the woods with a flashlight. It was Mark. "What's going on? I heard noises coming from the street."

"Mark? What in God's name are you doing here?" Will asked.

"Will? How in the hell did you get here?" asked Mark.

The stranger cut in. "He was trying to get himself killed, that's what he was trying to do."

"Will, I want you to meet Max Whitfield. He used to be with the FBI. Now he investigates on his own and was sent to us by the state police," Mark said.

"I specialize in murders like your brother's. Your brother's killer has a profile that I've been tracking for months. I'm here to catch the son of a bitch."

Will stood in complete silence. After a moment Will asked, "What kind of profile are you chasing?"

"A vampire."

Will stood now in disbelief at what he just heard. "A vampire? Like Count Dracula, drink-your-blood kind of vampire?"

"Yes. Your brother was attacked by a modern-day vampire," Whitfield said.

Will gave Mark a glare.

"Will, about two months ago, the same kind of vampire killed my wife and took my daughter. The killing was at night and unlike your brother, my daughter's body was never found. Trust me, Will, this is no joke."

Will turned to Mark. "Can I talk to you for a minute?"

Will and Mark began walking down the street, about twenty feet away from the vampire hunter. "What in the fuck is going on? A vampire hunter? How in the hell could you not tell me this?"

"Will, I thought you were heading back to Boston. I was hoping Max would only stay for a few days, take off and everything would be back to normal. I never thought you two would meet," Mark said.

"Mark, please tell me you don't believe all this vampire nonsense?"

"I didn't know what to think at first. But if you look at all of the pictures and the evidence, well …"

"Oh c'mon, Mark. You of all people are buying into this con-artist's bullshit. This guy's a fucking flake and you trust him?"

"Will, remember the blood drop you found on the collar of Eric's shirt?"

"Yes."

"It came from a puncture wound on his neck. There were two small pinpricks on his jugular vein. The blood came from there."

Will had no idea what to think anymore. He began to walk away from Mark, but then turned back after a few steps. "How could you keep this from me?"

"Will, I knew you'd never believe it, so why put you through this?"

"'Cause you're my best friend, that's why. I mean, for all you know, this asshole came to town and killed Eric himself."

"No, Will, he didn't. He has an alibi the day your brother was killed. He's here to help."

"Fuck you, Mark. If you believe this clown, well, you're a bigger dipshit than I ever thought you could be."

As the two were talking, Max approached them. "Will, when I catch the vampire, then you'll know I'm right. I don't expect you to believe all of this. But trust me, you'll sleep easier once I catch this monster."

Will stared at Max and replied with as stern a face he had. "There is no such thing as a vampire. And when I catch the killer, a mortal being, I'll expose you for being the fake piece of shit you are."

With that, Will turned away and headed for home. Neither Max nor Mark tried to stop him.

When he arrived back at his mother's, Will sat on the steps of the front porch. Vampires in Alden? he thought. What a joke. Not only were clues to catching the killer few and far between, but now the only person Will trusted had been brainwashed by an outsider.

Will sat on the steps for hours. If he was going to catch the killer, he was going to have to do it by himself. If Mark believed in vampires, there's no telling if maybe the whole town did.

Chapter Twenty

The Janzforth factory was now a target for the police, although Mark dismissed it as the main host of evil in Alden. And even though Mark, Will and the two boys did not take notice, they were being watched while investigating the factory grounds. The short man was there, in the trees, watching very closely every move the men made, making note of everything the men said.

They snooped around the grounds. Matt was there, in the factory, looking out the windows, watching the men, hearing their every sound. He wanted to scream out to them, but he could not. Matt could hardly whisper or whimper. The men in the factory made sure of that by cutting Matt's tongue out.

After the long-haired man sank his teeth into Matt's neck, Matt fainted and did not wake up until he was being carried out of the room. He could hardly move, let alone speak.

He was finally moved to a room further down the hall. He was laid down very carefully on a table. His eyes were open, but he had no idea exactly what he was looking at. The long-haired man looked lovingly at Matt, and said, "You are now in the family of darkness. You are one of us."

Matt stared at the man and watched him as he left the room. Matt closed his eyes, but that only magnified the pain. He focused on it. He opened his eyes and gazed up half awake at the ceiling. The tiles were molded over, stained with water marks, turning the tiles into a light shade of brown. Some were a dark green and were falling apart at the corners. Matt's nose worked just fine, as the room was overpowered with a damp and musty odor. He raised his hand and touched it to his mouth. It was at this point that he realized he could not open his mouth. Wire sealed his mouth shut.

Matt also noticed that his nails were unusually long. They were almost an inch long now and were sharp and a light shade of yellow.

He was not himself anymore. He felt awful, the dim light in the hallway hurt his eyes. He was not scared, but rather, was thirsty. The blood he drank before passing out was still lingering in his mouth. And he craved for more. It was all he wanted.

He took another look around the room and realized he was not alone. In one corner of the room was a girl, about eight or nine. She was lying down in the corner, with an eye open, looking at Matt. Her eyes were yellow, the same as her fingernails, also as long as Matt's. Her hair was a mess, a light shade of brown with some white in it. Her skin was gray, covered in scrapes and bruises. Matt thought at first that she was dead, but knew she was not after she closed her eye.

In another corner of the room was a young boy, no more than five or six. He too had the long nails and the yellow, glowing eyes. About five feet from the table was another body, that of a teenage boy. His eyes were closed. His pale skin told Matt all he needed to know.

Despite his surroundings, despite the fear Matt had felt before his initiation to death, he was not afraid. He knew he was not in danger, for the other beings in the room were hardly interested in him. He felt safe alongside them. He was at peace lying on the table. With that, he dropped his arms off the table and closed his eyes. Within seconds, Alden's newest vampire was fast asleep. He would not wake again until he heard the sounds of his old friends outside the building in the daylight.

Chapter *Twenty-One*

The next morning, Will woke up in his room, drenched in sunlight. He had not slept well the entire night. He tossed and turned, thinking about Mark, Max and what had been said the night before. He even found himself looking out the window every once in a while, waiting for someone to be there looking in at him. Will was starting to believe the nonsense Max had told him, even though he knew vampires did not exist. They couldn't exist. His brother was killed by a mortal adversary, and Will was going to prove it.

Will got out of bed, showered and dressed, following his normal morning routine. He went down for breakfast and ate by himself (his mother had resumed work to take her mind off Eric). As he was washing the dishes, he heard a knock at the door.

It was Mark. "Hey, Will. I was hoping to talk to you. I need to apologize and explain some things to you."

Will thought for a second before pushing the screen door open. "Have a seat."

Mark sat in the recliner, Will was on the couch across from Mark. Mark cupped his hands and thought for a moment before speaking. "Will, I'm sorry for not telling you sooner. I knew you wouldn't believe me. So I kept it from you. Hell, I'm not even sure I believe this damn story. But the state police are convinced it's got some truth to it, so I trust it too."

"Mark, you're gonna sit there and tell me you believe in vampires?"

"All of the evidence points in that direction."

"Then why was he struck in the head? A vampire has no need to do that."

"I don't know why he was killed that way. It makes no sense to me."

"What if it's someone who only thinks they're a vampire? What if there's some whacko out there who's impersonating a vampire to cover his ass. You know, play the insanity card."

"I'm following you. The next step, though, who is it?"

"I don't know. What does Max think?"

"Max thinks the killer is staying with someone here in town, someone who is protecting him and helping him."

"Anyone come to mind?"

Mark didn't answer. He and Will were both going over a list of Alden's top suspects, when Will finally came to a person that fit the description. "What about the girl at the funeral, you know, the one who was smiling?"

"Angela Raines?"

"Yeah, she seemed to think something at the funeral was funny. Not to mention, she had a crush on Eric."

"She and her family haven't even lived here a year. It's possible they are hiding him, moving from town to town."

"She's as good a suspect as we've got."

"But how could she be out in the daytime if she's a vampire?"

"Oh Christ, Mark. For the last time: she's not a vampire! She's acting like one to protect herself."

"Let's hope so," Mark said as he stood up and headed for the door.

"Where are you going?"

"Let's head over to the Raines place and ask her a few questions."

Will got up and headed out the door, making sure he locked it on his way out. He and Mark were not as excited as they had been the day before, but they had a feeling they were on to something.

The Raines house was about nine or ten blocks from the police station. The lawn looked like it hadn't been cut in a couple of weeks, but the house itself was in good shape. The entire block was your typical suburban neighborhood, complete with white picket fence at the house on the corner.

They pulled in the driveway, and as they stepped out of the car, they both made sure not to slam the doors.

Mark rang the doorbell and the two waited. He rang the bell again. No answer. Will then walked around to the side door and knocked. Mark also walked around to the side door, but again, no answer. They both walked completely around the house, but it appeared no one was home. Will stepped up to one of the side windows and peered inside the house before being interrupted by the sound of a woman's voice. "Can I help you boys with something?" said the woman. She was short, borderline dwarf. She had long blonde hair with streaks of white in it. Her face was covered in wrinkles, but she still had an attractiveness to her, even in her forties or fifties.

"No, ma'am," Mark said. Will stepped away from the window as inconspicuously as he could. "We were just looking for the Raineses, Mrs. Strye."

"Oh, well, deputy, the only one still around is the daughter, Angela. Her folks, Mr. and Mrs. Raines went away on vacation a month or two ago."

"They went away for a couple months and left their sixteen-year old daughter all by herself?"

"Well, that's what Angela said. Kind of a strange girl, don't you think?"

Will cut in. "Strange? What do you mean?"

"I'm sorry, Mrs. Strye. Mary Strye, meet Will Sandwith," Mark said.

"Oh, I'm terribly sorry to hear about your brother," she said.

"Thank you," Will said.

"What were you saying about Angela? We don't really know her that well," said Mark.

"Well, I don't keep constant tabs on her, but she keeps some odd hours."

"She comes in late?" Mark asked.

"She sometimes leaves early in the morning and then comes back at five or six the following morning. Sometimes she leaves for two or three days at a time," she replied.

"Do you know where she goes?" Mark asked.

"No, I have no idea."

"Is she dressed like she's going somewhere in particular? Perhaps to a job or a party?" Mark asked.

"No. She dresses different all the time. Sometimes she's dressed very shoddy, like she has nowhere to go at all."

Will asked, "Does anyone else ever come to the house? Any friends or classmates?"

"Not that I've ever seen. It's always just her."

"Well, thank you for your help, Mrs. Strye. We'll be going now."

"Is she in some sort of trouble?"

"No, probably nothing. We're just checking up on anyone who might know something about the murder. Thanks for your time."

Will and Mark made their way to the squad car and got in. Mark started the car.

Will said, "She keeps odd hours, but looks as though she has nowhere to go? Seems like we may be on to something."

"Don't get carried away. She could have a very good reason for her hours. Let's face it: she could have a guy or girl on the side that she's been seeing. If she brings them here, the neighbors will surely see them."

"Yeah, but we should still try to question her. Sounds like the best lead so far."

"We could stake her out," Mark said.

"You'd be willing to do that?"

"Well, I'll run it past the chief, but it shouldn't be a problem."

"I'm up for it."

"Tell you what. Stay here, walk up and down the street or

something. I'll go to the station and switch this car with my pick-up. That way, she won't notice the police car. When she shows up, we'll talk to her."

"All right, man. Hurry back. I won't talk to her alone."

Will got out of the car and watched Mark turn off the street and head back towards the station. Will was tempted to check the house again, but without Mark there, he could blow the whole case if Angela were to catch him.

Will strolled up and down the street twice, but Mark was not back yet. Will walked up the driveway, checking in every direction making sure there were no cars coming. He saw no one walking the street. In fact, he didn't even see anyone on their lawns or looking out their windows.

He got to the side door and checked to see if it was open. It wasn't, so Will went around to the back of the house. He turned over a garbage can and peeked in what was apparently the kitchen window. There was nothing out of the ordinary on the table, floor or countertops. He checked again to his left and right, but there was no one there.

He then made his way to the other side of the house and took a look in the window he checked out the first time before he got caught by Mrs. Strye. He was uneasy. But he had to go on now.

Will looked in and figured it to be the living room. There was a pile of mail on the coffee table, and a stack of newspapers on the floor next to the TV. Will tried to adjust the way he was standing so he could see into the next room, but was interrupted yet again. "What are you doing?"

Will looked to his left, where the voice came from. Will soon realized it was Mark. "Dude, you scared the shit out of me," Mark said.

"You're scared? I thought I was busted for sure."

"I told you to stay out on the street. Jesus, Will. What if Angela came back? Or if someone else would have seen you and called the chief?"

"I know, I know. I had to check. Something just didn't feel right about this place."

"Well I don't care. We'll wait for her, talk to her and then decide if we should go on from there."

The two got into Mark's truck. Mark picked up some provisions. The two could be there all night if what Mrs. Strye said was true.

"What do you think? If she's the killer, who's she working with?" Will asked.

"I don't know. Like I said before, if she's got a boyfriend, well, there we go."

"Mark, did people like Eric? I mean, was he popular? Did he have a lot of friends?"

"Will, you knew Eric. He was on the football team, he played hockey. He had a popular girlfriend. He was a straight arrow. He couldn't have a lot of enemies. Too many people would have had his back."

"I hoped so. But if that's true, the list of suspects should be real short."

"Yeah, but you never know if a drifter came through town or if someone from Buffalo came to town, like Darren's buddies."

"I hope this broad gets us somewhere."

"She's a pretty safe bet right now. But we'll see. Hey, listen. I was up pretty late last night, so I'm gonna take a nap. Wake me if she comes back. After a while, we'll switch. That way we're both alert and awake in case she pops in late."

As Mark drifted off, Will made sure the only time he took his eyes off the Raines house was to check the street in case she was walking home. He wondered, if she was the killer, along with someone else, would she ever admit to it? No one in the neighborhood could know if she was home or not that night. It was almost a week ago. Not even her parents were around to question.

After about an hour went by, Will saw a girl walking up the street. She looked normal, so Will wondered if it was her. She had on a light blue sweatshirt and a pair of windbreaker pants. She had brown hair pulled back in a ponytail. As she got closer to the house, Will's heart was beating faster and faster. She got one house from the Raines place, when Will was about to wake Mark. But the girl kept going. She went almost to the end of the street before entering one of the houses near the corner. Will then realized that he must not get excited at the sight of every person on the street.

Will could not take his eyes of the house. There was something strange about it.

He wanted to get out of the truck and go in the house, but knew he must not. Mark would never let him. But if Angela did not let them in, how would Will and Mark ever get any clues? Would Will be able to keep himself from going into the house without Mark? The more Will processed what Mrs. Strye had said, the more he was convinced she had to be the killer. She and someone else, a man. For who could deliver the death blow with one solid shot. Sure a woman could do it, but a sixteen-year old? Not likely.

Almost two hours went by before Angela Raines came home. It was after two in the afternoon. The sun was hidden behind the clouds. A cool breeze was in the air and it whipped Angela's hair around her head. She approached her house and looked all around. She got to the front door and opened it. Before going in, she checked one more time to make sure she had gotten home safe and unseen.

Will tapped Mark on the arm to wake him up. "Mark. Mark! Wake up, man. She's back!"

"Where is she? I don't see her."

"She went in the house. She kept looking around as she went in, like someone was following her."

"Let's go. We'll go to the front door and knock," Mark said.

Mark and Will made their way quickly to the front door of the Raines place. They weren't running, but they tried their best to get to the door as fast as they could without arousing suspicion, from Angela or her neighbors.

As they walked up the steps leading to the front door, the door opened and a figure stepped out, practically knocking Mark off the steps.

"Whoa! What's your hurry?" Mark asked.

Angela's dark hair was long and shiny. She had light-blue eyes and a small nose. She was petite, but not curvy. Will now understood why Eric chose Lindsay over Angela. She wasn't unattractive, but she was no prize either.

Finally, she responded. "I'm sorry, I was on my way out."

"Angela? I'm Officer Thornton and this is Will Sandwith. You might have seen him at his brother Eric's funeral?"

Again she had a blank look. "Yeah, I'm sorry about Eric. I really liked him. He was a great guy."

"Thank you," Will said.

Mark quickly jumped in. "Angela, do you mind if we come in and ask you a few questions?"

"What kind of questions?" she asked, running her hand through her hair which was now covering half of her face. "Am I a suspect?"

"No, no," Mark said. "We're just going around asking some of his classmates if they know anything that might be helpful."

Angela thought for a second. "Sure, I've got a couple minutes. Come on in."

The house was dimly lit. The only light entering the front hallway was coming in through the front window. There was another window in the kitchen, but the room still had very few shadows. There was a stairway ahead on the right and the living room was to the left. Will could see a corner of the kitchen just beyond the living room, which had been painted a shade of light green. There was a small stand just inside the door with two sets of keys on it and a pile of mail on the floor next to the stand.

Angela walked into the living room and motioned for Will and Mark to sit on the couch. She started to walk into the kitchen before turning around. "Can I get you guys anything to drink?"

"No thanks," Mark replied.

"No, no," Will added.

As Will sat on the orange sofa, he looked around the room. There was a picture on one wall with Angela and her parents. Her father was bald, with only a comb over to show for his hair loss. Angela's mother was a heavier woman with dark hair and blue eyes. On the wall next to the kitchen was another picture with Angela and another guy, perhaps her boyfriend. He had dark hair, like Angela's and a pale complexion.

Angela came back into the living room and sat down in the recliner across from Mark and Will. She had a can of Coke and sipped it slowly.

"Angela, how well did you know Eric?" Mark asked.

"Well, we talked a few times, he was in my business class. We sat next to each other, so we'd talk every once in a while."

"Did either of you have feelings for the other?"

"No, no. He had Lindsay, and I was seeing somebody for most of the school year."

"Angela, where were you the night of the murder?" asked Mark.

She thought for a second before answering. "I was here. I was out running and came home around nine. I took a shower, watched some TV and went to bed."

"Where are your parents? Are they coming back soon?" Mark asked.

"They went on an extended vacation. My father had some sick time built up over a few years and decided to use it up this summer. He and my mother went on a trip across America. They should be home later next month."

Mark stared at Angela. "Angela, if you know anything about this case or have any information that you think may help us, please call me."

Mark handed Angela his card and got off the couch. Will also stood up and both made their way towards the door. Mark turned around and faced Angela. "Eric was fond of you, Angela. He told Will about the new girl in his class. Anything you think can help us is crucial."

Mark and Will made their way towards the truck and got in. A few minutes later, they were in Will's driveway. "So what was that crap you fed her about Eric thinking she was a great person?" Will asked.

"I'm hoping she'll buy it and feel guilty about being involved in his murder. If she's innocent, well, no harm done."

"So, do you think she's innocent?" Will asked.

"Well, we have no reason not to believe her. I mean, how can we prove if she's guilty or not?" Mark looked at Will and saw a grin on his face. "What are you smiling at?"

"Well, we might be able to prove if she's guilty."

"How?" Mark asked.

"We could go back and check things out for ourselves." Will took a set of keys out of his pocket.

"Whose keys are those?"

"I don't know."

"Where did you get them?"

"Angela's."

"You took a set of keys from the Raines place? That's stealing, you know? I could arrest you for that."

Will was still smiling. "You don't have to do that, Mark." He put the keys back in his pocket and stepped out of the car. "I'm gonna put them back tonight."

"What? What in the hell are you talking about?"

"I'm gonna go back there tonight and after I let myself in and look around, I'm gonna put the keys back on the stand where I took 'em."

Mark got out of the truck. He was careful not to raise his voice. "Theft is one thing, Will. But breaking and entering? I can't allow you to do that."

"Then don't come with me. Look the other way. I don't care. Mark, if my gut is right, then I'll find something, anything that might implicate her. If I don't take that chance, then I'll never know, no, we'll never know if she's the killer or not. Mark, please, let me take a look in there, even if it's just for a few minutes. It's the last law I'll break, I promise."

Mark put his hands on his hips and looked Will dead in the eye. "Fine. I'll go with you and keep watch. But if you get caught, I can't save you."

"Caught? I'm not gonna get caught." Will smiled and hit Mark in the arm. "Get me around nine."

Mark got back in his truck and watched Will go into his

mother's home. He sat behind the wheel wondering if he should let Will go into the Raines place. It was dangerous, and could cost him his job. But Will was right. If Angela was in on the murder, this was the only way they'd ever know. It would be another long night for Mark … just not too long he hoped.

Chapter *Twenty-Two*

Will had dinner that night with his mother, one-on-one, for the first time since the funeral. She had spent the previous night at her sister's house to get away from her own home. The thought of spending the night of her son's funeral at home, alone, was too much. She was depressed. She was not suicidal mind you, just sad about the events of the past week. Her religious beliefs would not allow her to take her own life. Even with Will in the house, she did not feel safe. For the first time in her fifty-plus years living in Alden she made sure her doors were locked at all times … and she was not alone in that way of thinking. Many people who bragged about the safety of the town were now locking up tight and checking the locks twice.

As Will and his mother sat down for dinner, Will noticed that his mother seemed preoccupied. Her answers were short and sharp. She didn't smile. She seemed annoyed with Will and his questions. Will worried for her and what may happen to her when he left for Boston.

"Mom, have you given any thought to coming with me, to live in Boston?"

"Will, we've talked about this. I work for the town. If I move, I lose my job. I can't just transfer to another city. I lose all of my seniority, my benefits, everything if I go. I can't."

"Mom, I don't care about your job and money. I'm concerned about you. You need to get out of here. This place is pulling you

103

down. Soon there will be nothing left of you but fear and despair." Will went over and knelt down next to his mother. He grabbed her hand and looked into her eyes. "Mom, I'm worried about you. Forget about this place. Come with me to Boston. You can live with me until you find a job."

A tear rolled own her cheek and as she looked deep into Will's eyes. "Don't worry about me. I overcame your father walking out on me and I will overcome this. I have the church, I have my sister. I'll be all right."

The doorbell rang. Will got up. It was too early for Mark to pick him up, but he thought maybe Mark had some news on the case that he had to give to Will.

It was not Mark, and Will had thoughts of slamming the door in the visitor's face.

"Will, hey, can I talk to you?" said Will's father.

"What are you doing here?"

"I just wanted to talk to you."

"Talk to me? What do we have to talk about? You had twenty years to talk to me, but didn't seem to care. Why on Earth should I talk to you now?"

"Will, I know you hate me, and I don't blame you. I just wanna talk to you for a few minutes, that's all. C'mon, please, just five minutes?"

Will opened the screen door and stepped outside. It was a cool night, unusual for Alden in August. "All right, what do you want to talk about?"

"Son, I wanted to tell you that not a single day went by that I didn't think about you boys. I wanted to call, but I had nothing to say. I couldn't find work for a while and I was drinking a lot. I wasn't proud of myself."

"Did you come here looking for pity? Because if you did, you might as well leave."

"No, Will. I'm not looking for sympathy. I'm telling you that I didn't keep in touch with you guys because I wasn't proud of who I was."

"You could have called to tell us you were alive."

"I didn't think you cared."

Will thought for a second. He looked at his father. The wrinkles around his eyes consumed the sparkle of his brown eyes, and he hadn't shaved in a day or two. Will remembered that look from his childhood. Will thought about all of the times his father wasn't there: football games, birthdays, his graduations. "Dad, I did care. I cared for a long time. All it would have taken was a phone call or a letter."

Will's father began to sob. "Will, I'm sorry. I'm so sorry."

Will put his arm on his father's shoulder. "You know, Dad, it's not too late. All you gotta do is try."

Will's dad wiped a tear away from his eye and grabbed Will's hand. "I'm gonna make it up to you, boy. I'm gonna prove to you I can be a father to you after all these years."

Will shook his father's hand and turned to go back into the house. "Son?"

"Yes, Dad?"

"I love you and I'm never gonna let you down again."

Will watched his father walk down the steps and down the driveway to the street. This was the man who abandoned him and his mother all those years ago. But Will knew that his father was sincere in his apology, and that he may need his father's love and advice someday.

Will went back into the house and went back into the kitchen. His mother was washing the dishes. "Who was at the door?"

"Oh, it was Lindsay. She just came over to talk for a minute." Will had lied to his grieving mother, but he figured it was better than telling her the truth.

Will went into the living room and watched TV for about an hour, before Mark finally showed up. All he wanted was to take his mind off what his father had just said to him.

Mark seemed irritated.

"Hey, Mark. Thanks for coming to get me."

"Yeah, no problem. It bears repeating that I really don't approve of what we are doing tonight, so I'd like to be on our way as soon as possible."

Will didn't know if it was such a good idea anymore, breaking into the Raines place. "I understand. I'll tell my mother I'm going and we'll be on our way."

Mark went out to his truck and Will went into the living room to say goodbye to his mother. "I'll see you later, mom. I'm going out with the guys to Neighbor's Bar to have a few drinks."

"Okay. Lock up before you leave. And don't stay out too late."

Will leaned in and kissed his mother before heading out the door, checking to make sure he locked the door. He jogged down the driveway to Mark's truck and got in. He slammed the door and they were off.

"Mark, I don't mean to be a pain in the ass, and I'm sorry for putting a lot of pressure on you lately. By next week I'll be gone and you can put this case behind you."

Mark continued to stare at the road. "Will, I'm not pissed at you. I'm just upset at the fact that with all of the overtime I've been putting in lately, we just don't seem to be getting anywhere."

"I promise you, if this doesn't produce anything tonight, I'll drop trying to solve this case. I'll let you and the chief do your thing and I'll help out if I can."

A minute or two later, Mark and Will arrived at the Raines residence. Mark parked the truck and the two sat in the truck motionless, staring at the house. Mark broke the silence. "Will, I'll watch the house from here. If I see anyone coming to the house, I'll honk the horn like crazy."

"All right. I'll be listening."

"And Will, be careful. If you get caught, it's your ass."

Will nodded. "I know, I know. I'll be out of there before you know it."

Will hopped out of the truck and walked slowly up the driveway. As he got closer to the house, his pace got slower and slower. He stopped at the front door and stood. He rang the doorbell and waited.

No one answered. He rang it again and knocked on the door this time. Still no answer. Will reached into his pocket and grabbed the set of keys. He fumbled through them, trying three different keys before finally finding the one that unlocked the door.

He opened the door enough for himself to get in. He took a step inside and looked around.

He was in the hallway and with the same cautiousness, closed the door and locked it. Will didn't know where to look first. He pulled open the closet door in the hallway and peeked in. There were the usual coats, shoes, umbrellas, but nothing even remotely resembling a murder weapon.

Will closed the door and looked around. He decided to go upstairs. Will had to coach himself here: "One foot in front of the other, Will. You can do it. You must do it." Will got up the two stairs, but at the third step, he heard the wood creak beneath his foot. He looked in every direction, making sure no one saw him. Will gathered his courage yet again and proceeded up the stairs. The hallway at the top of the stairs was dark, completely dark. Pitch black was more like it. Will put his hand out to make sure he didn't knock anything over and felt his way through the darkness.

The first room he came across was the bathroom. He left the john and made his way down the hallway. The next room was a bedroom. As to whose it was, well, Will guessed it was Angela's. He didn't want to put any lights on, so he squinted as best he could to see things that would let him know for sure.

The dresser held a hair brush, a jewelry box, a few pictures. One picture in particular caught Will's eye. It was of Angela with her parents and another person, a man. It was the same person in the picture with Angela on the living room wall that Will had seen earlier in the day. He figured he could show it around and see if anyone knew who the guy was. Will put the picture in his pocket and made his way towards the doorway.

He went across the hall into another bedroom, only it looked more like a storage room than a bedroom. There were clothes scattered all over the bed and boxes lined the floor. Will almost tripped over a box as he entered the room.

Just then, Will heard a car horn beeping. 'Holy shit!' Will thought to himself. Angela had returned home. Will looked around and dropped to the floor. He pushed aside some of the boxes and crawled under the bed.

He carefully pushed some of the boxes around to conceal the floor beneath the bed. Just then he heard the door open and someone walking up the stairs. Will held his breath and lay perfectly still. The creaking of the stairs had stopped and Will knew whoever came home was upstairs. Will closed his eyes and prayed. He had not prayed in years, but it was all he could think to do.

A light went on from across the hall and he heard some rustling coming from across the hall. He inched out slowly to perhaps catch a glimpse. A few seconds later the light was gone. Will waited to hear the stairs creaking again.

The light came on again, only stronger and brighter; the light was coming from inside the room. He looked to his right and saw a pair of feet. The person was inches away from Will. He held his breath.

The person shut the light off and rumbled down the stairs. Will listened as best he could and heard the door slam. He waited, then finally got out from underneath the bed.

He made his way downstairs. He got to the bottom of the stairs and was about to go outside when he noticed the pile of mail next to the living room. Will began sifting through the pile and found mostly junk mail and bills. He made sure not to disturb the pile too much, as Angela would surely notice that. He came across the occasional magazine and then found an envelope from Automated Industries, Inc. Will was about to pass over it, when he noticed that it had been postmarked First Class. He opened it, with no regard for the envelope (anything he opened he was taking with him at this point). It read:

Dear Mister Roger Raines:
We are sending this letter as your final reminder that with your recent termination from Automated Industries, Inc., your health insurance and benefits have also been terminated.

Will read no further, put the letter back in its envelope and put the letter in his pocket. He sifted through the pile a bit further and came across another envelope that caught his attention.

It from was Autumnview Mental Hospital, located in Watertown, New York, about three hours northeast of Alden. Will opened the envelope and quickly put it in his pocket.

Will then pushed the mail back together as best he remembered it to look like before he started going through it and put the keys back on the stand. He locked the door and closed it hard. He ran as fast as he could, not looking back at the house.

He got to the truck and jumped in. Mark took off down the street before Will even shut the door.

"What in the fuck were you doing in there, man? I thought you were dead for sure!" Mark screamed.

"Holy shit, dude. I thought I was dead too."

"Will, I saw her approaching that house and almost died. I thought you were had."

"Was it her?"

"Yeah. She wasn't in there very long. What was she doing?"

"I don't know. I was hiding under the bed like a little girl when she came home."

"Well, did you find anything at least?"

"I'm pretty sure. I found a letter here that states Angela's father was shit canned at his job."

Will handed the letter to Mark. Mark read it over. "So all that talk about an extended vacation was a crock of shit. Anything else?"

"Yeah, this."

Will handed over the letter from Autumnview. "Wanna take a road trip tomorrow?" Will said with a smirk.

Mark read the letter over and handed it back to Will. "What time should I pick you up?"

PART II

Looking for the Sun

Chapter *Twenty-Three*

August 15

Mark and Will left the Raines' street and headed back to Will's house. The two said nothing on the drive; both were too excited about the information they found in the Raines' house. Were they positive they had the ID of the killers? No, but they were as confident about this lead as any. They had a start point and another potential killer that otherwise would have gone unnoticed. Will wanted to head to Watertown that night, but it was a moot point. Mark had to work the day shift tomorrow.

Mark pulled the car into the driveway and shut the lights off. He turned and faced Will. "All right, here's the plan. I get out of work at four-thirty tomorrow. I'll change at the precinct and head over here. Be ready at about five o'clock."

"I'll be here."

"Will, promise you won't go back to the house, okay? Promise to stay out of trouble until I get here."

"I'm not doing anything without you there. This is getting a little intense. You're the professional here. You gotta be here."

Will was about to get out of the car when Mark stopped him. "Hey, Will?"

"Yeah."

"I've been thinking about it. We won't get back here tomorrow night until after dark. Go and find Max tomorrow and tell him to keep an eye on the Raines' place."

"Where is he staying?" Will asked.

"He's at the Alden Motor Lodge, off Lincoln street. Pretty sure it's room 12."

Mark pulled away. Will stepped inside and locked the door behind him. He fell into the recliner by the TV and thought about what happened tonight. First he broke into someone's house and then almost got caught. He then thought about going to see Max. He didn't like Max and certainly did not want to talk to him. Will disliked Max because of his cocky attitude, and the fact he polluted Mark's head with vampire nonsense.

Will also wondered what Max was up to tonight. He probably slept during the day and prowled the night like a thief. 'To catch a vampire you have to work at night, right?' Will thought. He was interrupted by a light from the kitchen. It was his mother.

"Oh, I thought it was you. Where were you tonight?" Morgan asked.

"I went out with Mark and some of the guys. I wanted to get a chance to say good-bye to them."

Morgan sat upright. "When are you going? You didn't tell me."

"I'm not sure when I'm going. I mean, it could be two or three days from now, it could be a week."

The two sat in silence for a moment. She obviously thought Will was staying longer than that, to help her get through her tough times.

"Mom, why don't you come with me to Boston for a while? You've got some off-time coming to you, right?"

She smiled and wiped a tear from her eye. "William, my life is here. I have to get over this, and even though it may take years, I have to keep living my life. I can't just up and leave work, or the church or my other responsibilities."

"Mom, I'm not telling you to move to Boston permanently, just for a while, you know, until you're back up to speed."

"Thank you, but I'll visit you soon, how does that sound?"

"Fine, Mom. Tell me when."

Morgan got up and gave her son a hug. She stepped off, stopped suddenly and turned to Will. "By the way, Mira called here again tonight. She said you were supposed to talk tonight."

Will had forgotten. He nodded.

"Will, you better start treating that girl like you love her and not some buddy of yours you can ignore."

"Yes, Mother. I'll give her a call right now."

"Keep this up and you'll be single all over again," Morgan said shaking her head as she went to her bedroom.

Will went over to the phone and dialed Mira's number. He let it ring a few times, but there was no answer. He figured he'd just give her a call in the morning. He figured he would see her soon, but there was no guarantee of that. He got up and made his way to bed.

Chapter *Twenty-Four*

May 21

About fifteen minutes outside Watertown, Donald Jackson was at work, performing his usual sanitation duties at Watertown Mental Hospital. He was truly in the minority in Watertown, for there were only four black families in the entire community. Donald had served as a janitor for the past seventeen years (head daytime janitor for the past seven) and much to his credit, had never called in sick. In fact, he had never even been late. He took his work very seriously, too seriously some thought at the hospital. But his work was what kept him going.

Donald's wife and two daughters were killed in an automobile accident nine years ago. It was an icy, arctic night that her car hit a patch of black ice and slammed head first into a tractor-trailer. Donald always thought it was fitting that he was at work when he got the call that his family had gotten into a fatal accident.

Donald's new family included the workers and residents at the Watertown clinic. He took time each day to get to know the patients; their history, medical conditions, learned how to be their friends. And over the years, many of the patients who recovered from their mental illnesses would come back to see him and tell him how much he meant to them.

On this particular Monday morning in May, the sun was shining, yet a gloom had been cast over Donald's day from the word 'Go'. One of Donald's friends was being released. David Raines, a patient at the clinic for the past two years, was on his way out of Watertown, much to the dismay of Donald. He had grown quite attached to David over the time they interacted together. David was not like many of the other patients; he was smart, mischievously brilliant. Donald wondered sometimes what David was doing there. Donald would spend his lunch breaks sitting in David's room, picking his brain, trying to figure out what made David tick.

Donald was in the front corridor at the hospital when David was on his way out. David's parents were there, signing the paperwork that would give them their son back. David was by no means cured of his personality disorder, but the medication he was prescribed would certainly keep him in line. Donald went over to the bench where David was sitting and sat down.

"Well, Davie, I'm gonna miss you," Donald said.

David looked at Donald, his face blank, hardly a muscle moving. The medication sucked the life right out of David.

"It's okay, you're gonna be just fine. You'll be better off with your folks," Donald said getting up.

Mrs. Raines walked over. She was a rough-looking woman, her face wrinkled, her breath and clothes reeking of cigarette smoke. She was short, with graying blonde hair. Mr. Raines, too, had the smoker's complexion; he was short as well, though taller than his wife. His black hair was combed over his head and his glasses were nearing the end of his nose. He looked like he was at his wits end and wanted nothing more than to be on his way out of the clinic.

"Can I help you?" Cheryl Raines said with a sharp tongue.

"No, ma'am. I was just saying goodbye," Donald said.

"Honey, are we ready?" Arthur Raines said, grabbing David's bags of clothes.

"Yes. C'mon, David. It's time to leave."

As the three walked out the doors and into their car, Donald stood and watched. He wondered if he would ever see David again. He hoped not, for it would mean David was back in the clinic, and once again, not in his right frame of mind.

Chapter Twenty-five

August 15

Will was right about one thing: Max did move at night. He slept during the daylight hours and only went about his business at night. He made certain to stay out of sight and be as invisible as he could. He would camp out in his car for hours, checking out anything unusual. He had gotten the lowdown on the major players in Alden from Mark and the chief, so he knew who to keep an eye on. There were the burnouts, but they were already questioned by the police. There were the partiers, mainly the high schoolers, but Max figured they were out as suspects seeing as they would have been in school when his family was destroyed.

The one place that Max always made a case of driving by was the old industrial district down Route 33. Max kept an eye out for anything suspicious, and occasionally he saw a few of the local kids hanging out there, but he never saw any violent activity. He mainly drove around and kept an eye on the town, basically a second set of eyes on the night shift.

This night he followed Steve Murphy and Darren Banyon. Despite already being questioned by Mark, they were the closest suspects they had. They often skipped school and disappeared for days at a time (usually to refill their stash), and a trip to Pittsburgh certainly was not out of the question.

Max waited outside Steve Murphy's home, which was a dump. It was in an older neighborhood. The houses were falling apart and Max wondered if there was anyone in this part of town that wasn't doing drugs or fighting an alcohol addiction.

Just as he had the past few days, Darren Banyon showed up right on schedule. He pulled up, Steve jumped in the car and they were off like a shot. Max made sure to stay a safe distance behind them, keeping his lights off and pulling over to the side of the road.

After almost fifteen minutes of driving, they parked the car right next to the old Janzforth factory. Max parked across the street and prepared himself. He loaded his pistol and put his hunting knife in his boot. He took a look for the boys, but they were gone. He scanned the area and finally caught a glimpse of the two as they rounded the corner to the back of the factory.

Max slowly got out of the car and ran across the street as quietly as he could. He got next to Darren's car and followed their path to the back side of the building. He got around the corner and made sure to stay as close to the building as he could. But the ground was covered in louse stone and gravel, so he walked carefully.

Max's senses were on high alert. He was looking in all directions as he walked. He heard nothing. The air smelled awful. Max was sweating a bit and his hands were clammy. He gripped the gun even tighter and stopped.

He heard a sound come from the field about ten yards off. He turned and pointed the gun. He took a deep breath and moved a step towards the sound.

From his right, from behind a tree that was growing just a few inches from the building, a person lunged out and tackled Max to the ground. He dropped his pistol and flung the attacker off of him. He reached out and grabbed his gun. He pointed it at the assailant and then noticed a second person coming from the field. He pointed the gun at him, but kept an eye on the first person. Both were perfectly still.

Max pulled the knife from his boot. "Stay right there." Max was nearly out of breath. "All right, who are you two? What are you doing here?"

"Who the fuck are you?!" the man on the ground replied.

"I'm with the FBI. I'm one of the good guys. Now answer my fuckin' question."

"I'm Darren," the boy said getting up off the ground.

"And I'm Steve," the other boy said.

"We aren't the killers. We're here to catch a killer."

"What are you talking about? What do you know about the killings?"

"Listen, man. All we know is that this was our secret place. We did our dealings here with our clients. Now, kids are disappearing, and this place is being taken over by someone else," Darren said.

"By who?" Max asked.

"I don't know. That's what we're here to find out."

Max composed himself and put his knife and pistol away. The boys dusted themselves off and huddled towards Max. "Okay, guys. Go home. You've done enough tonight. I'll come back with the chief tomorrow and check it out."

"Don't tell him we were here or we're in some deep shit. We aren't supposed to be anywhere near this place, okay?" Steve pleaded.

"Don't worry. You're only trying to help. I won't tell anyone you were here. Just go home and I'll be in touch with you guys after we've checked things out."

The boys got into their car and headed off. Max got into his car and sat there for a minute. He decided to get some stakes out of the trunk and try to find a way in.

Max was about to get out of the car when a bright light was flashed on him from just outside the driver door. A tall figure stood there making sure to shine the light directly into his eyes. "What are you doing here, Max?" The chief took the light off Max and was now examining the contents of Max's car.

Max got out and leaned against the car. "I'm just into being prepared."

"Prepared for what?" the chief asked.

"Chief, there is something going on around here. Can't you smell it in the air?"

"Max, this isn't exactly the best part of town. It hasn't been for the past thirty years or so," the chief replied. Max didn't respond. "Let me tell you a story. That factory over there, the Janzforth factory. The man who owned and ran the place committed suicide when the business started going under. Before that, though, he was one of the most respected men in Alden. That factory, despite it being run down, is a symbol of how great Alden once was. The town has considered tearing it down, but we don't. If anything, it is one of the other buildings that houses criminals."

Max stood up straight and looked right at the chief. "And what about the kids that hang out around here? Wouldn't they know best where there's something strange going on?"

"Oh, you mean the burnouts? I wouldn't trust a word they say. It's a constant struggle with them. I'd love to run them all out of town, but I can't. They'd love to get rid of the police. Believe me, they'll say anything to get us running around chasing our tails."

Max was about to reply when the chief cut him off. "Listen. I don't believe this vampire nonsense for a second. And we let you stay here with the understanding that you won't interfere with our investigation. When we need you, we'll tell you. So, go back to the motel. We'll contact you tomorrow."

"And who is keeping an eye on these buildings?"

"I'm on watch tonight. And I'll be patrolling this area several times tonight. Go to the motel, and if I catch you around here again tonight, I'll run you out of here so fast your head'll spin."

Max gave the chief a look and got back into his car. He drove off and looked back in the rearview mirror. The chief was still standing there. Max knew that he had to get into the Janzforth factory.

He decided not to try during the day though. There were too many police about in the daytime.

Chapter *Twenty-Six*

Will awoke the next morning and stretched out. He had gotten a good night's sleep and felt refreshed and ready to face the day. He had nothing to do except meet Max, and the later he did that the better. Then, he and Mark would take the trip up to Watertown to do some real detective work. They weren't sure if the people at the institute would even cooperate with them, but they had to try.

Across town in the bowels of the Janzforth factory, Angela and David were discussing their next move while Simeon slept the day away in his coffin.

"David, it's getting crowded around here. Those two losers were back here again, along with the FBI guy and the police chief. It's only a matter of time before they figure out we're in here."

"Don't worry, sis," David said, pulling his long, dark hair back and putting it in a ponytail. "Tonight we unleash our evil on the town. We'll start with those two that are creeping around here and then go for the special agent. I have a feeling he's going to walk right into our grasp."

"Why do you think that?" Angela asked.

"Because we have something he wants. Tonight we let his daughter out for the first time. All of our subjects will quench their thirst for blood."

"Now go home and rest. We have a busy night tonight. Come back here at sunset. Simeon will be waiting for you."

Angela retreated to their parents' house and David was alone. He went down and checked in on their recruits. Matt was still on the table, lying flat with his hands at his side. Max's daughter was sleeping by the wall and the teenage boy was on the floor under an old desk. David noticed his eyes were open and staring right at him. David walked over and knelt down by the boy.

"Don't bother trying to move. Your powers are so weak while the sun's up that it would be as though moving in slow motion."

The boy's mouth was sewn shut, so there was no chance of an argument. David continued. "Tonight you will be set free to ravage the town. Tonight you will taste human blood and make your power known to all."

The boy closed his eyes and was soon asleep. His mouth was lined with dried blood. It was David's job during the day to make sure that none of the vampires tried to get free of the factory and go off on their own. They needed to be trained by the master. It would be tonight.

Will meanwhile decided he might as well go and see Max. He didn't really want to, but the sooner he got it out of the way the better. Will had to put aside his disdain so he could talk to Max and let him know where he and Mark were going and where Mark wanted Max to be that night.

Perhaps it was the way Mark held Max in such esteem that bothered Will. The only reason Mark even took Max seriously was because he was an FBI agent. Max was talking about vampires and the undead and all Mark was paying attention to was the badge Max held. Somebody wanted the murder of Max's wife and daughter to look like a vampire attack and Max fell for it, and hard.

Will thought for a second. What if someone was trying to disguise the murders as some kind of ritual killing with vampires as the scapegoats? He walked through downtown Alden, taking in the sights and sounds, but the only thing that sounded different from his childhood years was the silence. There was almost no sound. No hustle and bustle. No one eating or drinking outside the coffee shop. Will walked faster and faster trying to get to the police station as fast as he could.

After what seemed like an hour, though it was actually about fifteen minutes since he left home, Will finally got to the station. He walked in and went to the front desk. The receptionist was not familiar to Will. She had reddish hair with streaks of gray in it. It was shoulder length and despite sitting behind the desk, he could tell she was on the heavy side.

"Can I help you," she asked.

"Uh, yes. My name is Will Sandwith. Deputy Thornton said there were some pictures of the crime scene from my brother's murder I could look at. I was hoping to take a look at those."

She looked at Will with sad eyes. "Oh, I'm so sorry to hear about your brother, but I can't let you see any pictures without either the chief or one of the deputies with you."

Will turned around and was about to walk away from the counter when the chief walked up to the counter. "Sheila, it's all right, let him see the pictures." The chief looked at Will and sighed. "I'm not sure exactly what you think you're gonna find, but don't spend too much time looking at those things. We looked 'em over quite a few times. I don't think you're gonna do anything but drive yourself crazy."

"I know, Chief, I won't spend a whole lotta time looking. Maybe there's something we missed."

Will went down the hall into a small room at the back of the station. The receptionist came in shortly to give Will the pictures. He opened them up and studied each of them closely, but nothing jumped out at him. He thumbed through them over and over and was about to hand them back in when he looked at the picture where he could see the blood drop on Eric's collar. He wanted a closer look at Eric's face and neck, so he found the dark room they used to develop some of the pictures. Will took a magnifying glass into the room with all of the pictures and sat down.

He looked first at the picture with the blood stain. He put the magnifying glass over the stain and then moved up to the neck and face. He was about to look at his face when he went back to Eric's neck. Will noticed that the skin was discolored just a little on the jugular vein. There were two specks of light red, hardly visible even with the magnifying glass. Will put down the glass and sat back. He had the pictures scattered on the table and was deep in thought as he stared at the table. Was Max right? Were there vampires out there somewhere in Alden's landscape? And if so, why didn't Mark mention it to Will before?

Will looked at the picture again from a distance and noticed a sparkle, like glitter, next to Eric in the dirt. He looked at the other pictures and noticed the same speck of light. He took the magnifying glass again and put it over the sparkle. Even with the glass he couldn't tell what it was. He looked at some of the other pictures, but again, there was no way to tell what the speck was.

Will sat back in his chair and leaned back. He put his hands behind his head and sat deep in thought, staring at the pictures on the table. He knew that the police had combed the area and all of the clues had been collected. But what if the police didn't realize they had a potential clue?

Will put all of the pictures into a pile and slipped them back into the envelope. As he passed the chief's office, he poked his head in. "Hey, chief, I'm turning in the pictures to your secretary. I checked them out, but I didn't find anything. So, I'm gonna head off."

"Thanks, Will. We'll be seeing ya."

Will gave the envelope back to the receptionist and headed out of the station. He knew if he told the chief about a speck on the ground and that he couldn't even make out, he would get laughed at. And there would be absolutely no way he would be let anywhere near the scene of the crime. Will headed off towards Route 33 and set off for the crime scene.

It was a gloomy day in Alden. The sun was hiding behind the gray clouds of an oncoming storm. There was a sharp cool breeze in the air. Will walked as quickly as he could; he was underdressed for the weather. He figured his timing to head out to the crime scene could not have been better. Another few hours and the rain might have washed away perhaps the only clue left to be found.

Will could see the tape from the scene of the crime and wondered if the police were ever going to take it down. All it was at this point was a constant reminder to anyone who saw it that a murder had been committed and the safety within Alden's borders had been violated.

Will stepped through the tape and walked cautiously around the scene. He knew exactly where Eric's body had been and made sure not to step through that area. He thought back to the pictures at the station and took as good a guess as he could as to where the speck would be. He knelt down and began skimming his hand over the dirt, keeping a keen eye out for anything metal.

The wind was getting cold now. His hands were shaking a bit as every so often he thought he felt metal, but he was only fooling himself. He leaned forward a bit and almost fell. At that moment Will felt a sharp pain surge through his hand and up his arm. He immediately yanked his arm off the ground and began shaking it. There was a stream of blood no wider than the line of his hand now heading for his forearm.

It was nothing more than a pin prick and that's when Will looked directly to the spot where his hand was. Sticking out of the dirt no more than half-an-inch was a piece of metal. Will slowly took the end of metal and pulled it from the dirt. It turned out to he about two inches long and appeared to be a needle. The end that pricked his hand was rounded, but the other end was jagged, as though someone cracked it. It had to be a hypodermic needle. It was thin and smoothed yet extremely sharp.

The wind picked up and nearly caused Will to drop the needle. He put it in his wallet.

On the way to the motel to see Max, Will thought about whether or not to tell Max about what he found. Max was working on his own agenda and wouldn't believe a thing Will told him, so he decided to keep the discovery a secret. He would tell Mark when he saw him later, but for now, Max didn't need to know. It could only make the rift between Will and Max even wider.

Will passed through town again and now it was downright creepy. It looked like a ghost town. The Opera House, which also housed the town offices, looked empty and old. The café closed early with the impending storm getting closer and closer by the minute. Will felt the sprinkle of a few rain drops on his head as he now quickened his pace. He was just a few blocks away from the motel and began to jog.

As he reached the motel parking lot, he saw Max's car, or at least what he thought was Max's car based on the Pennsylvania license plates. He stopped to catch his breath and looked for Room 12. He wiped the rain and sweat off his brow and straightened himself out. He didn't want to even so much as look at Max, let alone talk to him.

Will knocked. He waited a few moments, and finally, Max came to the door.

"Will, what are you doing here?" Max asked. He looked like hell. He hadn't shaved in a few days. It looked like he had been sleeping in his clothes, his hair was messed up.

"Mark wanted me to come by and deliver a message."

"Come on in," Max said as he walked back into the room.

Will followed him in and stood in the center of the room. Max sat himself down in a chair in the corner and lit a cigar. "Take a seat, Will."

"That's okay. I won't take up much of your time."

"What's up then?"

"Mark and I are heading up to Watertown tonight to check out a suspect. We were hoping you could keep an eye on a particular house tonight until we get back."

Max took a drag of the cigar and sat up, looking directly at Will. "Where the hell is Watertown and who in the fuck is a suspect there?"

"It's a town about three hours from here and they have a mental institution there that may have been the home of one of our suspects."

Max stared at Will with a look of confusion mixed with fury.

"Fine, let me explain. We went to a girl's house here in town, Angela Raines. While we were there, she acted as though she was hiding something. While we were talking to her, we discovered that she has a brother that was being treated at a mental hospital in Watertown. We're hoping that if he's there, he can give us some answers."

Max looked at the floor.

"We're hoping you can keep an eye on the Raines place until we come back. You know, just make sure she doesn't leave the house or follow her if she does."

Max leaned back in his chair and took another drag of the cigar. He exhaled and looked at Will. "Will, we don't need you running off all over the state looking for clues. The killers are right here in this town. The vampires are sleeping as we speak in the bowels of this town. They're getting ready to strike again and you're leaving. It's no wonder your brother's dead. This town's full of cowards."

Will took a step toward Max and pointed at him. "Enough. Enough of this vampire bullshit! Goddamn it, Max. You're an FBI agent. You know that vampires and ghosts and goblins are just stories. Made up stories to scare people. There are two or three people out there working together to cover up the murders and make it look like vampires."

Max now got up out of his chair and walked over towards Will. "Were you there the night my wife was killed? Were you there when I came home to find my daughter gone? Don't come in here and tell me what to believe. You can tell Mark that I am not watching some fucking house tonight. Instead, I'm going to find me some vampires and get my revenge while you two are jerking off upstate. They're hiding in that old fuckin' factory. I know it." Max walked back over to his chair and sat down. "Now get the fuck out of here."

Will was about to step outside when he stopped and turned to Max. "When Mark and I catch the killers, you'll see how shitty of an agent I know you are."

Chapter *Twenty-Seven*

May 21

When Arthur and Cheryl Raines left Alden to come and collect their son from the Watertown Mental Hospital, they had left their daughter, Angela, behind to watch the house and study for her final exams, which were fast approaching. They packed their tan Saturn with enough clothes to get them through the weekend and planned on staying in Watertown for a few days after picking David up so they could enjoy the scenery with the son they hadn't seen in months.

They had picked David up the day before and took him out to dinner. He didn't say much, being so heavily medicated that he could barely stay awake. They booked a room at the Watertown Ramada for a week, but didn't plan on spending a whole lot of time in the room. At about eight-thirty in the evening, they headed back to their hotel room to relax, get plenty of rest and get an early start on the following morning.

David was propped up in his bed watching TV while Arthur and Cheryl went out to the car to get David's bags.

"I don't know, hon. I think we should only give him one pill tonight. I mean, he's going to be sleeping anyways," Arthur said.

"Art, the doctors said to give him two pills every time we give him his meds. And you're going to disregard that advice the very first day," Cheryl said, shaking her head.

"Cheryl, he's a zombie. We can't even talk to him. If we give him two pills every time, well, we might as well have left him in that godforsaken clinic."

"He's our son. Two pills are what's best for him right now. In a few weeks, if he's making progress, then we can take him down to half the medication."

"Okay, okay. I'll go along with that," Arthur said.

They went back up to their room and started to unpack David's things. At about ten o'clock, Cheryl was getting ready for bed. She walked into the bathroom and shut the door. Arthur, who was sitting in his bed watching TV with David, was startled by his wife's yelling.

"Arthur? Arthur? Give David his medication!"

"Where is it?" Arthur asked without taking his eyes off the TV to look for David's pills.

"It's in my purse, right on top."

Arthur got up and found the pills. He opened the bottle and took out two pills. He was going to give David the pills when he began to think about his argument with his wife. He then carefully put one of the pills back in the bottle and sat down on the bed next to David.

He took the glass of water that was on the stand next to the bed and gave David his pill. David placed it in his mouth and chased it down with the water.

David settled back down in bed and closed his eyes. Arthur went back to his own bed and lay down. A few minutes later Cheryl came out of the bathroom and got into bed.

"Did David take his pills?"

"Yeah," Arthur said, annoyed.

"All right, I was just asking." Cheryl rolled over. "Good night, honey. Good night, David."

As expected, David did not reply. Arthur didn't either.

Arthur was awakened by a hand covering his mouth with a damp cloth. As he inhaled, he took in a harsh smelling fume, got light-headed and passed out. A moment later, Cheryl Raines suffered the same fate. David then carefully tied their hands behind their backs and tied their feet together. He gagged them both and wrapped them in sheets.

About twenty minutes later, there was a knock on the door. David peered out of the peep hole and smiled. He opened the door slowly and a woman entered the room. She sat on the bed and David sat next to her, both of them gazing at the sight of their parents tied up on the bed across the room.

"Did they put up a fight?"

"No. No, they are weak. It was too easy."

"Now what do we do with them?"

"Well, we must get them out of the room tonight while it's still dark outside. If we wait until morning, we might as well turn ourselves in."

"Okay, we'll load them into the trunk of the Saturn. I'll follow you in the Buick and we'll dispose of their bodies."

"All right, but be careful. The back exit is just down the hall."

With the help of the darkness provided by a moonless sky, Angela and David carried their parents' bodies to the Saturn and placed them in the trunk. David then drove off in the Saturn, followed by Angela in the Buick. They drove along route 7-A through the countryside for almost forty-five minutes before David pulled off on a dirt road leading into the woods.

They both shut their lights off and drove very slowly down the bumpy road. As they got deeper and deeper into the woods, they found it tougher to see exactly where they were going. David finally stopped the car and popped the trunk. Angela parked the Buick and walked towards the Saturn.

"Did you remember to bring the shovel?"

"Yeah, I got it in the backseat."

Angela went to get the shovel while David got his father out of the trunk. He dragged his body about twenty feet into the brush and set him down. He then did the same with his mother. Angela stayed by the car and kept an eye out for any other cars. No one was around and David started digging. The ground was soft, as it had just rained two days earlier.

Angela stood perfectly still and watched her brother dig. She wasn't really sure how it had come to this, that she was an accomplice to the murder of her mother and lather. She had fond memories of her mom and dad. She thought back to all of the Christmases and birthdays that she had enjoyed as a child. She thought back to how her eighth grade graduation and how proud her parents were of her.

The one thing that remained the same in all of her memories involving her parents was that her brother was not there. He was always in some hospital or mental clinic being treated for a mental disease that no doctor could quite put their finger on. That was how she had gotten herself into this. That's why she was leaning up against a car keeping an eye out for passing cars while her brother buried her parents alive: she felt sorry for her estranged sibling. He had been drugged for the better part of his life, and yet, she felt there was a sanity hidden within his madness. He had extremely deep thoughts, almost philosophical. He wasn't a bad student; he just seemed uninterested. Perhaps, just by some off chance, her brother really was the re-incarnation of a vampire killed long, long ago.

David was constantly rambling about how he was betrayed and slain in a previous life and how he was going to bring darkness into the modern-day world by helping some vampire named Simeon. He was always so convincing. His plans were always so well thought out, his vision always so clear, his determination always so hard to dismiss as insanity.

About an hour later, David had dug a hole roughly six feet deep and four feet wide. He stepped out of the hole and leaned down next to his parents' bodies. He placed his hand on his father's chest and put his head down near him. "You two will now pay for what you have done to me. You left me to rot in a goddamn hospital. I must be one with the night to survive. Good night, father."

David then rolled both of his parents into the hole, his father first, then his mother. He then shoveled the dirt and muck on top of his parents, moving faster and faster, racing against the sunrise. Angela heard her mother let out a cry for help at one point, but said nothing. If David had heard it, it did not phase him one bit.

When he finally finished, he walked back towards the car and stared at it.

"What's the matter?" Angela asked.

"We must get rid of the car. If the neighbors see the car without parents, they will know something happened."

"How are we going to ditch it?"

"We need to find a dock around here somewhere. We'll push the car into the water and let the current take the car away."

"There was a boat ramp off 7-A a few miles from here. There were hardly any lights, so we should be able to get rid of it unseen."

"Perfect. You lead the way. And drive carefully. We're almost home free." A few minutes later, they were at an old boat ramp. The water was perfectly calm, and the moon was still hidden behind the clouds. David sat in the driver's seat and revved the engine a few times. Then, he released the brake and the car went flying into the water. As it got a few feet into the water, it slowed the car down, but got a little further out into the river.

Angela watched from the ramp. The car was now completely submerged. She was clenching her hands, praying oddly enough that her brother would come out of the water. Seconds later, David popped up out of the water and swam back to shore.

"The current is strong here. Our work is done. Let's get back to the hotel room before the sun comes up. We haven't much time."

The two got into the old Buick and drove back to the hotel, racing the sunrise that was now just beyond the horizon. They pulled into the parking lot and David practically jumped out of the car and ran into the hotel.

They had made it back in time. The shades in the room were drawn. The Do Not Disturb sign was on the door. David would rest throughout the daylight hours while Angela kept a watchful eye out for anyone. Even though her brother was not yet a vampire, he acted like one; when he was called to the order of the undead, he would be ready. She too would rest up and get ready for another busy night.

As the final few rays of the sun broke through under the blinds before it set for another day, Angela, who had dozed off, awoke to find her brother sitting up on the other bed, staring in the mirror. She sat up and rubbed her eyes.

"Sister, it is time to head back home," David said, looking down at the floor.

"What is our next move?"

"We head back to Alden and get our headquarters in order. We have one subject, but we still need others. Our work is nowhere near complete. And Simeon will be here soon.

David got up and walked towards the door. He turned and looked directly at Angela. "We are so close to revealing our power to the entire world. You and I are invincible. And the people of Alden will be the first to know."

Angela followed David out of the room and to the car. They got in and did not stop until they reached Alden. They did not arrive back into town until after midnight and the roads were empty. The car finally stopped outside the old Janzforth factory and the two got out.

David unlocked the trunk and opened it. He and Angela looked in at a young girl no more than four, sleeping with her hands and feet tied and a gag in her mouth. Her face was dirty and her hair a tangled mess.

"Who is this?" David asked.

"A new recruit. I picked her up in Watertown before I came to get you."

David smiled. "Great work, sis."

David picked her up and carried her to the back door of the factory. Angela unlocked the door and opened it. They walked down the corridor and before they reached the end, turned into one of the dimly lit rooms. David set her body on a table and as she hit the table, she let out a whimper. Angela glanced at David with a look of terror on her face. Next to the table was a cart with a knife on it with a cup of blood next to it.

"You know what to do," David said looking at Angela.

"She will be one of us by morning."

"Good. I'm heading down state to look for our next victim."

"Will you at least try to stay out of the sunlight?"

"Yes. It is more important for our master to have disciples than me pretend to be him."

"David, be careful. If anything happens to you, I won't be able to carry out the mission. I cannot do this without you. I don't want to let the master down."

"I've waited my whole life for this opportunity. The chance to go out and fulfill my destiny. And I'll be damned if I'm going to let the sun stop me now."

David turned away and left the room. Angela was alone with the young girl and began preparing her for her rebirth into the world of eternal darkness. David had told Angela exactly what to do on the ride back to Alden about a hundred times. She had gotten all of the supplies he had asked for in the letters they wrote to each other, and she had found the perfect spot for a vampire to make his home. Alden was quiet enough for them to move unde-tected, but close enough to a big city to take thousands with them.

Chapter *Twenty-Eight*

August 16

Will arrived home and went directly into the basement. He undressed and hung his wet clothes on a wire by the washer and dryer. He grabbed his wallet and his pager from his pants pockets. He headed upstairs with nothing on but a towel around his waist. He got to the top of the stairs when the phone rang. Will hurried to get the phone before the answering machine picked it up.

He was a bit out of breath when he answered. "Hello?"

"Hi, Will?"

"Yeah, it is."

"Will, it's Mira. Why are you out of breath?"

"I was downstairs when the phone rang so I had to run upstairs to get it. How are you? I miss you."

"Oh. Don't start our conversation off with a lie. You were supposed to have called me the other day at nine and then you leave a message at one-thirty. You must be beside yourself with a burning desire to see me."

"Yeah, I'm sorry about the other night, but I went out with some of the guys and lost track of the time. It's a lame excuse, but it's the truth. What's new with you?"

"Not too much. Just work, work and more work. How are you guys holding up down there?"

"We're hanging in there. My mother is still in shock, but she has some great people around her helping her get through it."

There was a brief pause at the other end of the line. "Will, when are you coming back here? It seems like you like being there without me."

"No, no. It's not that. Mark, you know, my good buddy, the cop? Well, we've been checking out a few leads, but nothing of any substance. I'll be home in a week at the longest."

"Okay, well I'm at work, so I have to run. Call me later and be on time, please."

"I will call you at eleven tonight."

"Okay. Love you."

"I love you, too."

Will stood by the phone staring at the floor for a moment thinking about Shannon, and the kiss and how lie lied to Mira. She was the best thing in his life and he was about to screw that up. He knew he couldn't just keep chasing lead after lead with Mark.

Will was upstairs changing when he heard his mother downstairs. She came home for lunch each day and today was no different. Will finished dressing and went downstairs. His mother was in the living room eating a sandwich, watching TV. "What? Did you just get up?"

"No, Mother. I've been up for several hours. I've already been out and about all over town."

"Where did you have to go today?"

"I went over to Henry's for a little while. Nothing major, just some catching up."

"Did you talk to Mira yesterday? She called looking for you."

"I actually talked to her not even fifteen minutes ago."

"Are you going back to Boston soon or did you lose your job?"

"Oh, you're in a terrific mood today."

Will got out of his chair and headed into the kitchen.

"What? All I did was ask a question."

"Yeah, that's all you've done since coming home."

She looked away, shaking her head in disgust.

"To answer your question, Mother, I'll be going back to Boston in a few days to resume working at the paper."

"I was just wondering. You spend all your time with Mark and the guys and I wasn't sure when you were going back."

"You're right. I have been ignoring the family the past few days, but—" Will's pager beeped. "I'll be home all day tomorrow so do you want to go out for dinner?"

"Don't you have to check that?" Morgan said pointing at the pager.

"I'll check it in a minute. Are we on for dinner?"

"Yeah. Just think about where you want to go so we can go as soon as I get out of work."

Will nodded and headed in to the kitchen. He checked the number on the pager but already knew it was the paper. He picked up the phone and dialed. His boss, Mike Parker, answered.

"This is Parker."

"Mr. Parker, this is Will. You paged me?"

"Yeah, Will. When are you coming back to work? The stories aren't waiting for you, ya know?"

"Yeah, yeah. I will be back next Monday, I promise. We're tying up some loose ends on my brother's case, so I'll be heading back on Saturday or Sunday."

"Call me before you leave so I know when you'll be back in town. If you come in Saturday I'll have some stuff for you on Sunday."

"No problem, I'll call you before I leave Buffalo."

"Great, I'll talk to you then."

Will headed back upstairs. It was a little after one in the afternoon and Mark wasn't coming by until after five, so Will decided to take a nap and catch up on some sleep.

It was about quarter to five when Will woke up from his nap. He thought about falling back asleep, but not only would Mark be at the house in half an hour, but also Will's mother would be home in twenty. And if she came home and found Will asleep, he would never hear the end of "how nice it must be to have nothing to do all day."

He lay in bed for a couple minutes before finally sitting up and tossing off the covers. He got up and walked over to the window. The rain had passed, but gray clouds lingered. It wouldn't be dusk for a few hours, but the sky had a reddish-orange tinge to it just above the horizon.

Will got dressed and decided to go downstairs and wait for Mark and his mother. He turned the TV on and flipped through the channels for a few minutes, until Morgan came home.

"Have you done anything today?" she said.

"No, not really."

"Where are you off to tonight?"

"Didn't I already answer this question today?"

"Humor me."

"Mark should be here any minute to get me and we're going out with a bunch of the guys. You know, just one more time before I head back."

Morgan was sifting through the mail on the kitchen cupboard hardly paying attention to what Will was saying. Just then, he heard a car horn coming from the driveway.

"That's Mark. I gotta go, Mom," Will said as he passed her on his way out of the house. Will shut the front door behind him as he left the house, making sure to lock it.

He opened the truck door and got in. "Ready to roll?" Will asked.

"Yeah, did you go see Max today?"

"Yes."

"Well, what did he say?"

"Let's just say I don't think he's gonna be watching the house tonight."

"What? Why not?"

"He claims he knows exactly where the vampires are and he's not wasting any time staking out a house with no one but a teenage girl in it. He said we were cowards for running out of town and chasing these leads."

Mark gripped the steering wheel. "You know, the guy hasn't done shit since he got here, yet the one time we need him to help us out for a few hours, he turns all fucking macho."

"He claims he knows where the killers are."

"Where?" Mark asked.

"In the old business district by the Janzforth factory."

"If that Raines girl does something tonight and Max comes up with nothing out there, I'll run his ass out of town myself."

Will stared out the window. For whatever reason, he wasn't as confident with this lead as he was earlier in the day. What if David Raines was still in the hospital? Their lead would be completely shot and they would have no clues left to cling to. Then Will remembered the needle in his wallet. "Hey, I almost forgot, I found something today at the crime scene."

Mark looked at Will. "What could you have possibly found there? Hell, what were you doing there in the first place?"

"I was at the police station today just to look at the pictures on more time when I noticed the same glimmer in the dirt in all of the pictures in the same place each time. I couldn't tell what it was, so I decided to go take a look."

"What did you find?"

"I was combing the dirt with my fingers when I got pricked by a needle."

"What kind of needle?"

"I have it right here," Will said taking it out of his wallet. "It looks like a broken needle, like you'd see at a hospital."

"Or like a diabetic would use for insulin. Will, this could be a great clue or just some litter. I wouldn't put a whole lotta hope on that."

"It fits the crime, though. There were two red dots on Eric's neck, barely visible as though done with a needle."

"Okay, but—"

"There are no vampires and this is the clincher."

It would be more than two hours before they got to Watertown, so Will dozed off while Mark cooled off. Will slept pretty much the whole way through. He fell asleep just outside of Rochester and didn't wake up until Mark parked the truck in the parking lot of the mental hospital. "I'll give you a minute to wipe the drool of your face and get composed before we head in," Mark joked.

"Thanks," Will replied, checking his appearance in the mirror on the sun visor

"Now, Will. There's a very good chance these people won't tell us a damn thing. They don't have to and if they have a solid confidentiality policy, their lips are sealed."

"Even if we're investigating a murder?"

"It doesn't matter, man. They don't care. Unless a judge orders them to talk, they probably won't. I'm hoping because it was your brother that was the victim, they'll be a little more sympathetic."

"It's worth a shot."

They entered the institute and made their way straight to the front desk. There were two people behind the desk: a black man leaning on it and a nurse seated at the desk. The nurse seemed startled.

"Can I help you?" she asked.

"Hi, I'm deputy Mark Thornton of the Alden Police Department and this is Will Sandwith. His brother was murdered about a week ago and we have reason to believe that a young man who was being helped here may be a suspect. Is there a doctor or nurse that we can talk to?"

The man immediately left the room. The receptionist sat up straight and stared at Mark. "How do you know the suspect was in here?"

"We were talking to a young lady that we believe is involved in the murder when she said her brother was having mental problems and that she was visiting him the night of the murder."

"I don't really know what to tell you. We can't give out information about our patients without a court order. They have rights in this building, even after they leave."

"If I give you his name, could you at least tell me if he's still here?" Mark asked.

"I'm sorry. Sorry about your brother," she said looking at Will, "and as I said before, I can't tell you anything. I'm sorry."

Mark and Will left the building. They had barely made their way to bottom of the steps leading to the walkway when they were approached from behind. "You two looking for someone?" a man asked.

Both Will and Mark turned around and saw the man was the same man from the office. "Yeah, we were," Mark replied.

"Come here," the man said motioning to a bench under a large willow tree. The bench was off to the side of the building, out of sight from any of the workers inside. "My name's Donald. I'm the head janitor here. I can tell you just about anything you want to know."

"Are you sure? The woman at the desk made it sound as though that would be punishable by death," Mark said.

"Listen, they know the patient's names. I know the patients themselves. If I can help you and them, well, I'll tell you what I can."

"Do you know anything about David Raines?" Mark asked.

The man sighed and thought for a second. "Yeah. I knew him. What's his trouble?"

"His sister is a suspect in a murder in Alden, New York, where we're from. I'm Mark, a deputy in Alden, and this is Will. His brother was the victim of a recent fatal attack."

Will finally jumped into the conversation. "We're just trying to figure out first if David is still in here. And second, if he is linked in anyway to his sister and the murder?"

"To answer your first question, no. David was released about two or three months ago. His parents came to pick him up."

"What was he here for?" Mark asked.

"David had a split personality disorder. One moment he's a good kid, the next, he's a vampire." Mark and Will looked at each other. "Split personality to the max."

"What do you mean by a vampire?" asked Mark.

"David had a fascination with vampires and the undead. He believed he could become one. He always talked about their eternal life and their power."

"How did he think he could become one?" asked Will.

"He felt that you had to act like one and believe in it enough. He talked to the Devil quite a bit." Will and Mark got confused looks on their faces. Donald didn't even have to wait for their questions. "He felt that if God answered people's prayers for good purposes, why not Satan for evil deeds."

"Were his parents going back to Alden?" Will asked.

"Oh, I don't know that. I suppose they were goin' back there."

"Well, thank you so much for your time, Donald. I can't tell you how helpful you've been."

Before Will and Mark left, Donald stopped them again. "Excuse me, fellas?"

"Yeah, Donald?" Mark replied.

"I answered your questions, now can you do me a favor?"

"Name it."

"If David is involved in the murder, please try to spare his life? He was on medication when he left here, you know, to help his disease. He's a good kid when he's taking his meds. He was my friend."

Mark put his hand on Donald's shoulder. "I promise you that unless one of our lives is in danger, we will take him alive."

"Thanks guys. He really is a good kid."

Mark and Will got into the truck and waved to Donald as they drove off. Will could contain his emotions no longer. "I'll kill him if I catch him, whether he's medicated or not."

"I know. That's why I gave Donald my word and not yours. It would be a lot to ask from you, you know, to let Eric's killer live."

"When we stop for gas, I'm gonna call my mother and tell her to get out of town. That son of a bitch and his sister are the killers and she could be a potential target."

"I'm gonna give the chief a call as well and tell him what we found out," Mark said.

It was almost eight-thirty now and they had an almost three-hour drive ahead of them. It would seem much longer than that.

Chapter *Twenty-Nine*

June 6 – Pittsburgh, PA

Max Whitfield was on his way home from the office when his cell phone rang. He checked the call number and saw it was from his home.

"Hello?" Max said.

"Hey, honey, it's me," the woman said at the other end.

"Yeah, what do you need? I'm almost home."

"Tonight, for the dinner, what dress would you like me to wear?"

After arguing with his wife for a few minutes, Max ended the call. He sat behind the steering wheel, shaking his head in disgust. His wife always asked him those kinds of questions, knowing full well she didn't really want his opinion, at least that's what Max always thought.

Max and his wife, Kelly, had been married for almost fifteen years. Max met her shortly after he joined the FBI out of Pittsburgh, they dated for a year before getting married and had been living happily ever since. Sure, they had the occasional argument now and then, but after the birth of their daughter, Susan, the fighting seemed to lessen by the year. He did his best to leave his work at work, but with some of the creeps he had to deal with on a daily basis, it wasn't always easy. He would stay up at night sometimes, thinking about just how safe he and his family were, reaching over to wake up Kelly so they could talk, but always stopping himself just before he touched her, to make sure she slept, so she wouldn't have to worry about what he was dealing with.

Susan was the pride and joy of both Max and Kelly. Kelly had had complications while birthing Susan, and as a result, Susan would be their only child. She was almost four, and a beautiful, healthy child. Max knew every time he looked at her that she was the only child he ever needed and that if his work could help save other children like her, he was doing the world itself a great justice.

Max had worked with the Pittsburgh FBI dealing with kidnapping cases since he joined them. He was not the best in the field or the captain of any special units, but he showed up for work every day, knew the profiles of countless offenders and was moving his way up the ranks. He would work a lot of overtime and sometimes go out of town for weeks at as time, but it was all for the greater good, or at least that's what he would tell Kelly when she got on his case about it.

Neither he nor Kelly would talk much about 1995, the rockiest year of their marriage. Max and a team of about nine special agents went roving around the northeast looking for a kidnapper who it seemed was baiting them, leading them on a chase that never ended. They went from state to state looking for the person responsible, finding clues but never a killer. Body parts would be found, pieces of clothing, toys and stuffed bears that belonged to the children. Then finally, the kidnapper slipped up and left himself exposed.

As the team went through the house, they found blood stains on the floors and the carpets. They found the children in the basement, or at least what was left of them, and it was Max who found the latest victim. She had been tortured, but wasn't dead. As Max held her, she said nothing. She was in shock, and as Max held her in his arms, she died. He could never get that image out of his head. The only possible survivor and Max let her life slip away. People around him always tried to convince him it there was nothing he could have done, but it didn't do him any good. He still saw her in his mind and could still feel her cold skin on his hands. He'd wake up at night with those visions in his head.

As he arrived at home, Susan was watching cartoons. He went up to her and kissed the top of her head. He walked into the back of the house and Kelly was almost done getting ready. She was putting the final touches on her makeup.

"Max, it's almost six. Dinner's at seven so you'd better hurry."

"Yeah, yeah. I'm going, I'm going," Max muttered.

He showered, got dressed and was finishing with his tie when he heard Kelly giving instructions to the babysitter. He splashed on some cologne and made his way to the kitchen where Kelly was sitting with Amy Wells. She was about thirteen or fourteen and lived just down the road. She had black hair, extending half way down her back, and ice-blue eyes. She was a good kid, a cheerleader, smart, and she made a great sitter for Susan.

"Now, if you need anything, call this number, it's Max's cell phone number."

"Okay, but we'll be all right."

"You can use the phone if you want, but don't let anyone in. No one."

"I know, Mr. Whitfield. I've done this before," Amy said with a smile.

Kelly got up from the table and picked up her coat. "We should be back here before eleven. But if not, just wait."

Amy and Susan watched out the front window and waved to Max and Kelly as they pulled out of the driveway.

"I hope everything goes all right tonight."

Max looked at Kelly with an annoyed look and said what he always said when she said those words. "Nothing ever happens, Kell. She'll be fine. She's got the number."

Because of his work, Max was a keen observer of his neighborhood. As they got closer to Amy's family's house, Max noticed a green Buick parked in front of the house in the street. It had New York license plates, but he couldn't make out the numbers and letters from the rear view mirror. There was a girl sitting in the driver's seat and it looked like she was reading. "I wonder who that is?" Max wondered aloud.

"I'm not sure, hon. She was there the other day too. Maybe she's a friend of Amy's," Kelly said.

"Well, whoever she is, she could try to at least stay out of sight 'till we're gone."

"Max, please. Amy's a good kid. I'm sure they'll sit around and watch TV." Max and Kelly argued the whole way to the dinner downtown.

Chapter Thirty

While Max and Kelly were at their dinner with Max's colleagues from the FBI downtown, Amy was at the Whitfield's keeping both eyes on Susan.

Angela Raines was the girl in the green Buick parked out front of Amy's house, and she had planned on paying Amy a visit that night, but was surprised to find out that Amy was not at her parents' home. Angela used to spend summers with her aunt, who lived just down the street. Amy would always pick on Angela and David, and Angela never forgot that. She waited for nightfall before making her way out of the car. Amy had put Susan down for the night, or at least she hoped, and had settled down in front of the TV. As she scanned the stations, a figure was watching her very closely.

Angela made her way from the side of the house to the back. She made certain to stay out of the light and be as quiet as possible. The next-door neighbor's dog was standing on the other side of the fence. It stood at attention, but Angela stayed perfectly still. Soon she heard a man's voice coming from the house. "C'mon, Noco. C'mon, girl. Get in here, and hurry up."

Angela waited for the dog and the neighbor to be gone, then made her way towards the window. She stood on her toes and peered in through the kitchen window. She couldn't see Amy clearly, but could see part of her.

Angela began to turn the knob on the backdoor when she

became the one to be startled. Amy got up off the couch and went to the front door. She opened it and watched as Amy let in another girl, a homely-looking girl who had to have been a classmate of Amy's.

Angela let go of the doorknob and stepped away from the door. She would not make her move tonight. Rather, she would wait it out and get her victim on another night.

Two hours later, Max and Kelly came home and found Amy alone. Even though the other girl was gone, and there was no sign of anyone else being there, Max had to ask the question that had been on his mind for hours.

"So, Amy, how did things go?" Max asked.

"Just fine. No problems."

"Did anyone come over here tonight after we left?"

Amy knew she was caught. "Yes, sir."

"Who was it?" Max asked.

Amy sat rubbing her knees. "It was a girl from school. She had nothing to do, so we just hung out."

Max was satisfied with her answer. "Okay. Just tell us next time you're going to have someone over. We would like to know who's in our house when we go out."

"Yes, sir."

With that, Amy left and Max went to the fridge to grab a beer. It had been a long day. Work, then a business dinner, then finding out a stranger was in his home. He heard Kelly upstairs talking to Susan. That was all Max needed to hear to turn a bad day into a good one. He grabbed the remote and checked the baseball scores.

Chapter *Thirty-One*

June 15

Max got out of work early every Wednesday and today was no different. It was the perfect day for him to do some lawn work or to just lounge around and do absolutely nothing but catch up on some TV. Wednesday nights were when Max and some of the guys from work met up at Willie's, one of Max's fellow employees, to do some card playing and shoot the shit. They would always start off talking sports or family issues, but, as always, it got onto the topic of work. They all went through similar situations at some point during their tenures as special agents, it was just during different years or different places. Max never heard anyone tell a story comparable to his, but he actually never told anybody other than Kelly about his "living nightmare." He didn't know how the guys would react. He thought about telling them just about every time they met up, but he couldn't get the words out of his mouth.

After he got home, around three in the afternoon, he laid down on the couch and put the TV on. Two hours later, Kelly came home from her sister's house with Susan and woke Max up from a sound sleep.

"Honey? Honey, wake up. It's almost five o'clock."

"I'm up, I'm up," Max said, rubbing his eyes and sitting upright.

"I'm gonna get started on dinner. It should be ready in about and hour." Max walked back to the bathroom and thought about what needed to be done outside. He went out the backdoor and went to the shed to get the lawnmower. He checked the oil and the gas and began to push the mower out front. As he passed the back of the house, something from the flower garden caught his eye. He walked over and checked the ground. There, in the soil, he found several footprints. One was so clearly imprinted in the earth that he could see the shoe size. He looked around the backyard and began to try and figure out in his head who had a shoe that size and why they were in his backyard. What really alarmed him, however, was that the footprints were right under the kitchen window.

Max went in and found Kelly. "Kell, do you know how we got footprints under the kitchen window?"

She looked up from the newspaper and gave him a puzzled look. "What are you talking about?"

"Right under the kitchen window in the flower garden, there are footprints in the soil."

Kelly got up and went outside with Max. He showed her where the prints were and she just stared at the ground. "The only person I can think of is Amy. She's probably about that size."

It made sense, but Max wasn't entirely convinced. Kelly knew she'd have to give a better explanation. "She probably came out here with Susan to play with her and had to go in the flower garden to get something."

Max thought it over for a moment. "I don't know. Right under the window? It's too perfect. I mean right under the window." Max began to walk towards the mower again. "Tomorrow after work, I'm going to the hardware store to buy one of those security lights. And when you get a chance tonight, call Amy and see if she did go outside with Susan."

Max pushed the mower to the front lawn and began making lines in the grass. As he got closer to the street he saw the same green Buick parked in front of Amy's house. He thought nothing of it, but he couldn't help looking at it every time he got close to the street.

After dinner, Max showered, got changed and got ready to head over to Willie's. Kelly was on the phone, but not with Amy.

Rather, it was her mother. Max knew she would be on the phone
for hours, so he went into the living room and bent down by
Susan.

"I gotta leave now, honey. Can I get a kiss?"

Susan didn't even take her eyes off the TV. Max leaned in and
she planted a kiss on his cheek. Max went into the kitchen and
looked at Kelly, and he was annoyed now. She put her hand over
the mouthpiece and spoke softly to Max. "My Aunt Linda is sick.
Mom's really upset. I'll see you later." She went back to talking to
her mom. Max shrugged his shoulders and walked out to his car.
As he drove off, he could see the green Buick in the distance and
saw someone sitting behind the wheel. He couldn't make out who
it was, but he figured it was the girl they saw the night before.

It usually took about twenty minutes to get to Willie's and
when he got there, he called home. The phone rang and rang and
rang until Max hung up. He knew that Kelly was on the phone
and because it was long distance, she wasn't checking the other
line. He sat down and promptly lost ten bucks.

Across town, Kelly was on the phone with her mother and,
every so often, checked in on Susan to make sure she was okay.
She was very quiet when she got into one of her cartoons. It was
probably about quarter to nine when she finally ended the conversation with her mother. She opened the fridge to get Susan's
bedtime snack together, when she realized that there wasn't any
milk. She thought for a second about making Susan something
else and waiting till tomorrow to go, but it was a perfect night
outside and she would just head to the corner store, pick up a few
odds and ends and be back in no time. Plus, Max needed milk for
his coffee and she'd never hear the end of it if she didn't get him
stuff he liked so she could talk to her mom for a few hours.

Kelly got Susan into the car and they headed off to the store.
A few minutes later they pulled up and Kelly got Susan out the
car and held her hand as they entered the store. Kelly grabbed a
basket and quickly made her way around the store. As soon as she
was in, she was out. She grabbed the items she needed for tile
morning and headed back for home.

Kelly pulled in the driveway and parked the car. Susan was sleeping, so Kelly grabbed two bags and made her way to the backdoor. She heard a loud noise coming from the house and through the window she could see the TV on. She put the key in and turned the knob, not realizing that the door was already open.

She put the bags down on the kitchen table and raced into the living room. She grabbed the remote and turned down the volume. Kelly began wondering how the TV could have gotten that loud. She walked back into the kitchen and began to make her way to the back door to go get Susan. She almost got out the door when the TV got extremely loud again. Kelly knew she was not alone and thought for a second about going to the car and getting Susan.

Kelly slowly made her way into the kitchen and peeked into the living room. The other entrance from the kitchen to the back of the house was clear. The remote was exactly where she left it. There was no sign of anyone being in there, so Kelly decided to defuse the situation by turning the TV off. She set the remote on the table and was about to go into the kitchen when the kitchen light turned off. Kelly was scared now. The light didn't flicker or burst. It shut itself off. She knew she would have to go through the kitchen to get to Susan.

Chapter Thirty-Two

"Assholes, show your cards." Willie turned into a real smartass when he was winning at cards, but it was his house and he was a good sport, even when he was losing. It was about ten-thirty and Max was almost out of money. He laid his cards on the table and hoped for the best. Next was Ken. And then Rob. And then Carl. They all looked at Willie to see what he had.

"You guys can all kiss my ass," Willie said with a million dollar smile. He spread his cards out and all of the other players hopes were smashed in a mere second. The royal flush ended Max's night and a few other guys were sent packing as well. Nick was watching the Pirates' game having run out of money about an hour ago. He didn't want to go home though, so he got comfy on the sofa.

"Let's play just a few more hands. I'm feeling good," Willie said.

Max got up from the table. "I'm done. You took everything I got."

"Sure thing, Maximus," Willie said.

Max went to the couch to catch the score of the game when he heard Willie again. "Quitter."

Max looked at Willie and he flashed that smile again. Max sat next to Nick and got settled in. "Who's winning?" Max asked Nick.

"Not the Pirates, man. Hell, nothing new there."

"I here ya. I'm not sure they'll ever win again." Max and Nick sat for a minute or two not saying a word, just watching the game. The two got along just fine, both in and out of work. Max decided to break the silence, but was quiet about it.

"Hey, Nick? Did you ever take part in a rescue or an investigation that you just couldn't get out of your head?"

"What do ya mean?" Nick said hardly looking away from the TV.

"I mean, do you ever have nightmares or think about a case still to this day that you can't get away from?"

Nick looked at Max and leaned in a bit. "Max, we're in a field where we have to remember just enough so that we're better prepared for the next time, but forget just about everything so we don't have the nightmares and the cold sweats. You have to know where to draw the line. Some guys can, others struggle with it."

"I know, you're right. But there's one case I think about every day. Hell, I think about it every hour on the hour practically," Max said hanging his head.

"Let me guess, the Dennison case. Max, I was there. I know how bad it got in that house. I realize that you got it worse than any of us. You gotta realize, though, there was nothing more you could have done."

"Could I have done more? I mean, what if we got there sooner or if we had gotten to her quicker?"

"No!" Nick said, checking behind him to see if the guys at the table heard him. They didn't. "Max, we got there as fast as we could. The girl should have been dead before we even got there. She was hanging by a thread. You gave her hope for a moment at the end. That is the only thing you could have given her." Max stared at the floor. "You're right. You're absolutely right."

"Max, we all take things to heart that we shouldn't sometimes. It's the nature of the beast. You can't forget it all. Do everything you can to help the victims and leave it at that."

Max got up and extended his hand to Nick. "Thanks, man. I needed to hear that, especially from one of you guys."

Nick went back to watching the game.

Max went to call Kelly. All he wanted was to hear her voice. He hadn't called since earlier when he didn't get through. The line was busy. That usually meant somebody was on-line at the house. He hung up the phone and sat back down on the couch next to Nick. The game was almost over so Max decided to wait until it ended to go home.

Chapter Thirty-Three

Kelly should have screamed. She should have yelled as loud as she could. At least then the neighbors would have potentially heard her. She hadn't seen anybody in the kitchen, but, without any doubt, knew somebody was there. It was not possible for the light to have shut off by itself. There was no way the volume on the TV could have gone up a few moments earlier without someone doing it manually.

The kitchen was set up with two ways in and out. Kelly took the direct route from the back door straight through the kitchen and into the living room. The other doorway went from the far end of the kitchen to the back of the house. Both entrances led to the living room, but Kelly needed the one going directly out to the backyard.

Kelly looked around the room as quickly as she could. She couldn't find anything useful to use for an attack. She looked back at the kitchen and heard the creaking of the floor, confirming her idea that someone was in there. There, on the coffee table, was a small pair of sewing scissors. They would do nothing more than perhaps pierce the skin, but it was better than going in with nothing.

She slowly and as quietly as she could made her way to the table. She leaned over and carefully grabbed the scissors. She stood up and was going towards the kitchen, when it was Kelly who was alarmed.

She heard the screen door leading out of the kitchen slam shut, as if somebody left. For the first time since the light went out she thought that perhaps Susan got out of the car and came into the house. She did know where the light switch was and could have gotten in and out of the house.

But why didn't she say anything, or make any noises or even come in crying? Plus she had woken up out of a deep sleep and would definitely not have been in a good mood. And how did she turn the volume up on the TV?

Kelly moved as quickly as she could towards the doorway. She got closer and closer, but it seemed to take a few minutes. She was holding her breath and finally got to the doorway. She peeked her head in and didn't see anyone. She then got her whole body into the kitchen when she saw somebody running at her from her left. Before Kelly could even scream, the person slammed into her from the side, full force, sending her flying into the kitchen table. Kelly's body hit the floor and the table fell over, partially on her. She was squinting from the pain and barely had her eyes open, when she saw the feet of the attacker next to her head. She tried to scream, but the person punched her right in the throat. Kelly could hardly breathe. She got to her knees, wheezing, barely getting any air in.

She heard one of her cupboard doors slam and looked around to see what the person was doing. She spotted the person walking towards her and as she tried to move was kicked in the side, sending her onto her back. She looked up and saw the face of the assailant. It was a girl. She had to be around Amy's age, Kelly was thinking, when she realized that it was the girl from the green Buick.

The girl stood over her, staring at her with any angry look on her face. She finally decided to talk to Kelly. "You've seen my face. And we can't have that." The girl held a bottle of bleach which she then poured into Kelly's eyes. Somehow Kelly got enough air to scream, but the girl put her hand over Kelly's mouth, so it was little more than a whimper.

Kelly couldn't see the girl but could hear her breathing by her ear. "We don't need you. You're far too old to be of any value to us.

Your daughter is perfect, though. We can teach her everything. However, we can't have you going around telling people about me. So, say goodbye."

Kelly screamed as loud as she could, but it wasn't much. Susan heard her mother call to her, but didn't see her. She closed her eyes and nodded off again …

It was about eleven-thirty before Max finally left Willie's. He rolled the window down and let the wind hit him. He wasn't drunk at all. He was tired and had to get up for work in the morning, but it was a boring ride home. Unfortunately he had to wake himself up in order to make it home in one piece.

It was almost midnight when Max finally arrived home. He noticed that the Saturn Kelly used was parked in the garage and the driver side door was still open. He pulled in the driveway very slowly and pulled up right before the garage. He got out of the car and looked around. He walked cautiously to the Saturn and closed the door, being careful not to slam the door. He was about to step away from the car when he noticed Susan's favorite doll on the floor of the car in the backseat. He thought for a second that Kelly just forgot the doll, but then realized that Susan wouldn't have gone to bed without it.

As Max stepped out of the garage, he looked over towards the house and was confused that the light over the back door was on. They never kept it on, so it was unusual for Kelly to have forgotten about it. What really tipped Max off that something might be wrong was that the while the screen door was shut, the wooden back door going into the kitchen was wide open.

Max got to the screen door and peered in. There was no sign of Kelly or Susan.

There was no sound coming out of the house. Max pulled the screen door open and stepped into the kitchen. He held his breath for a second before calling to Kelly. "Kell? Kell, are you awake?"

There was no response. Max assumed that Kelly was sleeping, but there were too many reasons to be cautious. He looked over to his left and saw that the papers that were on the kitchen table were scattered all over the kitchen floor by the wall, as if someone cleared off the table with their arm. He also smelled a hint of bleach. It was the drop of blood on the floor by the table that made Max's heart leap up into his throat. He reached under the back of his sweatshirt and pulled out his gun.

His senses were running on pure adrenaline. The only sound he heard was the sound of his breathing. He made his way to the living room and carefully made his way around the corner. He took a look into the room and saw nothing out of the ordinary. Everything was where it normally was and there was no sign of anyone having even been in the room all evening.

Max then took a look down the hallway and saw nothing. The lights were off and the doors were shut. He made his way to the hallway and walked down. Max got to end of the hallway and got to Susan's room. He stood directly in front of the door. His palms were sweating. His trigger finger was shaking. His left arm inched towards the door. He swung the door open. As the door hit the wall he lunged in the room and hit the light switch on the wall. Susan was not in her bed. The bed hadn't been slept in at all.

Max then turned around and headed straight across the hall to his and Kelly's room. Again the door was shut. He supposed at this point that Susan and Kelly both fell asleep in his bed and that they simply forgot to lock up.

Max engaged the safety and put the gun into the back of his pants. He opened the bedroom door. He stepped in and before he could even flip on the light, a harsh odor hit him. The lights went on and there, on the bed, spread out as if hung on a cross was Kelly. Her throat had been slit. The sheets were drenched in blood. Her eyes were open staring directly at Max.

Max ran over to the bedside screaming at Kelly. "Kell! Kelly, talk to me, honey!"

Max was in hysterics, holding her, brushing her hair back away from her face. He wiped the blood off her face with his shirt. He was sobbing uncontrollably now. He rocked her back and forth, only saying her name over and over and over again …

It would be a half hour before the paramedics and the local police showed up. Max's co-workers also showed up. There was no sign of Susan. Max was out on the front porch talking to one of the officers when Nick, his buddy from work, showed up.

"Max! Buddy, I got here as fast as I could. How can I help? What can I do?" Max stared at the ground and didn't even blink an eye or look at Nick.

After a moment he said, "Nothing, man. There's nothing any of us can do. She's dead." Max started shaking his head. "She's gone."

Nick sat down on the step with Max and decided to have the second heart-to-heart of the night with his co-officer. "Max, you can't help Kelly. But your daughter is out there somewhere. You have to pull yourself together for her sake."

Max looked at Nick with a piercing glare. "My wife is dead. My daughter is missing. Excuse me if I'm a little fucked up right now!"

Nick wasn't shocked by Max's reaction. He'd seen it a hundred times with other fathers of missing children. "Max, you're an FBI special agent. You do this everyday. You of all people must know how crucial these first few hours after an abduction are." Max said nothing. He just kept staring at the ground.

"Max, was there anything suspicious around here the past few days? Was there anything out of the ordinary around here?"

Max didn't say anything at first. He mumbled to himself a little, but it was nothing that Nick could make out. Nick hammered Max with questions a second time. "Max, do you have any idea who could have done this?"

Max finally started talking. "I don't know for sure. I mean, I didn't see anyone around here lately that was out of the ordinary."

Nick gave Max a moment to think.

"Wait a minute, wait a minute. There is something that may help us. There were footprints under the kitchen window in the flower beds. I found them earlier today," Max said.

"Max, stay right here. I'm gonna find the local police chief so you can talk to him," Nick said as he ran to the back of the house. A few moments later, he came back with a middle-aged man, probably in his fifties. He had black hair and a clean shaven face. He was well built and had a large brimmed hat on. "Max, this is Chief Devereaux. I want you to tell him exactly what you told me."

"Well, Chief, I was telling Nick that I found some footprints in the flower bed under the kitchen window today. They were about a size five or six."

"You didn't see anybody around here though that might match that description?" the chief asked.

"No, no. The only person I know with feet that small is the girl down the street, Amy, but she babysits for us. She couldn't have possibly done this."

"Well, Max, we'll talk to her and we'll judge what her capabilities are. Is there anything else you can tell us?"

Max thought for second and his face lit up. "Yes, Chief, there is. There's a green Buick that's been parked down the street for the past two weeks now. There was a girl sitting in the car the one day, not a whole lot older than Amy. And the car had New York license plates on it."

"All right. It seems like you've given us a few good leads to work with. Now Max, we'll look into these leads tonight and tomorrow, but in the meantime, I want to you to stay with someone tonight. A friend perhaps, or a close relative. We're gonna be in and out of here all night and I want you to try and get some rest. Do you understand me?"

Max rubbed his face and nodded. How could he argue? He'd given that speech to parents of kidnapped children quite a few times over his career. "Yeah, Chief. I'll give one of the guys a call."

Max didn't stay in his house that night. But he didn't get any sleep either.

Chapter Thirty-Four

June 21

Almost a week had passed since the death of Max's wife and the disappearance of his daughter. With each day, hope grew slimmer and slimmer that Susan would be found. Max was put on leave indefinitely by the bureau, which he protested vehemently. He was told by his superiors that he needed some time away from the job to put his feelings in order and organize his life.

Max stayed at Willie's for the first few nights after the murder, but once the funeral was over, he decided to go back home and start moving forward with his life. The dust had not settled yet, and there was Nick at Max's door. Max let him in and said nothing as lie led him into the living room.

"Max, I know you have been taken off duty for a while, but there are a few things you should know," Nick said.

Max looked up at him, but said nothing.

"First of all, we checked with your neighbors about the green Buick you told us about."

"And?"

"It turns out that the car belonged to Daisy Raines' niece who was in from Buffalo. She'd been visiting for about two weeks."

"Is she gone? Did anyone talk to her?"

"Yes and Yes. She left the other day to go back home. Willie and Tommy talked to her the day after the incidents. They said she seemed like a pretty good kid. They said she acted a little strange at first, but her story checked out."

Max took his eyes off Nick and gazed out the window. "I lost 'em both, Nick. The kidnapper's a few states away by now. And to top it off, I've been put on leave." Nick stared at Max. Finally, he found enough guts to tell Max what he really came over to tell him.

"Max, there's something I think you should know about Kelly's death. In fact, you need to know."

Max glared at Nick.

"You came home and found Kelly on the bed. Her throat was obviously cut, but did you notice anything else unusual about the wound?"

"No. What did you find?"

"You have to promise to hear me out."

"I'm not promising anything."

"Okay then. Her throat was cut pretty deep and she did die of blood loss. However, the coroner found two tiny holes on her jugular vein. He guessed that the skin was punctured before she died, but we have no way of knowing."

"What are you trying to tell me, Nick?"

"Well, Max, I'm not one to believe in the supernatural or ghosts or evil beasts or anything like that, but two holes on her neck coupled with significant blood loss? You tell me what to think?"

Max sat back in his chair. "Are you saying that a vampire attacked and killed my wife?"

"I'm not saying anything. I'm telling you the facts. You can go whatever way you want with it."

Max stared out the window again, then looked over at Nick. "Maybe I haven't gotten enough sleep lately or maybe I need a good explanation for what happened, but is it possible that vampires do exist? I mean, there are some real psychos out there, I don't need to tell you that."

"Max, I don't know about vamp—"

"She was attacked at night. And it was a random attack. Maybe there are creatures of the night out there."

Nick didn't say a word.

Max stood and motioned to Nick that it was time for him to go. "Well, Nick. Thank you for telling me about this. You've shined a whole different light on this case." Nick could Max was planning something.

"Max, please tell me that you are going to take it easy for the next few days. You aren't going to do anything rash are you?"

"Nick, what am I going to do? What you've told me is a lot to take in, and I'm just tired. I promise I'm not going anywhere."

"All right. Call me if you need anything. Okay?"

"You'll be the first to know."

Max made his way to the living room. He lay down on the couch and thought about everything Nick had just told him. The facts don't lie. He began to evaluate his life and what he believed in. Maybe he was so narrow-minded and focused on what he knew to be true that he didn't see the ever-growing evil in the world around him. He knew about underground cults and groups that practiced ritual killings and sacrifices, but it wasn't his field of expertise.

Vampires in Pittsburgh? He questioned everything he ever believed in now.

Chapter Thirty-Five

It was nearly sunset. Max was still asleep on the couch. Max opened his eyes and looked out of the living room window. He couldn't see the sunset from his house, but he could see the colors changing in the sky over the trees across the street. The maroon and orange were becoming blue and purple and the moon was visible now. Max stood there and just stared ahead. He wasn't necessarily looking at anything, just watching the sky. The neighborhood was quiet. No one seemed to be going anywhere.

It occurred to him that what happened to his wife and daughter affected not only Max, but everyone around him.

Max stepped away from the window and made his way to the back of the house. He went into his bedroom and got changed. He put on casual clothes, jeans and an old gray tee-shirt, hooded sweatshirt and a pair of old hiking boots.

He looked over at the bed, the same bed he found Kelly in just a few days earlier. He sat down on the bed exactly where he had the last time he held Kelly in his arms. He closed his eyes and played the moment over and over again in his head to the point that even the smallest detail seemed crystal clear. Her neck was covered in blood but he couldn't tell if there were any markings on her neck. However, if Nick told him that there were, then there had to be.

He got up and looked into the mirror. He was staring directly into his own eyes and thought, You couldn't save them, but you can save others. He took a deep breath and gave himself the same tough guy, macho stare that countless criminals had seen so many times before.

He went back into the kitchen and out the back door. He stopped and looked at the sky one more time. Any hints of orange and red were gone now. Only darkness remained, blue and black. The stars were out and the moon illuminated some of the darkness.

Max went into the garage and turned the light on. He grabbed a few items and placed them into the trunk of his car. As he drove off, he looked back at the house and wondered if someone would be there waiting for him when he returned. He didn't lock any of the doors as if inviting the world into his home.

Max drove slowly as not to draw any attention to himself. He drove around town for an hour or so doing nothing but people watching. He saw couples walking hand-in-hand, a few joggers, and even a few dog-walkers. It was a quiet, summer night.

Max was about to head for home when he came to the cemetery that Kelly had been buried in just a few days earlier. He stopped at the gates and put the car in park. If indeed his wife were a vampire or a member of the undead, then she would be coming out of the grave to do it. Max couldn't think of his wife in that way, being a creature of pure evil. He had to put those thoughts aside. She was dead.

He sat in his car for a few minutes. The gates were not locked. He could pull the car right in. However, the police would be patrolling the area at least twice and his car would most certainly be seen. If he left it out on the street, however, it would definitely be noticed.

Max put the car in drive and took the lights off. He slowly made his way into the cemetery, surrounded on either side by rows of trees, hundreds of years old perhaps, their branches hanging over the road blocking out all moonlight. He could hear the stones from the gravel road crunching under the weight of the tires and was worried that perhaps the caretaker of the cemetery might see or hear him.

Max turned the lights on once or twice so he stayed on the road, but he was safe. To his right, beyond the trees, was a stretch of land that the cemetery had not used yet. Beyond that about twenty feet was a stretch of field that he could hide the car in. He pulled off into the field and got out. He popped the trunk and grabbed the items he took from the garage. A cool breeze was in the air. There was no light whatsoever. The moon was blocked out and the flashlight would surely give him away. His eyes adjusted a little to the darkness and he made his way to the gravesite. There was no grave stone, but the mound of dirt was fresh. The flowers he placed at the head of the grave were still there.

He became obsessed with the idea of vampires. All he could do was think about killing them, running them through with stakes. They messed with the wrong guy. He was no longer an FBI agent. He was now a vampire hunter. It was his passion. As shavings of wood fell to the ground, he felt better and stronger about his cause. He was a modern-day crusader, newly programmed to exact revenge on those who took his family. Two hours had passed and Max had about five stakes within his reach. But there was no sign of Kelly rising from her grave. The only sounds he heard were from the crickets in the field and the breeze blowing through the trees. Clouds had moved in and an occasional sprinkle of rain fell.

He couldn't take his eyes off the grave. He stared at the grave as if in a trance. The breeze turned into full blown gusts of wind. It whipped up some fresh dirt from the grave and swirled it around Max. He squinted to shield his eyes from the dirt, and if he hadn't been so enthralled by the grave, he might have heard the person coming up from behind.

"What are you doing here?" It was a man's voice, deep and discerning. As the question was asked, a flashlight was shone right into Max's eyes.

Max covered his eyes with his hand, but didn't know how to answer. He didn't even know who he was talking to.

"Sir, what are you doing here?" the man asked.

"I, I was just …"

"What is that on the ground?" the man asked as he shone the light on the wooden stakes.

"Oh, that. Uh, I got bored and found that wood. I was just sitting here, honest," Max said.

"Mr. Whitfield, is that you?"

"Yes, I'm Max. I'm doing work with the FBI."

The man finally introduced himself. "I'm Tom Wagner, of the Pittsburgh P.D. I was at your house the other night. I'm awfully sorry about what happened to you and your family."

"Well, thank you for the compassion, but it doesn't really help much these days."

"I understand that. What I don't understand is exactly what kind of FBI work requires you to sit by the grave in the darkness."

Max stood in silence and tried to come up with a good excuse, but couldn't. "Mr. Whitfield, I'm sorry about your wife, but you will have to leave now. If in fact you are on duty, you have to let the local police department know. Do you need a ride home?"

"No, no. I'm parked in the field over there?"

Max walked over to his car and exchanged a few more pleasantries before being followed out by the officer. He would have to wait until morning to see if Kelly's grave was disturbed. He figured the best thing to do was go home and get some sleep … on the couch of course.

Chapter Thirty-Six

August 9

It was still two months before school would start, and Eric Sandwith and Lindsay Adams were already bored with the less than exciting Alden nightlife. They had begun dating almost a year earlier, about a month before their junior year at Alden High. Most of the high school couples were nothing more than flings that lasted a month or so, but Eric and Lindsay were different. They had known each other for years, and because their older brothers were good friends, it seemed only natural that the two should fall for each other.

On this particular evening, Eric and Lindsay were at Eric's for dinner. Nothing odd there, except for Eric's mother. She was in especially good spirits today.

"All right, Mom. What's going on?" Eric asked.

"What do you mean?"

"Mom, you usually spend dinner doing your best to depress the two of us with stories about people at work with sick relatives or people with handicaps."

Lindsay did her best not to laugh and gave Eric a look that he knew meant for him to leave his mother alone.

"That's not true. I just tell you what's going on at work."

"Okay then. What happened today? You seem in happier than normal."

"Well, I talked to Will today," she said. She looked back at her plate and took another bite of food.

"And?" Eric asked. He was getting annoyed now by her stalling tactics.

"Well, he's doing well. He got the cover story at the paper the other day."

"How's his girlfriend?" Lindsay asked.

"Mira is doing well. Now what I'm about to tell you must stay secret, okay?"

"Yeah, mom."

"Your brother went ring shopping the other day. He's going to ask Mira to marry him soon." She smiled at Eric and went back to eating, knowing how much that irritated Eric. She waited for him to explode.

"Well, did he say when or how he was going to do it?" Eric asked, practically yelling.

Eric's mother finished chewing and wiped her mouth. "He's not sure exactly when. He hasn't even bought the ring yet. And he won't tell me how he's going to ask. It's his secret."

"He'll tell me," Eric said.

"Well, I think it's great that Will's that happy, no matter how he asks," Lindsay said.

Eric and Lindsay left shortly after dinner to go over to Lindsay's house.

Lindsay's parents usually went to bed early and left the TV in the front room for Eric and Lindsay. Eric's mother didn't like the idea of Lindsay going upstairs in her home, and unless Eric and Lindsay wanted to watch TV with Eric's mother, they had little choice but to go to the Adams home.

They drove along Route 33 to get to Lindsay's even though they only lived less than ten minutes apart. The drive was boring and the later into the day they drove, the fewer cars they saw. They drove along in Eric's car with the windows rolled down. The warm summer air felt soothing as it poured in through the windows.

Lindsay noticed a green Buick coming from the other direction.

"Look at that piece of shit car. It's actually worse than yours," Lindsay said.

"No, I still think mine's worse."

They looked to see who was driving it. The two cars passed and Lindsay saw Angela Raines. Angela gave them a glance as well.

"Oh, there was your girl, Eric." Eric said nothing.

"Eric, honey, are you sure you wouldn't rather be with her than me?" Lindsay asked sarcastically.

"Pooh Bear, you're the only girl for me."

"Smartass."

Eric smiled.

They arrived at Lindsay's house and spent almost the entire evening sitting around watching movies.

It was a little after 10:30 when Eric finally decided to head for home. His eyelids were extra heavy and Lindsay was half asleep for the past fifteen minutes or so. "Hey, Linds? Linds, wake up. I'm gonna get going."

Lindsay was sleep walking for the most part and walked Eric to the door. "What time is it?"

"A little after 10:30. And we have to wake up early for our run tomorrow." She kissed Eric good night and locked up. Eric got in the car and started it up. Eric rolled the window down and scanned the radio dial for something to help wake him up for the ride home. He got about a minute or two down Route 33 when he noticed something off to the side of the road. Whatever it was was waving at him, practically jumping out into the road in front of the car.

Eric slowed down to see who it was in the road. He came almost to a complete stop and realized that he knew the young lady in distress. It was Angela Raines. But he didn't see her car anywhere.

"Angela? What are you doing out here?"

"Oh, Eric, thank god you're here. I was walking my dog and he ran out into the road and was hit by a car. Please help me?" She had clearly been crying.

Eric pulled the car off to the side of the road and got out. Angela grabbed him by the hand and just about dragged him down the road.

"Hey, hey! Slow down, will ya?"

"I don't know how much longer he's gonna make it. He's right around here."

The two stopped and looked around. "I don't see anything. Are you sure we're in the right spot?" Eric asked.

"Yes, we're in the right spot. He must have gotten up and dragged himself into the woods," Angela said. She then took Eric by the hands. "Thank you for helping me."

"What are you doing? We have to find your dog."

"No. He's fine."

"What are you talking about?" Eric asked pulling his hands away from her and taking a step back.

"Eric, you didn't have to stop, yet when you saw me you did. That has to count for something?"

"Count for what? I would have helped whoever it was."

"Eric, you know I like you a lot, and I think you really like me too. You just *think* you need Lindsay."

"What? Angela, I love Lindsay. You're a good person, but I'm spoken for."

"Trust me, you're better off with me. He wants you too."

Eric was totally confused now. "He? Who are you talking about? And, no, I'm not better off with you."

"Good bye then, Eric. I gave you a chance."

Before Eric could respond, he was struck on the head from behind. The blow knocked him to the ground face first. He was already unconscious.

Angela watched as Eric hit the ground and then looked at the man. It was David, holding a piece of wood he found. "You didn't hit him too hard did you?"

"I don't think so," David replied.

Angela knelt down beside Eric's body and listened to hear if he was breathing. "I think he's dead."

David stared at Angela in horror. "Are you sure?"

"Yes, he's dead. You weren't supposed to kill him. I wanted him."

"I'm sorry, sis. But we must get going before someone drives by and sees us." David knelt down and checked Eric's neck.

Angela took her sweatshirt off and wiped Eric's neck. She and David then disappeared into the woods, leaving Eric's body by the roadside. It would be a while before anyone driving by noticed the first case of homicide in Alden's history.

Chapter Thirty-Seven

It was almost midnight when Mark got a call from the dispatcher at the Alden Police Station. "Mark? Mark, are you there?"

"Yeah, this is Thornton."

"Mark, I got a call from Mrs. Sandwith. She said Eric is very late getting home. Could you swing by the Adams place and see if his car is there?"

"Yeah, I'll swing by in a few minutes."

He approached the Adams and pulled into the driveway. He did not see Eric's car and all of the lights were off.

So he pulled out of the driveway and went down Route 33. He was checking out if anything was coming in on the radio from the neighboring towns, when he noticed a car off to the side of the road.

He pulled up. The driver door was still open and that the lights were still on. Mark pulled up behind and got out of the car. He had his pistol loaded and ready in one hand and a flashlight in the other. The license plate verified this as Eric's car.

Mark got up to the door and shone the light in the car. There was no sign of any struggle or blood, but there was no Eric either. He panned the light along the roadside and noticed a body lying face down in the stones about ten feet away. Mark put his gun away and ran towards the body.

To Mark's dismay it was Eric. Mark flipped Eric's body so he was on his back. His face was ghost white and his skin was like ice. Mark noticed a large puddle of blood near Eric's head. Mark stood there for a minute, confused and frightened. His best friend's brother was dead and Mark was alone. He scanned the area to make sure no one else was there. Finally, Mark got back to his squad car and called the dispatcher for assistance.

"Dispatch, send an ambulance to Route 33 between Connors Road and Willoughby Lane. And call the chief right away. Tell him there has been a murder." Mark then stood by his car and flashed the light on the body. Perhaps the murderer was still there, lurking in the shadows, waiting for another victim. Mark quickly turned to his right and left shining his light on the woods. All was still. Mark could hear nothing but a few crickets off in the distance. He was alone.

It seemed to take an eternity for the ambulance to show up. Chief McGillis got to the scene first. He was in uniform, but was pissed off to have been woken up out of a deep sleep.

"Mark, what in the hell is going on here? I heard something about a murder." Mark pointed his light on Eric's body. The chief knelt down beside the corpse. "When did you get here? How long have you been here?"

"I got here about twenty minutes ago. His body was lying there, face down. I turned him over to see who it was."

"Was he dead?"

"Yeah, he was cold as ice."

The chief was silent for a while. Then he got up and walked over to his car. He made a call to the Sheriff's Department to have them send out a few officers.

In the meantime, Mark was at the side of Eric's body, examining the head and the wound. The hair was soaked in blood and half of Eric's face was pressed in from being face down on the gravel. Mark then called over to the chief. "Chief! Chief, come here quick!"

The Chief ran over and knelt down next to Mark. "What is it? What did you find?"

"I was checking the wound and noticed these two marks on his neck. Here, on the vein."

On the left side of Eric neck were two pin-sized holes which would have been overlooked if not for crusted blood around the holes.

"What are those? How did he get two holes directly in line like that directly on his jugular?"

Before Mark could respond, the ambulance could be heard coming up the road. The two stepped away from the body and signaled for the ambulance to park.

It would be another hour before the emergency techs declared Eric dead and took the body away. Some of the officers from the Sheriff's Department and some of the Lancaster and Depew officers were there to assist. As most of them headed off, Chief McGillis walked over to Mark who was leaning against the door of his car. "Mark, do you want me to go over to the Sandwiths and tell his mother?"

"No, no. I'll do it. I should do it. I know her well enough that it might cushion the blow."

"Do you want me to come with you?"

"No, I'll do it. There's plenty of paperwork to work on, so there's no use in both of us going. Plus, I need to do this, for her."

As Mark drove along Route 33, he was trying to figure out what to tell Mrs. Sandwith. He got to her house and pulled in the driveway. He got to the front porch and rang the doorbell. The front light came on and Mrs. Sandwith carefully opened the door. She recognized Mark and opened the door wide.

"Oh, no. Mark, what's wrong? Where's Eric?"

"Mrs. Sandwith, please, can I come in?"

She stepped away from the door and walked over to the couch. Mark sat her down and sat down next to her. "Mrs. Sandwith, I don't know how to tell you this, but Eric is gone."

She stared at him, tears welling up in her eyes. She had no idea what Mark meant by that. "Where is he?"

"He's dead. He was attacked and was dead when I found him. He's gone." Mrs. Sandwith tried to say something to Mark, but could only stare at him. He could tell she was trying to process what he said, but she was silent. Her eyes then rolled back into her head and she collapsed on the floor.

Mark picked her up and laid her down on the couch. He called her sister and told her to come over to the house immediately, not telling her what happened. Mark then called the only person he wanted to give the news to less than Mrs. Sandwith. He found the number and called Boston.

Chapter Thirty-Eight

August 12

Max Whitfield was at home sleeping when Nick showed up at his door again. Max let him in. Nick sat down in one of the chairs and sat up rubbing his hands together. "So Max, how are you holding up? We can't wait for you to come back to work."

"I'm doing all right I guess. I'm holding up as well as to be expected under the circumstances."

"I stopped by because I heard about a case that might be of some interest to you. I was doing some research on Kelly's case the other day."

Max looked at Nick and stared at him with extreme interest. "What did you hear?"

"Well, we don't have an interest in the case seeing as there was no kidnapping involved, but there was a murder in a small town in western New York. The first murder in the town's history."

"And?" Max asked.

"Well, the killer struck the victim on the back of the head and left two unusual marks on the victim's neck."

"Pin holes on the jugular vein?" asked Max rising abruptly from the couch. Nick nodded.

Max began thinking when he asked another question. "What town was it in?"

"Alden, New York. It's about a half hour outside of Buffalo."

Max wasn't even paying attention to Nick anymore. "Max,

I'm only telling you this as a friend. If you get into any trouble, I'll pretend I didn't tell you anything. You must not take this lead too far."

"Don't worry, Nick, I won't rat you out."

Nick left and Max began packing his car for a trip to Alden. He was sure that the killer was the same and that he would be able to stay on his trail. He packed light. A few changes of clothes, some money and some wooden stakes.

Chapter Thirty-Nine

August 16

Max packed the stakes into his trench coat pockets and headed out to his car. He started it up and made his way to the factory. He had to park his car out of sight, remembering what the chief had told him. He would then set up shop in one of the trees outside the old Janzforth place and wait for activity.

Across town, Steve and Darren were hanging out at Darren's house (if you want to call it that, it hadn't looked like a house in years). The two were sitting in Darren's room, listening to heavy metal music. Steve was deep in thought, sitting at Darren's desk. Darren, though, was pacing back and forth, obviously nervous about the upcoming night's activities.

"Dude, calm down," Steve said. "We have to be calm and level-headed if we're gonna do this right."

"Calm? How can you stay calm? We're gonna break into that old fuckin' factory to look for killers," Darren said. He stopped for a moment, the first time he stood still in quite a few minutes and looked Steve. "Why are we goin' in there, anyway? I don't want anything to do with that place."

"Listen, dipshit. That's our turf. We own that place and some stupid fucks are trying take it over. We haven't sold shit in two weeks now. I have no money left. Maybe we can flush the bastards out."

"There's got to be a better way, man. I mean, let's tell the police we saw someone going in there. They'll take care of it."

"The police don't believe us. Hell, that dick FBI guy didn't believe us and he was piss-scared. We have to take care of this ourselves."

"Well, what's our plan?"

"We go in real quiet like and check things out. I took my old man's gun in case we get attacked." Steve pulled a handgun out of the back of his pants.

Darren couldn't believe it. "What the fuck are you gonna do with that? Kill somebody?" Steve said nothing. "And what about the car? Once the cops see it we'll get busted for trespassing?"

Steve put the gun away and stood up. "We're gonna walk. So we better leave now."

Reluctantly, Darren followed Steve out of the house and they made their way up the street. It would take the better part of an hour to get there. "In case you forgot, Eric was killed on the roadside, man. Maybe we should have driven?"

"There's two of us and we're armed. We'll be fine, dumbass."

The moon was still hiding behind the trees and the stars were not quite visible yet. The two were well hidden under the dark of night, but eyes were watching them, looking for them. They couldn't feel the weight of the stares coming from the trees and empty fields.

Unlike Darren and Steve, Will and Mark were hours away from the encroaching danger. And unlike Darren and Steve, Will and Mark were terrified. Not only did they know who the killers were, they couldn't get home fast enough to be of any service to the chief.

After driving for almost twenty minutes (spent in perfect silence) Mark stopped off at a gas station and began fueling his truck. Will went over to the pay phone and put in the necessary money for a long distance call to Alden. The phone rang twice before Morgan answered. "Hello?"

"Mom, it's me!"

"Yeah? What's going on?"

"Mom, listen to me. Mark and I found out who the killers are. They're still in Alden!"

"What are you talking …"

"Mom, there's no time to discuss it. You need to get out of town for a few days."

"Will, I can't leave work. I just went back."

"Mom, I don't mean to alarm you but the killers are still in town. And for all we know, they're watching you as we speak. You need to go and stay at Aunt Karen's for a few days, until we catch them."

"Will, we'll discuss it when you get home."

"Mom, don't think that just because they got Eric they can't get you. Please, I beg you, go to Syracuse and stay with Aunt Karen. If we can't find anything, I'll call you and you can resume living your life as normal."

There was a moment of silence at the other end of the phone. "Fine, I'll leave tonight. But you better be careful. Let Mark and the police take care of this. I don't need to lose you too."

"I promise I'll be careful and I'll talk to you tomorrow."

"I love you."

"I love you too, Mom."

Will hung up the phone. The killers were still at large, but at least his mother was getting out of harm's way. Will walked over to the truck, and got in. Mark had finished gassing up the truck and he too was on the phone. After a few seconds, Mark hung up.

"My mother's getting out of town tonight. She's heading to Syracuse. I'm shocked she listened to me," Will said in a monotone voice.

"I wish I had that success with my call."

"What do you mean?"

"I called the station and spoke with the dispatcher. She said the chief is staking out the old business district and is not taking any calls from you or me tonight."

"Why?"

"He thinks you're leading me on wild goose chases and that I'm so anxious to help you I'm neglecting my duties to serve the town first. She wouldn't even tell him I called. She said if I want to speak with the chief, it had better wait until morning."

"But it may be too late by then?"

"I'll tell him anything that hasn't been proven first and it turns to be crap, I'll be pulled from the case and put behind a desk. We can only hope the killers take a night off, or at least wait for us to get back."

Back in Alden, Darren and Steve were making good time on their way to the old factory. They spoke to each other every few minutes or so, but Steve was too focused on the task that lay ahead and Darren was too focused on his fear.

Chapter Forty

Mark and Will drove on. "Ya know, I can't wait till we find those two," Mark said.

"Yeah. They probably don't even know we're on to them."

"We'll follow them and when we know we've got 'em cornered, we're gonna run in guns blazin'."

"What? Isn't that when we call for backup? I mean, we want 'em alive, right?" Mark said nothing. "Mark, what are you thinking? It's like you aren't even listening to me."

"Will, there's something about that night I never told you."

"What night?"

"The night of Eric's death."

"Dude, what didn't you tell me?" Will sat upright and stared at Mark.

"About four years ago, almost right after you left for college, me and Hank and Hoss and Jay went into the woods by the old Janzforth building, ya know, to tip back a few beers, shoot the shit, all that stuff. We were in the thick of the woods, where you can barely see beyond your face. It was black. We were there for two or three hours, the fire was just about dead and the beer was pretty much gone. So, we were on our way back into town when we heard voices. There were a couple of different voices. Mostly guys. We heard a female voice every so often, but she wasn't talking. It was more like yelling," Mark said. "We all looked at each other in horror. No one said anything. We all got down on the ground as quietly as we could. Finally, we heard one of the guys let out a yell, like he was celebrating for some reason. It was Stan Carney, ya know, he was a few years ahead of us in school?"

Will nodded. Stanley Carney was two years ahead of them in high school, but didn't finish school. He got kicked out for drug dealing and spent some time in a juvenile prison upstate. He was known for his tough-guy image and for the gun he carried around in his back pocket. There were rumors he shot a man in Buffalo in a drug deal gone bad, but it was never proved.

"So there we are, praying none of the guys came over and found us there. If they did, we probably wouldn't have made it out of the woods alive. About five or ten minutes passed and we didn't hear any of the voices. I thought for a moment they were gone. Then we heard the girl scream again. She was yelling at them to let her go and to get off of her. The guys just laughed and told her to shut up. They raped her, Will. We heard it all. Every scream. Every cry for help. Every victory yell from the guys. And with every sound, I prayed harder and harder for them to go away. Just finish with her and go away.

"After about an hour or so, the sounds stopped. It was scary how quiet it was. I was about to get up and check things out. I got to my feet and heard some branches cracking a few feet away, coming from the direction of where the guys were. Standing there, not even ten feet away, was Carney. He was leaning against a tree, pissing. He was looking in our direction. I closed my eyes and prayed to God he didn't see us or come over any further. Alter a minute or so, he got done, found the other guys and left. I saw the lights of their car as they left the woods. I made my way over to where the guys had been and checked things out, you know, to see if they left anything behind. There were a few beer cans, some cigarette butts, but nothing else.

"We left shortly after and ever since, we've never breathed a word about that night, until now. I spent the next several months thinking about that night. I couldn't sleep. Every time I did, I heard those cries and those screams. I'd wake up sweating and would wait for the morning. I should have done something. I should have helped that girl. She was screaming for help and we were the only ones there to help her. I just stood there, paralyzed with fear. I couldn't even move. Instead of helping her, I lived for years with the guilt of not saving her. That's why I became a police officer. At least now I get a chance to save lives."

Will waited for a moment. "What does that have to do with Eric's death?"

"When I arrived at the scene, I leaned over and checked Eric for vital signs. I got up, went to my car and called for backup. And the whole time, I knew someone was watching me from the woods along the road. I went over to Eric and knelt down. I never even looked at him, though. I stared blankly into the woods, hoping to see something, anything. But for the second time in my life, I was praying for God to help me. I was frozen with fear. I didn't breathe. I waited for help to arrive so I wouldn't be alone. Will, the killers were there, I know it. They were watching me. All I had to do was get up and run into the woods. I could have caught them, at least caught a glimpse of them. And I let them get away."

Mark stared ahead at the road. "Will, I promise you, if it's the last thing I do, I'm gonna get these guys. I'm gonna chase 'em down if I have to. They will not scare me off. If it kills me, I'm gonna get 'em."

Will now knew he wasn't angry with Mark. He couldn't be. "Ya know, Mark, I'm gonna be there with ya. We are gonna find those two and when we do, we're gonna strike fear into them."

They were almost home. Mark was driving a little faster now.

Chapter *Forty-One*

Darren and Steve weren't the only ones out this particular night in Alden. Max Whitfield was staking out the old Janzforth building. Chief McGillis was driving from one end of Alden to the other in search of anything unusual. Angela and David Raines were not at home. And for the first time in several days, Matt Burton was not locked up in the factory.

Almost an hour had passed since Darren and Steve left for the Janzforth factory. The moon was popping in and out of the clouds.

The two boys were on Route 33 and the old factory was just a few minutes away. Darren in particular was starting to walk a little faster, hoping to catch the killers off guard.

They were close to the very spot where Eric Sandwith met his end. Off to their right was an open field, used for farming by Mr. Powell. There was a fog hovering over the wheat that was about waist-high this time of summer.

The two continued on their way when they heard an owl off in the distance. They stopped. A few feet further they heard another sound. Darren kept walking, but Steve stopped.

"Why are you stopping?"

Steve put his hand up, listening for a sound. Darren walked over to Steve. "Dickhead, let's g—"

The sound they heard was coming from the field, through the fog. It was faint, just audible to anyone on the roadside. "Steven … Steven. Come here …"

Steve and Darren looked at each other with wide eyes. They waited a moment and were about to run when they heard the voice again. "Steven … Help me … Please …"

They peered into the fog that covered the field. They scanned the open plain and finally fixed their eyes on a figure standing in the middle of the field. They took a few steps towards the field and squinted. In the field was Matt Burton. The two looked at each other again. "Steve, what in the hell is he doing there?"

Steve said nothing. He wasn't sure if he should be glad to see a buddy of theirs or to be terrified.

Matt called to them again. "Steven … My ankle's caught … Help me get out …"

Steve started walking into the field when Darren stopped him. "Steve? What are you doing?"

"I'm going to go help him."

"Why?"

"He's caught in a hole. He can help us get the killers."

"Steve, there's a search out for him. The police think he might be dead. Don't you think it's a bit strange he's right smack dab in the middle of a wheat field where everyone can see him?"

Steve turned to Darren. "He's a friend of ours. And he's obviously not dead. Let's give him a hand and then he'll give us a hand."

Steve was halfway across the field when Darren reluctantly started making his way into the wheat. He was keeping one eye on Steve and the other on Matt, when suddenly Steve disappeared from the landscape. "Steve! Steve! You all right?"

Nothing. Darren stopped for a second and listened. Matt broke the silence. "Be careful, Darren. The field is full of holes."

Darren started moving again and finally got to Matt. He turned and scanned the field, searching for Steve when he noticed Matt's feet, neither of which were stuck in any holes.

"Matt. What the fuck's going on here? You said you were stuck."

Matt didn't even so much as blink. Darren got right up to Matt, and inch from his face and asked him again. "Dude? What's going on here?"

Matt's eyes were open, but he wasn't there. What really caught Darren's attention were Matt's yellow eyes. Darren quickly deduced that if Matt wasn't talking, someone else was. No sooner than the thought crossed his brain, did he hear the voice one more time. "Hello, Darren … We've been waiting for you …"

Darren quickly turned around and there, between him and the road was a man in a black cloak. His eyes were yellow and his hands were clasped together. His finger nails were long and his skin was ghost white. Darren also noticed the fangs that covered his bottom lip.

Darren stood still, petrified of the figure. His hand slowly reached for the gun in his back pocket.

The figure spoke to Darren in a monotone voice. "I don't want to hurt you. I want to help you."

"Where's my friend?"

"He's sleeping in the grass. He's fine, I assure you. He agreed to help me."

"You killed him, didn't you?"

The figure walked towards Darren. Darren reached behind him and a second later had the gun drawn on the figure. "Don't move!"

The man stopped, but Darren heard the wheat moving behind him. He turned and saw another figure. The man had a bat in his hands and was about to swing at Darren. Instinctively, he ducked down and heard the bat slice through the air. In the process, however, he dropped the gun. He knew he had no time to look for it as he saw the men approaching him. He crawled on the ground a few feet and then got to his feet and ran for the woods.

He didn't look behind him. He ran as though it was Death itself chasing him and it might as well have been. He nearly tripped and fell flat on his face several times, but he got deep into the woods before finally stopping and hiding behind a tree.

All of the years of smoking finally caught up with him. He was wheezing, definitely loud enough to be heard from several feet away. He peered out around the tree every few seconds, but saw no one. He dropped down and was sitting on the ground. He put his head against the tree and stared straight up into the sky. "What was going on?" he thought.

Darren heard the cracking of branches coming from behind the tree. He got to his feet as quietly as he could. He looked down and saw a piece of wood that was quite thick. Darren leaned up against the tree and waited to hear the footsteps of his attacker.

Not even three feet away was one of the men. The man turned his head, saw Darren and was about to pounce when Darren swung the piece of wood and hit the man square in the face.

The man let out a whimper before hitting the ground. Darren stood over the body and was about to head off again into the woods when he stopped and stared at the body. Should he take off the man's hood and take a good look at his assailant? Darren was about to lean in when the man's finger flinched. Darren decided to turn and run. As he made his turn, he ran into something and landed on the ground. He looked up at what he thought was a tree. It was the vampire. Darren tried to scramble away from him when he grabbed Darren's hands and held them behind his back.

Darren struggled, but to no avail. All he could do was scream for help. The vampire knelt down and was inches from Darren's face. "I gave you a chance to come quietly, painlessly. Now you will taste pain."

Darren screamed as the vampire moved in, but the screaming stopped. Anyone who heard Darren's cries heard nothing but the crickets now.

What the killers did not realize, however, was that someone was listening. Perched up in one the tree tops like a hunter waiting for his prey was Max Whitfield, and he'd heard everything.

Chapter *Forty-Two*

Alden was the type of town that rolled up the sidewalks once the sun went down. Hilda Timmerman was of the belief that everyone should be inside, on the couch and ready for bed by nine o'clock. She was from the old school of thinking that Alden was not like other towns which had been corrupted by delinquents. She had the best of intentions when it came to Alden's squeaky-clean image.

It was like any other night for Hilda. She spent much of the evening with some of her friends down the road, gossiping and playing bridge. They would talk about friends long gone, problems facing the town, new folks encroaching upon the town.

Hilda left her friend Irene's house and unlocked her door. The moon was nowhere to be seen, most of the lights along the street and in the houses were off, the crickets seemed to be off in the distance. She looked around but saw nothing. Everything seemed normal she thought to herself.

She went through her usual evening routine. She went into the kitchen and put on a pot of water to boil for her tea. Then, she made her way to her bedroom and changed into the outfit she would wear to bed. She finished by settling into the couch in the living room, turned on the TV and waited for her water to finish boiling.

She sat in front of the television and began scanning the channels. The news wouldn't be on for a few more minutes, so anything light-hearted would do. She found a movie when she heard the tea kettle begin to whistle.

She finished making her tea and was about to go back into the living room when she saw out of the corner of her eye something moving in the backyard through the kitchen window. She slowly made her way to the window and scanned the backyard, but nothing looked out of the ordinary. The flowers were waving slightly with a light breeze and her garden gnomes were staring back at her.

She settled in on the couch and took a sip of her tea when she heard a noise come from the kitchen. Hilda turned her attention back to the television when she heard the noise again. She put her tea down and got up off the couch.

Hilda began to walk towards the kitchen when she heard the noise again. It sounded as though someone was knocking lightly on her backdoor. She walked over to the window and looked in the direction of the door. No one was out there, but the noise continued every few seconds.

Hilda thought about calling the police, but what if the noise turned out to be nothing? Everyone in the neighborhood would know the police had to come to her house and she would be the topic of town gossip.

She decided to pull open the curtain covering the window in her backdoor and see exactly what was making the noise. She looked out the window and down to the porch. The noise was coming from the screen door, which was not shut completely. It was opening and closing in the breeze, banging against the doorframe each time the wind blew. She opened the backdoor and pulled the screen door shut. She was shaking her head in disgust at herself all the way back to the sofa.

She settled in for the third time and was determined to enjoy her tea and get ready for bed. She was halfway done with her tea when she heard the same noise coming from the backdoor. She figured the screen door handle must have been broken and now she would have to go to the hardware store to buy a new handle and bring someone out to her house to install it.

She got up, went to the backdoor and opened it. She stepped out and reached for the screen door. She grabbed the handle and was about to close it when she was startled by a little girl standing about ten feet away on her back lawn. Hilda jumped in shock and let out a faint scream as she grabbed her chest. She sighed with relief as it was only a small child.

She looked at the little girl and called to her. "Hello, there. Are you lost?" The girl said nothing.

Hilda took a step towards the girl and asked again. "What's your name? Are you looking for your parents?"

The girl just stood there. She was staring at Hilda, but Hilda noticed that it was as though the girl was looking right through her. As she got closer, she noticed the girl's eyes were yellow. Hilda stopped and gave the girl a confused look. "Are you okay?"

The girl opened her mouth, showing Mrs. Timmerman her teeth, including two sharp fangs. She raised her hands, revealing long, sharp finger nails.

Mrs. Timmerman backed up towards the backdoor. The little girl continued to stand as still as a statue, which caused Hilda to move even faster. She backed up into something and turned around.

There was another girl, in her teens and wearing all black. Her face was covered. Hilda stood still between the girls.

The girl swung her arm around from behind her back, hitting Hilda in the face. The blow sent her to the ground. As she regained her senses, she noticed the two girls standing directly over her. She started to scream when the little girl leaned in and sunk the fangs into her neck.

Chapter Forty-Three

Darren awoke from his beating-induced slumber as he was being carried. Matt was holding his legs, and another guy, someone Darren had never seen before, was holding him by the arms. Darren looked around and was now in the wheat field again. Leading the way out of the woods was the vampire that Darren found himself face to face with earlier that evening. They were getting no closer to the road, but rather, were staying in the field, a perfect cover from traffic. They were heading towards the old business district, exactly where Steve and Darren were headed. Darren then remembered and thought to himself, 'Where's Steve?'

As he looked around, there, next to the vampire, was Steve. The vampire had his arm around Steve, as though he was giving him advice. Darren tried to scream, but he had been gagged. He tried to get free, but his hands and feet were tied together.

A few minutes later, they arrived at the Janzforth Factory. The two boys took Darren in and he watched as the vampire closed the door and locked it. The smell of the building made Darren nauseated. They walked down a corridor all the way to the end and turned the corner. They took that hallway to the end and the group entered a large room.

The boys set Darren down in a chair and waited for the vampire's instructions. The vampire told the two boys to leave the room. The vampire leaned in and stared at Darren for a moment before speaking.

"You're probably scared, are you not?" Darren couldn't even think.

"I'm not going to hurt you. Look there, at your friend. Does he look like he's in pain? Does he look frightened?" The vampire got up and walked towards Steve. He put his hand on his shoulder and turned to Darren. "My name is Simeon and I've been walking this world for centuries. This town is the perfect place to unleash my anger against man."

He walked over to Darren. "When my partners return, we'll initiate you into a new world."

Simeon left the room, closing the double-doors behind him. Darren did his best to call to Steve for help, but to no avail. If he was going to get free from his bindings, he would have to do it himself.

Perhaps Simeon knew Max was in one of the trees outside the Janzforth factory, perhaps not. Max could not believe what he was seeing as Simeon and the boys went into the factory. Max wanted to jump out of the tree and follow them, but decided a sneak attack would work better.

He waited for the doors to shut before climbing out of the tree. He slipped the backpack on and tossed the stake to the ground below. He moved as carefully as he could.

He got to the ground and knelt down. He picked up the slake and headed over to the door. He reached for the handle and stopped just before his fingers touched it. The breeze blew by his face.

He reached for the handle and pulled. The door wouldn't budge. They had locked the door from the inside. He had to find another way in. But with doors locked and windows barred, it would take some time.

Max backed away from the door and walked around to the back of the building. Perhaps there was another door or a window whose bars had rotted away. He went up to one window after another and could not find a single one that he could get through without making quite a bit of noise.

He was around his sixth or seventh window when he heard voices coming from his left, around the corner of the building.

He quickly made his way to some of the shrubs behind him. He knelt down out of sight of the oncoming people and waited to see them. He could hardly see them coming and when he did, the only thing he knew was there were two of them. There was what looked like an adult with a child. They were walking fast and went around the opposite corner of the building to the door Max couldn't get into.

Max stayed low to the ground and made sure to stay behind the bushes and trees. If he did make a sound, the breeze rustling the leaves of the trees would cover for him. He followed the two and watched as they unlocked the door and entered the building. Once the two were in the building, Max waited for them to lock the door again. They did not. Rather, the door was wide open. Max thought for a second about going back and getting McGillis, but the open door may only be open for so long.

Max stopped just before the entrance. The odor coming from the building hit Max and caused him to cough. He regained his composure and thought about Susan. She was in there.

Max charged into the building, but a few steps inside his courage began to fade. He looked back and the darkness outside seemed bright as day compared to the pitch black of the hallway.

He took a few more steps forward, but halted. He thought he heard more voices. They were coming from down the hallway. Max waited for the voices. He heard nothing and continued on.

If he stepped too heavily, there was a soft echo in the hallway, so he walked very slowly and with the utmost caution. As he walked, he could see into some of the rooms along the hallway. He could see outside through the windows.

Max was almost to the end of the hallway. It went both to the left and to the right. He looked in both directions. He decided to go to the right. It was just a gut instinct. He looked over his shoulder every few steps, but nothing seemed to be following him. It was just him and the night. He continued to peer into the rooms he passed, looking for something, anything. A smell, a sound, a light. He was about halfway down the corridor when he looked into one of the rooms to his right.

There, staring directly at him was a little girl sitting on the ground. Max was startled at first and didn't move a muscle. It was Susan.

Max put the safety on his pistol and put it into his back pocket. He ran over to her and hugged her. He began to weep, stroking her blonde hair, squeezing the breath out of her.

He let her go, stepped back and held her by the arms. The tears rolled down his cheek and he began to sniffle. He finally spoke to his daughter. "Susie! Oh Susie! I found you! I finally found you!"

She showed no emotion. She continued to sit there, staring into the hallway. Max hugged her again, rocking her this time. "We're going to go home, honey. We're going back home."

In one swing, Max was unconscious. Susan acted as though nothing had happened at all. She sat there in silence as her father's body slumped over and lay on the ground next to her. A man leaned in and touched Susan's cheek. Then, just as it was a few minutes earlier, Susan was alone in the room ... and Darren had more company with him in the cafeteria.

Chapter Forty-Four

Darren heard noise coming from behind him and stopped trying to free himself. He figured it was Simeon returning to finish him off. Instead, it was a young girl dragging a body into the room. She laid the body next to Darren and went across the room to get a chair. She set it next to Darren and propped the body in it. It was the FBI agent he and Steve had met the day before. He had a trickle of blood on the side of his face.

The girl tied the man's hands and feet to the chair and gagged him, As she walked past Darren she looked him in the eye. Darren knew the girl from somewhere. He thought for a moment, and realized it was Angela Raines. What link did she have to the vampires?

Darren was confused, but once he was sure he was alone, he began trying to free himself again. The knots around his hands were tight, but the rope was dry. He slid back and forth along the back of the seat. He figured to either wear down the ropes or the wood on the chair. The only question was whether he would have ample time to finish the job.

Darren was surprised at how much time he had to himself in the room. The agent next to him was out cold and Steve was sitting on another chair, awake, but motionless. After several minutes, he stopped rubbing the ropes on the chair and tried pulling them apart. They eventually snapped, allowing Darren to pull his arms around to the front. He untied the broken ropes from his hands and untied the ropes around his feet. He dropped them to the floor and got up slowly.

He slapped the agent's face to wake him, but with no success. He then went over to Steve. He knelt down and looked him directly in the eyes. "Steve, wake up, man. We gotta get out of here."

Steve sat there as though doped up. Darren gave up on trying to snap Steve out of it, and just figured to drag him out if need be. He walked around the room, looking for a way out and for any clues he could use to tie the criminals to the factory.

It was what was in the corner that caught Darren's eye. When it was time to shut down the factory, the cafeteria became a storage room. The gas cans, lawnmowers, snow throwers were all in there. Darren noticed the cans, covered in dust and spider webs. He went over and checked each of the cans. The first two were empty, but the last two were about half full. Darren concocted a plan.

He grabbed the cans and look out the plugs. He poured the gas along the floor the length of the room. He then took the ropes that were on the floor under his chair and picked Steve up out of his chair.

Darren took Steve into the room directly across the hall from the cafeteria. It was a boiler room, which didn't natter to Darren, just so long as the vampires weren't in it. He leaned Steve against the wall and took the lighter out of his pocket. Now it was just a matter of waiting.

With each second that went by, Darren wondered if his plan would work. Finally, he heard footsteps coming from down the hall. He hid behind the door, but checked to see if the people went into the cafeteria. They had.

Simeon looked around and then looked at Angela. He balled up his left hand into a fist, and he grabbed Angela by the neck with his other hand. "Where are the two boys? Why is there only one person in here?"

Before Angela could respond, Darren stepped into the doorway of the cafeteria and held up the ropes, which were now on fire. Simeon looked at Darren.

"I freed myself, and now, I will burn you to a fuckin' crisp you son of a bitch!" Darren tossed the ropes on the gasoline, which sent a line of flames straight across the room, trapping Simeon and Angela in the room.

Darren seized the opportunity to pick up Steve and run down the corridor. He couldn't make out what they were saying, but as he ran he could hear the two yelling at each other amidst the flames.

The building was old and the paint that was peeling off the walls revealed the drywall that made up most of the foundation.

Simeon ordered Angela to grab the agent and make for the hallway. Simeon jumped through the fire, while Angela burned herself pulling Max's body through the flames. She followed Simeon down the hallway. They did not turn down the hall and follow Darren out of the building. Instead they continued on, towards the end of the corridor, towards George Janzforth's office.

Darren could see the exit in the distance. Steve was getting heavy, though, and Darren's feet were starling to drag under the weight. Darren's legs finally gave out and he fell. Steve's body lay next to him. Darren was about to pick Steve up when he heard the explosion. The flames had spread to the boiler room and blew the roof of the back of the building. The blow shook the building's foundation.

Darren heard the windows shatter and looked up just in time to see a large chunk of the ceiling come down on Steve. Darren tried to get up but he too took a piece of ceiling tile to the head. The smoke was spreading throughout the building and the fire was still growing.

Chapter Forty-Five

Chief McGillis didn't often work the night shift. He had deputies for that. On this night, however, Nick felt he better keep his eye on the streets. After all, the previous night, he found Max Whitfield scrounging around the old business district. Nick was going to put an end to all of this nonsense. If it wasn't bad enough Max was lurking around, Mark Thornton was nowhere to be seen and told nobody knew where he was going. He was driving along the east end of town when he got the call from dispatch. "Chief? Chief, are you there?" the woman asked.

"McGillis here."

"Chief, Mr. Farewell reported an explosion in the business zone along Route 33?"

"An explosion?"

"He called and said he was sitting at home when he heard what sounded like a bomb go off. He looked out the window and saw flames and smoke billowing from one of the buildings in the old business zone."

"Did he just call?"

"Yes sir. Not even a minute ago."

"I'm on my way over there. Call the EMS and my deputies. Tell them to get over there immediately."

As he sped down Route 33, he saw an orange glow off in the distance, over the trees and under a crescent moon obscured by black smoke. He was the first to arrive and parked the car along the roadside. The roof was blown off half the building. He could hardly breathe without sucking in soot. The windows were nothing but empty frames and the fire was going strong.

He walked down to the west end of the building, the opposite end where the explosion went off. The door was open, yet still on its hinges. He looked into the building and saw little. He took a step inside and crouched down to the floor. It was the only way to keep from choking. He took a few more steps and heard sirens coming from outside. He couldn't tell if it was his backup, the ambulances, or the firefighters.

The heat was starting to get to him. He ripped the buttons off the front of his shirt and wiped the sweat from his forehead. It was getting tougher and tougher to see. He was feeling his way through the debris when he felt something grab his hand. Buried under the fallen ceiling was a teenage boy. He couldn't tell who it was, but he was alive. From behind him, Nick heard people yelling for him to get out of there. Nick, narrow minded as he was, dug the boy out from under the pile and dragged him out the door. Before he could set him down on the lawn, two emergency techs took him to one of the ambulances. Nick fell to his knees and gasped for air.

An EMT was asking him questions, but Nick wasn't listening. He looked around at the chaos. Firemen were dousing the flames, police from Lancaster and Corfu were there, Erie County Sheriffs were parked along the road, ambulances were pulling up from both directions. He watched as two of the firefighters went in to look for any other survivors.

Nick finally took some water from an EMT and sat down. He was still breathing heavily when he watched a wall along the west corridor collapse, falling over into the other wall, wiping out the hallway Nick was just in. He got to his feet and ran over to what was left of the wall.

He was about to give up hope when he heard a muffled cry coming from his right. He threw rocks off the pile and he saw a leg. One of the firemen was under there. Soon, two other men were throwing rocks and ceiling tiles to the side with Nick. The man was alive but bleeding profusely.

Nick was about to search for the other firefighter when he was corralled by two of his deputies.

"Chief! Chief! You're gonna get yourself killed! You found one of them. Step back before you die of smoke inhalation," one of the deputies said.

The deputies led him over to a tent the EMTs set up. He laid down as one the techs checked him out and put a mask over his mouth. The air filled his lungs, making him cough. He closed his eyes and soon was dozing off.

It was about ten-thirty when Mark and Will crossed into the Alden town line. Much like Nick McGillis just a half-hour earlier, they saw the glow of the fire in the distance. Mark saw it first. "What the hell is that?"

"Someone must have a fire going," Will said.

"That's more than a crappy bonfire. That's huge. Look at the smoke trail there, beyond the trees."

"Where is the smoke coming from, like, what area?"

"That's Route 33 West, out by Lancaster. The business district."

Will felt a lump rise up in his throat. "Max might have been responsible for the fire."

Mark nodded. "I hope the bastard's still there. I've got a few questions for him, especially after he wouldn't help us out tonight."

As the two approached the business district, they saw the blaze. The firemen had put out much of the fire, but there were still flames all around the building. The firefighters were ignoring the small fires outside the building, focusing their efforts on the east end of the building. There were countless police cars, which left Mark feeling horrible, as though he should have been there, the first one at the scene.

Mark parked the car and the two got out. They were greeted by a state trooper who asked them to step back.

"I'm Mark Thornton. I'm a deputy here," he said, showing the trooper his badge. "This is a friend of mine who's helping us out. He's with me."

The trooper let them pass. They entered a world of confusion. People going in and out of the tent, fire fighters were picking through the debris, police were talking with the neighboring farmers who were brought out of their homes by the commotion. Mark and Will walked up to the building and Mark pulled one of his fellow deputies aside. "Where have you been?" the deputy asked Mark.

"I just got back into town. What happened?"

"We don't know. About forty-five minutes ago, we got a call from a fella up the road. He heard an explosion and saw the fire. Most of us have been here for about a half hour or so."

"Where's the chief?" asked Mark.

"He's in the tent with the EMTs."

"Is he all right?"

"He got here first and went into the building. He dragged out a guy and then went and rescued a firefighter who got trapped under a wall. He had to be restrained by a couple of us."

"Is he gonna be okay?"

"He's getting oxygen right now. He took in a lot of smoke."

"Do you know who he dragged out?"

"Uh, it was a teenage kid. His name was ... Derek maybe."

Will jumped into the conversation. "Was it Darren?"

"Yes! That's it."

The deputy was then pulled away to help one of the EMTs. Mark stared into the blaze. Will looked at Mark. "You know Steve had to be with him," Will said.

"Yeah. And if the chief got Darren out of the building, Steve had to be right there as well."

Mark went over and found the deputy he was talking to before. "Where did the chief find Darren?"

The deputy pointed to the west end of the building, which was now a pile of rubble. Mark went over to Will and told him where Darren's body was found. "Apparently, that wall fell down after the chief was in there. And if that's true, Steve's probably buried under there."

Both Mark and Will began sifting through the debris. There

were broken pieces of ceiling tile, shards of glass from the windows and clumps of ash. It was several minutes later when Mark called to Will, who was a few feet away. "Will! Will, get over here!"

By the time Will got over to Mark, he had already uncovered part of a body. The first part seen was a leg. The shoe was missing and bloodstains covered the pants, now shredded. The two carefully took each piece of debris off of the person until, just as Mark thought, they identified the body as Steve Murphy. He wasn't breathing and his face was now cold and turning blue.

"Help! Help! We've got a body here and he's not breathing!" Mark yelled.

Three EMTs came over and began trying to resuscitate the boy. After a minute or two of failed attempts, one of the EMTs said, "He's gone."

Mark put his hands on his hips and hung his head. It was Mark though who finally broke the silence. "If I had been here, he might still be alive."

"Mark, you can't do this. You can't save everybody all the time. You weren't even on duty tonight."

"Yeah, but I would have gotten here sooner."

"And then what? Huh? Maybe get here in time for the wall to fall on you? You could have been the one to die."

"That's part of my job! I have a responsibility to put my life on tile line for others! Instead I'm off chasing a whacko in Watertown that we don't even know exists!" Mark turned around and was about to walk away when Will said, "And what about Eric? Mark, you have a responsibility to find his killers, too. And we're damn close. If you want to make up for some of the things that have gone wrong here, then make the problems disappear. Find the Raineses and put an end to the killings," Will said.

Mark looked away from Will and stared off into the dying fire, then turned and walked away. He went over to the tent where Chief McGillis was passed out. He grabbed his hand. The chief opened his eyes.

"Hey, chief. You turned out to be a hero. The boy you pulled out is alive."

The chief pulled the oxygen mask away from his face. "Where were you earlier?"

"I got here shortly after you saved Darren. Will and I were off on a lead that may find us the killer. We think we know who it is."

"Who?"

"Couple of local kids. I'll give you the details later, when you're feeling better," Mark said.

The chief laid his head back down and closed his eyes.

Mark was standing outside the tent when an EMT came over to him. "You're one of his deputies, correct?"

Mark showed him the badge.

"We're taking him to the Eric County Medical Center. He's going to be fine, but we want to run some tests."

Mark hadn't even responded and the man was off getting Nick into one of the ambulances. Will walked over and stopped in front of Mark. "I'm gonna get going. There's really not much for me to do here, other than get in the way."

"Actually, why don't you go and ride in the ambulance with the chief. That way, you can call me and let me know right away if anything happens."

"You want me to ride with the chief?"

"Yeah. I mean you were just gonna go home anyways."

"Yeah, I know, but he and I don't exactly get along."

"It's not like you gotta give him CPR. Just sit outside his room and let us know if anything changes. I'll come and get you in a little while."

Will looked at Mark with a blank look. "All right," he said turning away before getting into the ambulance.

Mark watched as it pulled away. He then began thinking. Steve was dead, that much he knew. But how? It would appear he died from all of the rubble falling on him and him not being able to breathe. But if that was true, then why didn't David or Angela kill him while he was in there? The EMT's were finished trying to save Steve and had laid him on a gurney when Mark walked back over and pulled the sheet back.

There staring right back at Mark were two small pin holes on

Steve's neck, right on the jugular vein. The skin around them was
a bit red and there was a little bit of crusted blood, but someone
had definitely pierced Steve's neck. And if someone had pierced
his neck, then they had to have been in the building.

Mark went over to the west end of the building. He began
searching for anything - a body, a weapon, a lighter - anything
that would give him a starling point. Mark's quest started off with
a flurry. He was going through the charred mess with a purpose.

But after a few minutes, his hunger for evidence began to
fade. He found it more difficult to keep hope alive with each piece
of rubble he tossed aside. He was starting to think his search was
in vain.

Then he found something. Under a ceiling tile was a badge:
Max's FBI badge. Mark now moved like a tornado through the
wreckage to find Max.

Once at ECMC, Will waited outside the chief's room while
the doctors and nurses worked on him. He was stable and things
were looking good. After a half-hour or so, one of the nurses came
out and asked Will a series of questions,

"Are you a police officer?" she asked. She was an older woman.

"No, ma'am. I'm a friend of one of the chief's deputies. He
asked to stay here in case anything changed."

"He inhaled quite a bit of smoke. Were you there when he
came out of the burning building?"

"No. No, I got there shortly thereafter."

"Do you know when one of the officers is coming in? They
will have to fill out some forms for us."

"One of the deputies will be here before morning, but I'm not
sure exactly when." Will could tell the nurse was getting annoyed
at his lack of knowledge about what happened earlier tonight.

"We'll let you know if there a drastic change. Otherwise, let
us know when one of the other officers comes in."

The nurse walked away leaving Will to his thoughts. All he
wanted to do was help, but he felt as though this was partially his
fault. He kept Mark away from his duties. He didn't find the killers in time. He didn't even know when Mark was coming to get

him. Will leaned his head against the wall and closed his eyes. He could see visions of the building burning, Steve's body, lying there in the rubble, Angela Raines lying, right to his face, when asked about the night of Eric's death. These thoughts would soon help Will doze off. It would be a couple hours before he awoke to more bad news.

Back at what remained of the Janzforth factory, Mark and the other officers and sheriffs sat down and gave an account of what they uncovered and the conclusions they came to about this past evening.

One of the sheriffs, a younger man but very serious, gave his thoughts. "So far, this has been a complete disaster. One survivor, a teenage boy saved by the Alden police chief. One firefighter lost. What looks to be another four young men, possibly teenagers. And finally, two young girls, no more than five or six. All but the firefighter and one of the teenage boys were burned alive. The cause of the explosion seems to have been some gas cans along with the help of an old boiler. Did any of you find anything else of note?"

Mark thought about telling him about the badge he found, but decided not to. One of the other deputies chimed in, however. "I'm not sure what it has to do with the explosion, if anything, but I found several boxes of fake fingernails and about forty to fifty bottles of depressants, all in prescription bottles."

"Any names on the bottles?" asked the sheriff.

"No, the stickers were peeled off. Some of the bottles were melted, anyways." The sheriff pulled one of the state troopers aside and began talking to him very quietly. Mark was trying to make out what they were saying, but couldn't tell. After about five minutes, the trooper came over to Mark and the other officers while the sheriff went over to talk to some of the news crews for the local TV stations.

"All right, gentlemen. Sheriff Jarvis and I have discussed it and based on the evidence here, we have come to the conclusion that this was a ritual killing. The two boys found in the corridor obviously were trying to get out of the building, most likely after the initial fire had started. The fingernails were to give the illusion that the victims were vampires, also evidenced by the marking found on the one boy's neck. The depressants were to keep the victims dazed while the two boys did God knows what to them. That is the statement we are giving to the press at this time."

The trooper walked away and joined the sheriff who was finishing up with the media. Mark was as confused as he had ever been. As sure as he was that Angela and David Raines were responsible for the killings and the explosion, the theory the trooper gave him made perfect sense. Moreover, if the Raineses were involved in tonight's events, where were their bodies? They were not found in the building and there was no proof they were ever even there. Disheartened, Mark told one of his fellow deputies he was leaving to get Will from the hospital.

"Hey, John. I'm gonna head off and get Will. He's at ECMC with the chief."

"Can you believe this shit? In one evening, the town gets a huge explosion, we unearth seven bodies and the killers hand themselves over to us without any chase whatsoever. What a night," one of the other deputies said walking back towards the building.

Mark got into his truck and gazed at the sight before him. The TV crews were beginning to pack up. The troopers and some of the county sheriffs had left and the ambulances were all but packed and ready to go. The yellow crime scene tape was stretched from every tree for hundreds of feet. The fire burned out, but the orange embers were still glowing. Nothing more to do but sift through the remaining debris. Some of the deputies were going to stay through the night, but the work was better saved for the light of morning.

When Mark arrived at the hospital, Will was sitting upright on a bench outside the chief's room. It was about two a.m. and Will was passed out. Mark walked over and sat down on the bench next to Will. He reached over and hit his arm, waking Will. "Hey, Will. Wake up."

Will, squinting from the light, looked at Mark. It took a second to register before he became familiar with his surroundings. "Oh, hey. What time is it?"

"It's a little after two in the morning. I'm gonna check in on the chief. Any news?"

"No, nothing I know of. The nurse said he was stable last I knew," Will said leaning his head back against the wall and closing his eyes.

Mark walked into the room, surprised to see the chief sitting up, watching TV. The chief noticed Mark, but continued to check out the news stations. "Hey, Mark."

"How ya feelin', Chief?" Mark asked.

"I'm better now. That smoke really fucked me up earlier."

"The boy you saved is here, second floor. He hasn't regained consciousness yet, but he's gonna be alright."

The chief turned the TV off and looked at Mark. "You want me to get going, Chief?"

"And where are you going to run off to this time?"

"What do you mean?"

"Where were you tonight?"

"Well, I just came from the crime scene, but—"

"I mean, where were you before all of the commotion?"

Mark stared at the floor and shrugged. "I was up in Watertown."

"What were you doing there?"

"Will and I were checking up on a potential suspect."

"But the killers were here in town all along."

"Yeah, I know, but—"

"Mark, you're maybe the best, most reliable deputy I've got. You're duty is to protect Alden, not leave the town behind."

"Sir, I, I was off duty."

"Mark, the killers weren't off duty. Why were you?" The chief sat up in his bed and gave Mark a stern look. "From here on out, you are not to leave the town without telling me or one of the other deputies where you are going. We needed you tonight. Thankfully, the killers were caught, so you're off the hook. But don't let it happen again."

"Yes, sir," was all Mark could muster.

"Now go home and get some rest. In the morning, go back to the site and go through the rubble, every inch."

Mark stumbled for his words at first, but remembered how strange it was that the Raineses were nowhere to be found. "Chief, I take it you saw the news tonight?"

"Yeah?"

"And you heard the theory the sheriff's came up with?"

"Yeah, makes perfect sense. I agree with it."

"There are a few things that don't add up. I mean, some of the ends don't tie together as nicely as the sheriff thought."

The chief lay down and closed his eyes. "Don't worry about it Mark. Get some rest and we'll talk tomorrow."

Mark decided now was the perfect time to throw the grenade. "The wrong people got framed. The killers are still out there."

The chief sat up and turned towards Mark. "Will told you that, didn't he?"

"What? No, we—"

"Is he here?"

"Yeah, he's right outside the door."

"Get him in here," the chief shouted. Will walked in behind Mark. "Yeah, Chief?"

"Will, I know you're not the killer. And I'm sorry about the passing of your brother. But I have to ask: when are you going back to Boston?"

Will stood in front of the chief, jaw dropped, shocked at what he just heard. He had no idea how to respond.

"Ever since you came back, you have distracted my deputy and things in this town have gone from bad to absolutely fucking terrible. I'm beginning to wonder if you have something to do with that."

"Chief, wait a minute. Will—"

"Mark, shut up. Will, if you're not out of this town in the next two days, I will arrest you for being a disturbance."

Will finally spoke up. "All right, sir. I'll leave tomorrow."

"Mark, go home and get him out of here with you." Nick rolled over and pulled up the covers. Mark and Will left the room.

In the truck, Mark said, "Don't listen to him, dude. He's just stressed out. I'll talk to him tomorrow."

"Don't bother," Will snapped back. "He's right. What good have I done? I came back and tried to help, but got nothing accomplished. And in the process, took you away from your job on the most horrific night in town history."

"Will, you found out about David Raines, the real killer. We're gonna get him."

"Mark, we have nothing on David or Angela Raines. We've never even seen him. We're going on the testimony of an old janitor who might have made everything up."

"That's bullshit and you know it. He's in town and when I catch him, I'll give him a shot for you."

Back in Alden, Mark dropped Will off and watched him slouch his way into the house. There were, though, other eyes watching Will go into his house.

Chapter Forty-Six

Will unlocked the door and stepped inside. The lights were off and Will quickly reached for the light switch. The room lit up and Will looked around to make certain he was all by himself. He went into the kitchen and turned that light on as well. He grabbed a Coke and went back into the living room.

He sat down and look a swig of pop. He didn't turn on the TV, but instead, sat in silence. He wasn't listening for noises or anything like that. He was still mulling over what the chief told him earlier this evening. Will had the entire night to get it out of his head, but it was still there. All he wanted to do was help, but he came out looking like a trouble-maker.

It was now pushing three o'clock and it was too late to call anybody. His mother made it to Syracuse hours ago. Mira was probably asleep. He stared at the ceiling, trying to convince himself that maybe the chief was right. Maybe the killers were Darren and Steve and he could go back to Boston.

Will told himself he would call the airlines after he got some sleep and leave as early as tomorrow night. As he finished his drink, he lay down on the couch and thought about Mark. He was hell-bent on going after the Raineses and if they were innocent, it would be Will's fault. He was the one who convinced Mark they were to blame.

After several minutes of deep thinking, Will's eyes got heavy. He thought about going up to his room for a minute, but he was comfortable and too tired to move.

Will woke up a few hours later as the light breaking through
the front window hit his face. He squinted, looked at his watch,
but the sleep was still fresh in his eyes and at first he didn't know
if it was night or day. He sat up and leaned forward, holding his
head in his hands. He remembered all of the calls he had to make
this morning. He finally got the energy to get up and go to the
window. He did pull the curtain back, however, to take a look
outside. There was nothing out of the ordinary.

Will turned and headed off for the kitchen when something
on the floor caught his eye. He was squinting again, but this time
it was to try and get a better look at what appeared to be a stain on
the carpet. Will slowly walked over and knelt down next to the
couch. There, right in front of the couch were he had spent the
night sleeping, were two footprints. The mud had dried, but there
was no mistaking the prints. The feet were large, as big as Will's
feet if not bigger.

Will got up and looked around. He could feel his heart racing. Someone had been in the house last night and had stood
right over him.

Will ran over to the front door and checked the lock. Will
went to the kitchen. It was clear, yet there were more footprints
coming from the den. He followed the prints to the back door. It
was wide open.

He went over and slammed the door shut. He locked it and
went back into the kitchen. He stood by the sink and took a glass
of water, gathering enough courage to head upstairs.

Will happened to take a look out the window above the sink.
The view stretched straight across the backyard to the willow trees
that lined the yard as well as the block. A couple hundred feet
away but in clear view, hanging from one of branches, was the
body of Max Whitfield.

Will didn't know what to do first. He reached for the phone
and called the police station.

"Alden Police Dispatch, Trish speaking, how can I assist you?"

"Is Deputy Mark Thornton in?"

"No, he's out of the station at the moment."

"Could you get a hold of him and send him over to Will Sandwith's house right away?"

"I'll call him right away. What should I say is the emergency?"

"Just tell him I found Max. He'll know what that means." Will hung up the phone and went to the back door. He walked back to the willow trees. As Will got within a few feet of the body, he could smell the flesh that was beginning to rot in the sun. He got as close as his senses would allow and checked out the body. There was no doubt it was Max. He was wearing the same outfit he had on at the motel.

Mark was at the crime scene when dispatch called him. The old factory had cooled overnight, but not even the morning sun could reveal any new clues. He was almost ready to give up when his walkie-talkie sounded. "Mark? Mark, are you there? This is Trish."

"Yeah, Trish. This is Mark."

"Mark, a friend of yours, Will Sandwith, called a minute ago. He wanted me to tell you he found Max. He said you would know what that meant."

"Thanks, Trish," was all he could say as he ran as fast as he could to the squad car. He hit the lights and the sirens, driving as fast as he ever had.

Mark pulled into the driveway at Will's house and ran to the front door screaming. "Will! Will! Where are you?"

Mark heard Will's voice, but he wasn't sure where it was coming from. It was faint, but he heard it. "Mark, I'm around the back."

Mark ran to back of the house and found Will sitting on the porch steps. Will didn't even acknowledge Mark when he ran around the house. He was just staring off into space. "Will? Where's Max? What's going on?"

Will just sat there.

"Will, what's going on? You said you found Max."

"I did," Will said.

"Well, where is he?" Mark said. He was beginning to panic.

Will didn't answer. He simply pointed to the willow trees.

"Oh my God." Mark walked back to the trees. He too was over-come by the stench of Max's body.

He took a look at the body and ran back to his car. He came back a minute later and sat down next to Will.

"I called for some backup and for an ambulance. Will, what happened?"

"I don't know."

"Well, how did you find him?"

"I was standing by the kitchen sink and took a look out the window. There he was."

"You didn't see anybody or hear anything?"

"Not a thing. I mean, I know someone was in the house last night, but I didn't see anybody."

"Someone was in the house last night? How do you know that?"

"Just follow the footprints. They go from the back door to the couch were I was sleeping. The back door was open when I got up this morning."

Mark was shaking his head as Will told him about the prints. "Aren't you a little concerned about this? I mean, you don't sound it."

"When I got back here, all I wanted to do was catch the kill-ers. I was going to find them, confront them and kill them. But now, I'm as scared as I've ever been. All I want is to go back to Boston. But I can't. Not only are the killers still out there, but now they want me. I mean, what if my mother had been here last night? She'd probably be dead. All I know is I don't care what happens to me anymore. I could die tomorrow, it doesn't matter. I just want this to end, one way or another."

Mark looked at Max's body and sighed. "I can't wait till we can cut him down and get him out of here. I don't want to see this."

After examining Max's body, the police realized that he did not die from hanging, but from a slashed throat. Apparently the killer hung him for effect. They also found a wound on the back of the head, exactly like the one Eric had sustained.

Just like the night before, the media ascended on the crime scene. Mark made sure they kept off Will's property and that they did not get the chance to talk to Will. As the EMTs put Max's body in the ambulance and drove off, the same trooper who collaborated with the sheriff on the Darren and Steve theory was about to speak to the media again. Will overheard him talking to one of the deputies. "Well, those two boys must have done this before the explosion at the factory. All of these killings tie together and those boys are at the center of it."

Will jumped up and made a bee-line for the trooper. "Are you fuckin' stupid? Those two guys are not the killers! The prints in the house were made after those two were pulled out of the building, so they couldn't have done it. The killers are still out there!"

"Are you a police officer? Don't tell me who's doing the killings. You're nothing but a wanna-be reporter who thinks he knows more than everyone else."

Will was separated from the trooper by two of the deputies. "You son of a bitch!"

The trooper went out front and told the TV crews his side of the story. For the second time in less than twelve hours, the police told the people of Alden they were safe. It was about noon when the yard emptied and the commotion was over. Will and Mark were the only ones left, and as they went into the kitchen, the phone rang. Will answered. "Hello?"

No one answered at first, but Will could hear someone breathing through the static. Finally, he heard a woman's voice. "Will, Will, Will …"

"Who is this?"

"You know who this is," the woman said. Her voice didn't change at all. She was very calm, almost as though they were drugged up, Will thought. "I'm the person you've been after, right?"

"What do you want?"

"I want to put an end to the chase. I want to kill you and your friend, just like I killed your brother," she said. Will could hear her laugh when she finished.

"Fuck you, bitch."

"No, fuck you, Will. Did you know you drool when you sleep?"

"Why didn't you kill me last night? Why did you leave?"

"What fun is killing you in your sleep? I want you to feel pain before you die. I want you to watch your friend die."

"Then why don't we get together and make this happen, whore."

"Don't piss me off. You don't know what I will do to you when I get my hands on you."

"And what about your dickhead brother? Do we get to kill him too?"

"He'll be here ... with the master."

"Yeah, we'll see about that."

"Tonight, come to the house. We'll show you what real pain feels like."

"If you're so ready, then how about we come over right now?"

"We didn't kill you in your sleep. Give the master the same courtesy."

"I don't give a shit about your brother. Maybe you should have taken me out when you had the chance."

"I've got a friend of yours here at my house. If anyone other than you and Mark show up at this house today or tonight, Lindsay dies. If you show up before sundown, she dies. Be here tonight, alone, or she'll be dead before you even get through the door ..."

Mark got up. "C'mon, Will. Let's go. We know where they are."

"We can't go yet," Will said running his hand through his hair.

"What do mean? Let's get 'em!"

"If we go now, they'll kill Lindsay."

"Lindsay? Why do they have Lindsay?"

"Think about it, Mark. Other than us, who has any clue the Raineses might be involved? Hell, Lindsay's the one who first told us about Angela to begin with."

"I wonder if Hank's all right?"

"She didn't say anything about him."

Mark came up with a solution. "Okay, you stay here and try to rest. I'll head over to Hank's and see if he's all right. I finish work at five. I'll call you and we'll come up with a plan."

Will nodded in agreement. "Yeah, yeah that sounds good."

"Talk to you later." Mark left the house and sped off down the street. Will didn't know what to do with himself. He wanted to go over and try to save Lindsay, but that would only get her killed. He wanted to lie down and sleep.

Chapter Forty-Seven

Mark hit the lights and the sirens and sped over to the Adams house. It was just a couple of blocks from Will's house, but he couldn't get there fast enough.

Mark turned onto their street and could see the house. Lindsay's car was still in the driveway, as was Hank's. Mark pulled into the driveway and ran up to the door. He knocked on it several times. He was about to try to force his way in when someone opened the door.

"Mark, what the hell are you doing here?" Hank said. His hair was disheveled and he was in his robe.

"Hank, is Lindsay here?"

"Yeah, I got home last night and she was already asleep."

"Have you seen her this morning?"

"Dude, I just got up. But her bedroom door was still closed, so I guess she's in there."

"Are your parents home?"

"No. They're up at the cottage on Lake Ontario."

"Can I come in and check if she's here?"

Hank let Mark in and led him to Lindsay's room. "Why do you need to see her?" Mark didn't even answer. He knocked on her door and waited for an answer, then knocked again. He stepped inside. "Lindsay?" he asked.

He glanced around the room. Her bed was empty and the window open. "Mark, what's going on?"

"Hank, I think your sister might be in some trouble."

"Why, do you think she's in trouble?"

"I needed to talk to her, but she took off sometime after you got home. Listen, Hank, here's what I need you to do. Go up to the cottage. Don't tell your parents that Lindsay's gone, though. I'll call you from here when I find her."

"Is she in serious trouble? I mean, I'll help you look for her."

"No, I need you to go to the cottage. You can't help me here. Just go and see your parents and act like nothing's wrong. When I find her, I'll explain everything to you." Reluctantly, Hank agreed. He packed a bag and shortly was in his car heading north. Mark followed Hank to the town line, making sure he didn't double back. The realization that Lindsay was in fact kidnapped made Mark feel sick to his stomach. This was one of his friend's sister. He watched her grow up.

Mark's thoughts were interrupted by the dispatch radio. "Mark, Mark? Are you there?"

"Thornton here."

"Mark, I just got a call from Madison Johnson of Wilshire Boulevard. She thinks something might have happened to Hilda Timmerman."

"What makes her say that?"

"She said that Hilda's always out of the house by eight o'clock and she tried calling Hilda and got no answer."

"Okay. I'll head over there."

With all of the real problems the town was facing, going to check on Hilda Timmerman was an annoyance to Mark. He knew it was his duty to do these types of things, but the last thing he wanted to do was check on an old lady who probably overslept or couldn't answer the phone because she was irregular this morning.

Chapter *Forty-Eight*

Will tried everything he could think of to put his mind at rest and forget about Lindsay, but nothing was working. He put the TV on and was catching up on the sports he had been ignoring for the past few days when the phone rang. "Hello?"

"Will. This is Mom. What is going on back there?"

"What do you mean?"

"Don't play dumb. Aunt Karen was watching the morning news and there was a story out of Alden about an explosion and some people found dead."

"Yeah, the Janzforth factory blew up last night. Some of the local kids were in there and set a fire. The whole building is destroyed."

"Were you there with Mark? I mean, did you see it or hear it?"

"No, no. We weren't here when it blew. I saw it afterwards. It's gone. You'll have to check it out."

"Yeah, I can't wait. Will, can I come home yet?"

"No."

"Why not?"

"Mom, the kids who blew up the building are still on the loose. The police have a suspect, but they have the wrong person. They'll know tonight if they have the right person."

"How do you know if the police have the right person or not?"

"Mark and I found some evidence that might point the finger at somebody else." Will felt horrible lying to his mother, but he had no choice.

"Will, I'm coming back home tonight."

"Mom! Come home tomorrow, just not tonight. Leave first thing tomorrow, but it's not safe around here now. Just one more night, okay?"

She paused. "All right. I'll be home tomorrow morning. Are you going to be there?"

"I hope so. I mean, I should be."

"Okay. I'll see you tomorrow. And Will, let Mark do his job. I don't need you getting into trouble."

"Yes, Mother. I'll see you tomorrow."

"I love you."

"Love you, too, Mom."

Will felt worse now. He lied to mother more than once during the phone call and may have even jinxed himself by saying he'd be home the next morning.

For the next hour, Will tossed and turned on the couch. He would fall asleep for a minute or two, but he was up again and unable to get comfortable. Finally, Will got up and began sifting through some of the old photo albums his mother had put together. He examined each one as though he was seeing them for the first time, perhaps out of fear that it may be the last time he saw them. There were pictures of his grandparents, dead and gone, but still living in his memory, his father (but these pictures were few and far between) and Will with his brother. Most of the pictures from his childhood had Will holding his brother up or tormenting him, but each one made him smile and think about how much he missed Eric.

It was then Will had a thought. What if he just ran away from Alden? Go to Syracuse, get his mother and go to Boston forever, never once looking back at Alden and the nightmare waiting for him and his family. He could keep on living, providing a new life for him and Mira and his mother.

Will ran upstairs and began packing a bag. He gathered all of the things he would need: clothes, some pictures, a few items of nostalgia. After ravaging through his room, he ran into Eric's room to see if there was anything he might want as a reminder of his brother. He began rummaging through his desk drawers when he glanced up at the shelf above his desk. Front and center was a picture of Eric in his football uniform. Right next to that was a picture that was nearly identical, except it was Will in the uniform. The same number, the same hair, everything,

Will picked the pictures up and looked at each one. He went over and collapsed on the bed. It was now that Will knew he couldn't run away from the Raineses. These people killed his brother. The whole reason he went after them in the first place was for revenge. To run now would mean letting them get away with killing his brother and watching Will run with his tail between his legs. No, Will had to stay. He would have his revenge. Hell, that bitch challenged me, Will thought. He would not run. He would stay and finish this once and for all.

Chapter *Forty-Nine*

The room was dark, the only light from a window near the ceiling across the room. Lindsay was terrified. She tried to free herself from the ropes keeping her tied to the chair. She squirmed a bit, but couldn't seem to get the knots loose. She looked around the room, tried to make out what some of the objects were lying on the floor or hanging on the wall, but she really couldn't see in the dim light. There was a musty smell in the air, which had a damp feel to it. She assumed by the odor that she was in a basement somewhere.

Tears were running down her cheeks and her cries were muffled by the gag in her mouth. Her hands and feet were tied to the arms and legs of the wooden chair, which had left her behind numb. She struggled with the ties binding her hands, but would get frustrated quickly. She stopped and tried to figure out why anyone would want to kidnap her.

Lindsay worked at the store owned by her father, usually cashing customers out or doing some bookkeeping or stock work. It wasn't what she wanted to do with the rest of her life, but until she got out of high school, it would have to do. She would look at Hank and how desperate he was to get out of Alden and realized she never wanted to feel that way, to feel trapped.

She had worked the evening shift, six to eleven. When Eric was alive, she hated that shift. But now that he was gone, it was a nice escape from being around the house all day, thinking about him and crying herself to sleep. The store was usually quiet at night, with most of the people of Alden already at home for the evening. Sometimes, she would catch up on some reading or paint her nails while waiting for anybody to come through the door.

She was flipping through the pages of one of the tabloids next to the register when Hank walked in. It was around ten o'clock. Usually she would have tried to hide the paper from him, but ever since the funeral, she stopped caring about what Hank thought of her laziness.

"Did you hear about the explosion?" Hank said as he stepped up and leaned on the counter.

"What explosion?" she asked flipping the page.

"Down Route 33, the Old Janzforth factory. It blew up! There are a ton of police cars, ambulances, fire engines. There's even a few TV crews there."

"How did it happen?"

"I don't know. I drove by and looked for Mark, but I couldn't pick him out of the crowd. I'll probably try calling him later."

"When you go in the backroom, turn on the TV. Put on one of the news channels."

Hank went into the back of the store and Lindsay put away her magazine. She stepped outside and went to the end of the parking lot, by the edge of the street. She couldn't see the old business district from the store, but she could see a haze over the moon coming from that direction.

She stepped back inside and spent her last hour getting harassed by Hank. When her shift ended, she grabbed her purse and headed for the door. Hank asked her if she was going to the cabin.

"Probably tomorrow morning," she said and yawned. "I'm really tired. I just wanna get to bed."

"I've got some inventory to do, but I'll be out of here by two."

Lindsay got into her car and drove home. She lived only a few blocks from the store, but even in the short time she was in the car, she noticed several troopers and police cars, even a fire chief from Corfu. She was tempted to drive by the factory, but was too tired.

She got home and unlocked the door. Ever since Eric's death, she was a little afraid to walk to her door at night, but even more so tonight. She put on all of the lights in the living room and the lights in the kitchen even though she was heading off to bed.

She finally convinced herself to go upstairs and get ready for bed. She changed out of her work clothes and got into a pair of shorts and a tee-shirt. She went into the bathroom and began washing her face. As she was scrubbing, she heard a noise from the hallway. She turned off the water and grabbed the towel next to the sink. She wiped her face and threw the towel on the floor.

There was no sound coming from anywhere in the house. She took baby steps towards the doorway and found herself shaking a bit. She got to the doorway and lunged out as quickly as she could. She looked around, but there was no one in the hallway.

Lindsay gathered her courage and began to make her way to her room. She got to her bedroom and pushed the door open.

No sooner than she pushed the door open, a girl was there in her room just beyond the doorway. Lindsay tried to scream, but the girl was already coming towards her.

Lindsay turned to run and that's when it all went black …

And that's why her head was throbbing the whole time she was awake. Each time she thought about the attack, the girl's face became clearer and clearer. She knew the girl, but at that speed, and in the darkness of the hallway, it took a while to figure it out.

It was Angela. Lindsay was sure of it. It all made sense. She wanted Eric and couldn't have him. Also, Will was asking about her after the funeral. Everything made sense. Lindsay heard someone talking upstairs. The voice was muffled, but it was a woman's voice. Lindsay stopped crying and tried to listen to what was being said. The girl was talking for a minute or two, but then it stopped. She heard a thud as soon as the girl stopped talking, like a phone being hung up.

Lindsay saw a line of light spread out on the basement floor. The sound of footsteps creaking down the stairs followed a moment later. There was Angela. She got to the bottom of the stairs and walked over towards Lindsay. She pulled a chair up and sat down directly across from Lindsay. Lindsay glared at Angela.

"I just called Eric's house. Eric wasn't home though," she said with a grin. "I talked to his brother. You know, your brother's buddy. Yeah, I told him to be a good boy today and maybe, if you're lucky, you may see him yet."

Lindsay again mumbled something, but it got caught up in her gag. Angela leaned over and took the gag out of Lindsay's mouth, allowing her to taste the must in the air. She licked her lips and finally told Angela what she thought. "Why are you doing this? Why did you kill Eric?"

"Hey!" Angela yelled getting up from her chair. "Eric's death was an accident! He wasn't supposed to die!"

"So it was you."

"Yes, but he was supposed to live. We needed him."

"What do you mean *we* needed him? He wanted nothing to do with you," Lindsay said.

"Yes, he did. He just didn't want to hurt you. But me, I have no problem hurting you. Yes, I'll hurt you."

"Angela, why are you doing this?"

"Why am I doing this? I am doing this because this is what Simeon wants."

"Who is Simeon?"

"He is the one, the only. He is the maker and the destroyer. He needs me and David to gather the weak and turn them into heroes in his army."

"What army?"

"His army of death."

"What the hell are you talking about?"

"You don't understand what we are doing yet, but you and Will and that cop buddy of his, you will all know what we are doing tonight." Angela sat down in her chair and got within inches of Lindsay's face. She whispered to her, eyes open wide, staring right into Lindsay's. "We're vampires, Linds. We are the undead. And all of you will find out tonight how powerful you all can be with our cold blood pumping through your veins."

Angela got up out of her chair and went to go back upstairs. Lindsay couldn't believe it, but she didn't want Angela to leave.

"If you're a vampire, how could you go to Eric's funeral?"

Angela walked back over and put the gag back in Lindsay's mouth. "I'm not a vampire yet. I'm helping Simeon gain strength in numbers until it is my time to join him. I will be at his right hand. I will control legions of his soldiers and I will be the queen of the world, a world covered in blood." She turned and went upstairs.

Chapter *Fifty*

Mark arrived at 34 Wolcott Boulevard, home of Mrs. Hilda Timmerman. Everything looked normal from the outside. Mark pulled his car into the driveway and got out. He took a look around. All was quiet. There were a few birds singing, an engine from a lawnmower humming. Mark was about to go the front door when he heard a woman's voice coming from his left.

"Officer? Officer? Sir, I made the call. Is Hilda all right?" asked Wanda Peeks. She was an elderly woman.

"I don't know if she's all right, ma'am. I just got here," Mark said as he took another step towards the door.

She got in close behind him. Mark turned to her and put his hands on his hips. "Ma'am, thank you for the phone call as well as your concern for your neighbor. But you are not allowed to go in the house with me."

She looked at him as though she didn't understand a word he said. Mark spoke louder. "Why don't you go back home and I'll let you know if f need anything else."

"Are you sure you don't want me to go with you? I should probably go with you in case she fell."

"Ma'am, if she fell, how could you help me?" Wanda said nothing.

"Go back home and I'll call you if I need your assistance."

She rolled her eyes at Mark and waddled back to her house. Mark checked several times to make sure she left before continuing his investigation.

He knocked on the front door and waited for a response. He tried again. He tried opening the door, but the door was locked and bolted shut. The killer couldn't have exited this way. He made his way to the back of the house and looked for the door. The backdoor, however, was wide open.

Wanda didn't notice the backdoor was wide open? Mark thought, shaking his head in disgust. He was about to go into the house when something on the grass caught his eye. Lying on the lawn was a doll, a stuffed doll like a little girl would have. Mark walked over and picked it up. There were blood stains all over it, and some mud caked into the doll's hair. It smelled moldy.

Mark put the doll back down on the lawn where he found it and stood up. He went over to the door and stepped inside the house. There was silence throughout the house and the air was stale. "Mrs. Timmerman! Mrs. Timmerman!"

Mark continued to walk to the back of the house. "Hilda! This is Officer Thornton of the police! Are you here?"

Mark searched each of the rooms before going to his squad car to call the station. He stepped out the back door and stopped. He stared down at his feet. On the cement was a single red drop. He knelt down and dabbed his finger on the spot. It was dried blood. Just as the single drop on Eric's collar, the killer left his calling card.

Chapter Fifty-One

Will finished looking at the pictures in his brother's room and decided to take a shower.

After the shower, Will dried himself off, ran a comb through his hair and got dressed. What the hell does somebody wear to a fight? He found a long-sleeved tee-shirt and put on a pair of jeans. He found an old pair of hiking boots in his closet and tried them on. They were snug, but he figured they would serve him better than a pair of dress shoes. He put his wallet and his pager in his pocket (just in case Mira was looking for him) and decided he should take a walk to help clear his head.

No sooner did Will finish dressing when he heard a knock at the door. He ran downstairs. Will got to the door and pulled the curtain back. There was Will's Father.

Will unlocked the door and opened it. "Hey, Dad. What are you doing here?"

"Well, I'm leaving later this afternoon and I wanted to see if you wanted to grab some lunch before I left."

It was the escape Will had been looking for all morning. "Yeah. You wanna go now?"

"Sure," Joe Sandwith said with a smile.

"I just gotta lock up," Will said. Joe headed off to his truck.

The two ended up at Towers, a twenty-four-hour diner near the Alden-Lancaster town line. Will and the guys used to end their evenings, or early mornings, here all the time back in high school. The food was terrible, but all anybody was looking for at three a.m. was some grease and meat on some bread.

Will and his father placed their orders and spent the next two hours talking about everything. From work to sports to the explosion to the family, they covered it. Will couldn't believe he and his father were getting along after so many years of separation and hatred. And yet, as comfortable as Will felt with his dad, there was a part of him that felt as though he was betraying his mother. She would be devastated to see Will eating lunch with his father.

"So what do you do at the paper?" Joe asked.

"Well, I do some sports on the weekends, but mostly current event stuff, political crap and the occasional murder."

"Murder? Do you cover the trials?"

"Sometimes. I can't really get into it though. It's not why I wanted to be a reporter. I wanted to be a beat reporter for a hockey team or a football team. This political nonsense drives me nuts."

"Well, for what it's worth, I'm proud of you. You're a man of the world. You earn a good living and are letting the world know what's going on out there."

Will raised his eyebrows at that comment. "What did I say?" Joe asked.

"You said I let the world know what's going on. I'd hardly call Boston the world," Will said with a laugh.

"You know what I mean. People look to you to be honest with them, keep them informed. Not everybody could do your job."

"Or wants to do my job." Will took a drink. "So what have you been doing all these years, Dad?"

"Oh, boy. Well, I left here and moved to Ohio where I worked for car parts company, you know, factory work. And then I ..."

Will noticed the lines around his father's eyes, the scars on his hands, and how even when he dressed up and tried to look proper, he came off as a blue-collar guy all the way. Will actually admired that about his dad. He learned his work ethic from him. Anytime Will thought about calling in sick to work or cutting out an hour early from work, he thought about how hard his father worked when Will was little. All of the overtime, the days off he gave up, the hot meals he missed so Will and Eric could have a nice home.

" ... and now I live near Jamestown."

"Dad? Why did you leave? I mean, why did you abandon us with no explanation?"

"Will, I don't have a good reason. At least a reason you'll be able to live with. I guess I just fell out of love with your mother. I needed to get away."

"But why did you have to get away from me and Eric? Didn't you want to be with us?

"No, no. I love both you guys. But I couldn't look at your mother. If I'd gotten a divorce, I wouldn't have been able to show my face around your mother again. On top of that, I felt like a failure. I was about to lose my job. I felt the only choice I had was to run. And I've lived with the regret every day of my life since. I'm sorry, Will. I don't know what else to say."

Will didn't know what else to say either. He had a million other questions, but all they would do is put his dad in a horrible spot. And considering it took fifteen years for his dad to come back, who knows how long he would be gone if Will pushed him away again. It was better just to change the subject and accept what his father said as the truth.

"Do you still go out hunting?" This was one area Will knew would keep his father talking.

"Oh yeah. I've got about fifteen acres of land, fourteen of which are woods and fields. I can go hunting anytime I feel like it."

"Yeah, but have you gotten anything lately?"

"I got a buck last year. I was in a bit a slump, but I'm out of it now."

"Shotgun or bow hunting?"

"Bow. That's the real way to hunt."

Will's dad went on and on for several minutes about the nuances of the hunting world. Will was interested, but only because his father had a passion for it. Once Joe got tired of raving about his kills, the topic changed in a direction Will never anticipated. "You're friends with one of the deputies, right?" Joe asked.

"Yeah, Mark Thornton. We've been friends for years. Why?"

"Will, I've read a few stories in the paper, but who knows how much of it is true. You of all people should know that. What happened to Eric the night he was killed?"

"Based on the evidence, well, what little evidence there was, it looks as though he was attacked from behind while being distracted by someone in front of him."

"In other words, the attack was pre-meditated?"

"Pretty much. All indications show Eric had no clue the hit was coming."

"Do the police have any idea who might have done it?"

"No. No, they don't. They had a few suspects, but none of the leads match up."

"Well what about those two boys who blew up the factory last night? The sheriffs believe they're responsible for some kind of ritual killings."

"They didn't do it."

"What do you mean? I mean, how do you know that?"

"Mark and I talked to those two guys last week about Eric's death and they sincerely didn't know anything. They may have been druggies and losers, but not killers."

"Well, if they aren't to blame, who is?"

"Mark and I have a theory that two local people are responsible. Unfortunately, we can't prove it. You see, there was a girl at Eric's school that had a crush on him, but he was dating Lindsay already. This girl has a brother that was in a mental institution because he thinks he's a vampire, but is nowhere to be found. And the girl keeps mysteriously appearing in and out of her house for no apparent reason." Will stared at the table shaking his head,

"What's the matter, Will?"

"I know they were at the factory last night, Dad. I know they were responsible for the explosion. I know they killed Eric and everybody else in that goddarnn factory. All of the signs point to them, but we can't pin anything on them."

"Did anybody see them there last night?"

"No. It's like they vanished into the night. There's absolutely no evidence to put them there. But they were there. They had to be."

"Maybe they used the back door," Joe said as he took a bite of his sandwich.

"What did you say?"

"They probably used the back door. You know, the back way out?"

"No, Dad. All of the doors were locked. There were only two or three ways in and out and they were all checked."

"The police didn't check the exit way?"

"Dad? With all due respect, what the hell are you talking about?"

Joe took a long sip of his drink and took a deep breath. "I'm surprised the police didn't check it out, or know about it for that matter. George Janzforth had a direct exit to the outside from his office."

"His office was in the middle of the building. There were no doors near his office."

"Yeah, it was a secret escape passage. Only a handful of us knew about it. You see, George had mistresses throughout his tenure as president of the company. In order to sneak them in and out of the building, he had the construction crew make a passageway from his office to his property. He would use it, too, as a means of sneaking out of the office to meet up with his women."

The wheels in Will's head were turning very rapidly now. That explained how the Raineses got out of the building without anyone noticing.

"How long was the tunnel?" Will asked.

"Oh, jeez, I don't remember that. A mile and a half maybe. There was a barn at the back end of his property that connected to the passage. That was probably close to two miles."

"Dad. I think you may have just solved the case."

Will got up and paid the check. He went back to the booth and put some change on the table. "Dad, we gotta go."

"What's the rush?" Joe asked.

"I'll explain everything later. Just get me home."

Joe pulled into Will's driveway and parked the truck. Will got out but didn't shut the door. He stood there, searching for the right words. "Dad, don't leave today. Just wait till tomorrow morning. I'll explain everything to you in the morning. I've got something to do tonight, but I'll be free tomorrow."

"Okay. I'll see ya later."

Will slammed the door and watched as his father drove off. That was the man Will remembered from his childhood. Joe Sandwith, a man of few words. Will made his living writing, using words as his means of survival and all his dad could say was "Okay."

Chapter *Chapter* Fifty-Two

Mark was in charge of the investigation at 34 Wilshire Boulevard. The troopers showed up, followed shortly by two men from the sheriff's department to join the three Alden deputies trying to keep everything together in the absence of their chief and leader. Mark was fielding the questions and got to speak to the press for the first time. He got done doing a mini press conference and was about to start wrapping things up when he was approached by a man in civilian clothing.

"Excuse me. Are you the chief of police here?"

"No, sir. I'm one of the deputies here. Just filling in till the chief gets out of the hospital."

"Nothing serious I hope," the man said taking a look around.

"No, he'll be fine. Is there something I can help you with?"

"Yeah, I'm sorry. My name is Nick Shelley. I'm with the FBI."

"The FBI?" Mark said. "I didn't think an old lady being abducted would get that much attention."

"Well, that's not what I'm here for. I work for a branch of the FBI that specializes in kidnappings. One of my colleagues was here in your town. A fella named Max."

"Yeah, Max Whitfield."

"You knew him?" Nick replied.

"Well, I wouldn't say I knew him. We spoke a few times, he helped out our investigation a little, stuff like that."

"Is he here?"

"No. I'm afraid you're a day late to talk to Max."

"What do you mean?"

"He was found dead this morning." Mark watched the color leave Nick's face. "I'm sorry. I don't know what else to say. We found him this morning. He was dead by the time we got to him."

Nick looked towards the sky. "How was he killed?"

"Hanging. The rope didn't break his neck. He was apparently attacked before he was strung up."

"Do you know who did it?"

"I'm sorry to say we don't. Every deputy, trooper and sheriff in the area is on the hunt, but we have next to no evidence."

Nick shook Mark's hand and thanked him. "Well, if there's anything we can do to help, any question you might have, give us a call."

"Thank you. We'll be in touch."

Once the excitement died off, Mark headed to the hospital to see how Chief McGillis was doing. He also wanted to brief him on what went on today.

"Hey, Chief. How are ya feeling today?"

"Oh, hey, Mark. I saw you on the news this afternoon."

"Yeah, did I look okay?" Mark joked, doing anything to lighten the mood. The chief didn't see the humor. He looked out the window again. "Everything alright, chief?"

"No. Nothing is all right these days."

"Chief?"

"Why is this happening, Mark? Why are these people doing this to me?"

"Who, sir? Is someone doing something to you here?"

The chief wasn't really listening to Mark, but was speaking to himself as if Mark just happened to be there. "For over twenty years, I served as a deputy and not once did we have to call for backup or troopers or sheriffs. We had one of the safest towns in America and no one bothered us. Now, I become chief and we have murders and vandalism and kidnappings and TV crews everywhere and I'm at the center of the storm."

"Chief, this could have happened to anybody. You can't blame yourself."

"Alden's crumbling and I can't stop it. Everyone is pointing their fingers at me. I'm responsible for the safety of our people. And they're dropping like flies. I don't know what to do. I don't know what to do."

Mark put his hand on the chief's shoulder. "Chief, we're gonna find these guys and bring them down. You'll be the hero again."

The chief rolled over. "They hate me. They hate me."

Mark walked back to the car. He sat in silence for a minute or two trying to figure out what to do next. It was still early in the afternoon, way too early to go to Will's. He looked over at the radio and called dispatch. "Dispatch? Do you copy?"

"Yes, Mark. We read you."

"Please let the other deputies know that the chief will be out of commission indefinitely. For the next few days, we'll be on our own …"

Chapter *Fifty-Three*

Will was rummaging through the garage for a flashlight. As much as he didn't want to look for the passageway, he had to. Who knows how many other bodies might be found. And he possibly might catch the Raineses off guard. If he didn't make it to tomorrow morning, maybe no one would find the tunnel.

The Janzforth estate covered about twenty acres, most of which were woodland. The land was farmland before George Janzforth purchased it, and the barn and silo were still standing, even if they hadn't been used in years.

The property would have to be accessed from the woods at the back end of the property. A wooden fence enclosed the front and sides of the land and the police tape at the factory lined off the back of the land, so Will would have to use plenty of caution.

He changed from his white tee-shirt and into a gray sweatshirt. He went down to the front door and checked to make sure he had all of the essentials: flashlight, a knife and at least a semblance of courage.

He found Eric's bike in the garage and rode down to the corner. He made the turn for the estate and headed off into the wind. The sky was gray and a breeze kicked up. After about ten minutes, he rode by the front of the property and was amazed at the size of the house. There were no mansions in Alden, but this house was pretty close. It was an intimidating mix of brick and white siding. There were two pillars towering up to the second-story roof and the lion statues at the end of the driveway certainly caught Will's attention.

He made sure to go down about fifty feet beyond the house and got off the bike. He crossed the ditch and placed the bike on its side another twenty feet inside the woods. He stood still and checked around in every direction. There was no one in sight and Will decided to make his way to into the woods.

Will was far enough from the house that it would be tough for anyone to see him, but close enough to keep it in sight. After a few minutes of walking it was nearly impossible to see the house and the wind was blowing around some leaves on the ground.

He wasn't sure exactly how far the barn was set back from the house, but he now walked a few feet closer in the direction of the house. A few more minutes passed and Will still hadn't seen the barn. He was starting to think he passed it but he saw a bit of red through the leaves and branches. As he took a few steps in the direction of the color he saw, there was the top of the silo. It was a about a hundred feet away and Will quickened his pace.

He was still looking around to make sure no one was there with him, but saw no one. He could see the entire barn and his heartbeat got faster and faster. He heard a dog barking and stopped. Coming at him, was a black Labrador retriever. He was about to turn and run when he heard someone tell the dog to 'Stop.' The dog stopped and stared into the woods. Will saw now the dog was on a leash. The owner, he supposed, was heading towards the house and the dog soon followed.

Will waited till they were both out of sight and began to approach the barn. He could see the clearing and stopped at the edge of the woods. He looked out one last time and could not see the dog or the owner. He listened as closely as he could but heard nothing.

He stepped out onto the dirt and walked as fast as he could to the side of the barn. He pressed his back up against the wall and grabbed for the flashlight in his back pocket. He walked to the barn door and pushed it open. It creaked a bit, but it wasn't very loud. He went in and closed the door behind him, and turned on the flashlight. The barn was enormous; two stories, at least eighty feet in length and fifty feet wide. On either side were stalls filled with old hay and grass. The smell was awful, a mix of feces and rotting grass. Sickles and machetes were hanging on rusted nails.

Will tried to find a trap door in the floor. He thought for a moment about George Janzforth and his mistresses and all of the times they went into this same barn. Were they as uncomfortable as he was, practically crawling through the darkness, looking for a door that Mrs. Janzforth was never supposed to find?

Will got to the back end of the barn when he saw what looked like a closet. It was a small room in the back corner with a door half off its hinges. Will slowly reached for the handle. He grabbed it and pulled the door back. He flashed the light inside and looked in. The room wasn't as big as it looked. More farming tools hung on the wall. Will stepped into the small room and covered the walls with light. He was about to step out when the light passed by the floor at the back end of the room.

At the base of the wall, he could see the floor clearly. The dirt had been swept away and there was a hammer on the floor in front of the wall. Will walked up and put his hand on the wall. It didn't budge, but when he knocked on it, he heard an echo. There was definitely space behind the wall.

Will ran his fingers along the edges of the wall with his free hand and pulled on each edge. The right side didn't budge, but the left side gave a little bit. Will figured if he got caught at this point, he was already in trouble, so the amount of noise he made didn't matter. He set the flashlight down and pulled on the wood with both hands. He gave a good tug and almost fell backwards.

The wood gave and opened up, revealing a small entrance into the wall. A rush of warm air hit Will's face. The smell was terrible. Will picked up the flashlight and shone the light into the entranceway. There were a few stairs leading down and there was a dirt floor with no sign of light coming through the walls.

Will gathered his courage and stepped forward. He shone the light, seeing nothing but cement. There were rat droppings along the wall and some dead mice. Will began asking himself just how far he would go into the tunnel before heading back. If he got to the end at the factory and saw nothing, then it would be good, but it would also mean the Raineses left no evidence behind.

He saw a rat a few feet ahead of him, but it was the increasing amount of spider webs that were making Will nervous. He hated nothing more than spiders. He was now more concerned by the webs hanging from the ceiling than the floor ahead of him. He nearly tripped on some pieces of cement that were piled on the floor. There were some spots on the walls where the cement had cracked.

Will walked along for a few minutes and was nearing the tunnel's end. He shone the light a few feet ahead and there was a huge pile of rocks, apparently where the roof caved in. The explosion must have caused it, blocking the passageway. Will walked up and was checking the pile, checking to see if he could climb over it when he almost tripped again.

He put the light on the ground at his feet. He. had almost fallen onto the body of Hilda Timmerman. Will staggered a few steps back with his hand over his mouth. Her eyes were still open, her skin pale. Will knelt down and noticed the lower half of her body was buried under the rubble. Someone was probably dragging her out when the explosion went off.

Will was starting to sweat. He was going to get up and run when he noticed something familiar: blood spots on her neck. There were two of them right on her jugular. Will shut her eyes.

Will got back up and made his way back down the tunnel as fast as he could. He kept the light forward and finally found the stairs.

He ran out of the barn and was so caught up in his fear he began running straight for the house. He got about a hundred feet from the barn and realized he was in plain view of anyone. He made a dash for the woods and got in. A few seconds later he stopped and leaned up against a tree.

The people of Alden were being picked off one at a time and there was no rhyme or reason to it. First teenagers and now senior citizens. What was the pattern? Will wondered.

Chapter *Fifty-Four*

Will found his way home, a bit shaken, but in one piece. He went into the kitchen and poured a glass of water and sat at the table. It was about four o'clock and the sun was still hanging over the trees.

Will finished his water and stepped out the back door. The clouds had broken up and a few faint rays of the sun had crept through. Will sat down at the picnic table next to the house.

After a half hour or so of thinking and drifting in and out of thoughts of Boston and Mira and his normal, everyday life, Will made his way back into the house. He went into the living room and flipped on the TV to kill the time until Mark showed up.

It was a little after six when Mark showed up. Will was in the kitchen again. Mark let himself in and pulled up a chair.

"Hilda Timmerman is missing. I spent a couple hours there today and all I found was a drop of blood."

Will kept his eyes fixed on the table. "She's not missing, she's dead."

"How do you know that?"

"I saw her today."

"Where?"

"I saw my father today," Will said.

"So?"

"He told me about a secret entrance from the factory that George Janzforth used to bring his mistresses in and out of his office."

246

Mark nodded. "Go on."

"I went to the old Janzforth estate and found the tunnel they used in the barn. I went in and practically tripped over her corpse." Will looked out the window. "Her eyes were open, staring at me. Her skin was pale and cold. They must have been trying to get her out of there, but her body was buried under a pile of rock. I left her there."

The two sat in silence for a time. "What's our plan for to-night?" Will asked.

"I don't know, man. I don't know."

"I figure we should stake the place out first. Maybe they'll leave for a few minutes, while it's still light out. We could sneak in, get Lindsay and call for backup. You know, take 'em in alive."

Mark shook his head. "They're not going anywhere. They'll know we're watching them. And even if one of them did leave the house, it would have to be a trap." Will sighed. He knew Mark was right. They would have to wait for the sun to go down before making their move. "I'm gonna go lie down for a little while. It's been a long day already and I want to make sure I'm ready for anything."

"One more thing," Mark said. "I went to go see the chief today. I told him about Hilda, you know, just to keep him in-formed. He's lost it, Will. He's gone crazy. He will be of no help tonight or any other night for that matter."

"Hell, we're crazy. We're going into the lion's den and no one even knows where we're going. All I want is for this night to be over." Will got up and put his hand on Mark's shoulder as he passed him. "And I'll sleep like a baby for days."

Will went upstairs to lie down. Mark sat in the kitchen for a while. It was about seven-thirty when Will woke from his nap. The sky was red and orange with a hint of purple in the east soon approaching. Will made his way downstairs to find Mark still in the kitchen and looking out the window at the dusk. Will noticed a few items on the table, organized as though it was evidence in a trial.

"What's the weapon of choice tonight?" Will said.

"We're going in guns a blazin', buddy."

"Didn't anybody ever tell you the only way to kill a vampire is with a wooden stake?"

Mark looked over at Will and grinned. "I've heard that. But I also heard you can kill humans with bullets to the head."

"That's true," Will said picking up one of the pistols. "Is this one mine?"

Mark grabbed it from him. "Jesus, man. Do you even know how to use one of these?"

"Sure. You aim and pull the trigger."

"I gotta get something out of the car. I'll be right back."

Will sat down at the table. There were two guns, two flashlights, a knife and Mark's cell phone. Mark came back in a few minutes later and sat down.

"Ready to go?"

Will looked out the window, then looked at Mark and smiled. "No, I'm not ready."

"You better be. I'm not doing this alone."

They drove eastbound. The roads were quiet. A few minutes into the drive they neared a mini-mart. Will just about jumped out of the truck. "Pull in here! I need to make a call!"

Mark pulled in and parked the truck. "Who in the fuck are you calling now?"

"Just wait here. I'll be right back."

About two minutes later, Will came back. He climbed into the truck and looked at Mark. "I'm all set."

"Who did you call?"

"Don't worry about it. I'll tell you later."

Mark pulled out of the parking lot and finally turned onto the Raineses' street. The truck crawled past the house. Mark went down a few houses and parked the truck. Neither moved a muscle. They just stared.

"This is it," Will said. "Let's go get 'em."

They got out of the truck and grabbed their weapons. Mark took one of the flashlights and grabbed the shotgun. Will took the pistol and his light. Mark hid the shotgun under the coat he put on, while Will ran with his gun waving in the air for anybody to see. He didn't know any better.

The two carefully walked up to the house.

As they got to the cement walkway leading to the front door, they both noticed one of the basement windows was illuminated. They walked slowly up the path and stopped right before the front porch. The front door was open just a crack.

Will caught his breath and tapped Mark on the arm. "They know we're here."

"How do you know?"

Will pointed to the window. The light that was on in the basement was now out. The house was completely dark.

Mark shared Will's concern. "I hope Lindsay's all right."

Will stepped in front of Mark. "Let me go in first. We have no idea what's behind that door and if someone's there waiting to get the first one in, it should be me. I've got nothing to lose. Hell, I dragged you into this."

"No!" Mark yelled. "I'm going in!"

Chapter Fifty-Five

In the basement of the Raines residence, Simeon stood by the window looking onto the front lawn, his black hair hanging around his face. His hands folded as if in prayer.

He stepped away from the window and stood in front of Lindsay. Her cheeks damp from her tears, the gag soaked with tears and snot running from her red nose. Her sobbing made its way through the gag. She had two red marks on her neck, the blood from the holes stained the collar of her shirt.

He knelt down and looked Lindsay in the eye. "Your friends are right on time. But even now they are too late. Don't worry. I'll wait here with you until they come in." He went over and pulled the cord dangling from the light bulb. It was totally dark. Lindsay's sobbing was the only sound.

Chapter *Fifty-Six*

Will watched as Mark ran up the stairs. He knew he should have been right there with him, but his fear had taken over. He watched in fright as Mark pushed open the door and disappeared into the darkness. He was listening for a sound. But it didn't come. Will walked up the steps and found himself on the porch. He peered into the house, hoping to see Mark.

Like a clap of thunder, Will jumped at the sound of Mark screaming in pain. The sound made Will's skin crawl. He heard Mark scream again and knew he was alive. He stepped into the house and waited to hear Mark's voice again.

Mark was writhing in pain. It was corning from the front room, the same room Mark and Will had sat and talked with Angela. "Mark! Mark! What happened!" Will was about to step in to the room when he heard Mark yell. "Will! Don't! She's right here!"

Will stopped and gasped, and from right around the corner, Angela came at him screaming. She carried an axe stained with blood. She took a swing at Will, which he avoided by falling backwards to the ground.

The axe went into the wall and stuck there. Angela struggled to get it out. It gave Will enough time to get his bearings. He took the safety off and aimed it at Angela.

She got the axe out of the wall and turned and faced Will. She was but a few feet away.

"You won't shoot me. You haven't got the balls. You're just like your brother, a fucking coward!" She screamed again and charged at Will. He pulled the trigger and shot her in the stomach.

She halted and the anger was flushed from her face. She turned a ghastly white and dropped the axe behind her. She fell to her knees and placed her hands over her stomach. She was trying to say something. Will stared at her, waiting for her to die. She hunched over onto the floor and passed out.

Will got to his feet and continued to fix his eyes on her. She wasn't moving, but Will gave her a wide berth. He stepped around her carefully and went into the front room. In a puddle of blood lay Mark. He was shaking, no doubt from the pain. He was holding his right arm.

"Mark! Mark, what happened?"

Will knelt down next to Mark and cradled him in his arms. Mark struggled to speak, but revealed what happened. "She came around the corner. I couldn't react in time. She got me in the arm."

The axe blade was dull, thankfully. It cut into the bone, but didn't take the arm off. It was useless at the moment and Will was beginning to panic. "Mark, I gotta get you out of here!"

"No! No. I'll live. You have to go save Lindsay. It's up to you now."

Will rested Mark down on the floor and got to his feet. He stared at Mark for a moment and then looked back at Angela's body. She was still in the same position. Mark was in pain but trying to get to the door.

Will went through the kitchen. He wasn't sure where the basement door was, but he found a doorway in the kitchen next to the back door. He went over and reached for the knob. He opened the door and took the gun out of his back pocket. With his other hand he took the flashlight and poured the light into the entrance and saw the stairs leading down.

Chapter *Fifty-Seven*

She opened the door and stepped inside her apartment. She set her keys down on the table and hung her coat up in the closet. It had been a long day and she was exhausted. It had been an awful day. A cup of tea and an early night were in order. She was about to go and use the bathroom when she noticed the red button on her answering machine was blinking. She went over and pushed the play button.

You have one new message. New message:

"Mira. It's Will. Whatever you do, do not erase this message. I want to start by apologizing for ignoring you these past few days. I've come to realize what an asshole I've been and I'm sorry. I love you more than anything. Honey, what I'm about to tell you is extremely important. Mark and I know who the killers are. We're going to confront them tonight and you are the only person other than Mark and me who knows this. If you do not hear from me by tomorrow morning, call the Alden Police Department and tell them to go to the Raineses place. Angela and David Raines have kidnapped Eric's girlfriend and are the killers. Please, know I love you. I'm praying I talk to you tomorrow ..."

Chapter *Fifty-Eight*

Will placed his foot on the first step. He took the light and scanned the wall for a light switch. He found it, flipped it, but nothing happened. Will put the light back down on the basement floor and saw clutter. Boxes, garbage bags, old furniture. But no Lindsay.

He got about halfway down the steps and bent down. He used the light to scan the entire basement. He was hoping to see someone moving, but it was perfectly still. Nothing was moving. There was no sign of David or Lindsay. The basement was almost the size of the house, full of posts at various positions supporting the house. There were windows near the corners on each of the walls, but no light coming in. There were shelves along the walls with old coffee cans full of nails and other crap. A sheet covered what looked to be a sofa near the wall to his right.

Behind the stairs was a furnace and a water heater. Will figured if he found Lindsay, he could get out without having to confront David.

Will stood straight up and got to the bottom of the stairs. There was a damp, musty smell, but nothing that compared to the tunnel earlier. He spun around hoping to catch David creeping up on him, but again, found himself alone.

Will finally decided to try and engage David in conversation. "David? David, where are you?" There was no response. "C'mon, David. I know you're down here. You guys called me over here and now you don't have the balls to come and face me?"

Will heard a voice from the opposite side of the basement. "Perhaps you're calling the wrong person?" It was a man's voice. Not particularly deep, but not a boy's.

"Who should I be calling for?"

"David's not here?"

"Then who are you supposed to be, David?"

"David is a weak boy. He has no business here tonight. I am the one you should be worried about."

Will was now making his way towards the voice.

"Who are you?"

"My name is Simeon. I am the one you're here to meet. I am the black in the night. I am the nightmare you wake up from in the middle of the night."

"David, I went to the hospital. I spoke with your doctors. I know about your problem. David, just turn yourself over and you won't get hurt. You can be saved." There was no response for a moment. Will was now flashing the light all around him. "David is not here!"

"David, you're sick."

"David is a weak boy! I am the end of you!"

Will went over to where he heard the voice last. "You're pathetic, David. A sick fuck. I don't care who you are pretending to be. You are weak. And you had your chance to surrender."

Will was now behind the stairs, standing still, waiting for a sound. Will's attention was caught for a moment on a chair with a sheet over it. Will kept the light on it, examining it.

Simeon was right behind Will. He had a knife in his hand and had it raised over his head. He was silent in his motions. He was ready to come down with the knife like a hammer on Will.

Will was a second away from death when his pager went off. The beeping was loud and echoed in the darkness. It was enough to startle Simeon. Will heard him, turned around and flashed the light right in Simeon's eyes.

Will fumbled with the gun and grabbed Simeon's forearm with his free hand. David tried to bring the knife down, but Will was able to fight him off. Simeon used his other hand to grab Will by the throat. He choked Will, who struggled to keep the light in Simeon's eyes. Simeon's face was a mess of shadows and yellow light. Will could make out some of his features, but it was the eyes that Will stared into. They were yellow. They were filled with hatred and he was ready to choke Will to his death.

Will was getting weaker. The knife was getting closer to his face. Will kneed Simeon in the gut, causing him to let go of Will's neck and drop the knife. Will then punched him in the face, sending Simeon onto the floor and into the darkness.

Will was right back where he was a minute ago. Simeon was at home in the dark and as long as Will had the flashlight, he was at a disadvantage.

Will's pager went off again. He picked it up and set it on the floor. It might distract his attacker long enough to give Will a chance to come up with a plan. Will felt his way through the darkness. He got to his feet and tried to walk towards the nearest wall. He tripped however on a box, making a loud crash. He heard Simeon laughing across the room.

Will sat down on the ground and tried his best to muffle the sound of his breathing. He put his hand on a chair next to him and heard what sounded like a girl's cry. He found Lindsay.

Simeon had hid her chair behind a pile of boxes in the corner. She was gagged. Will felt her face, and once he found her nose, he found the gag and took it out of her mouth. "Lindsay. Lindsay. Be quiet. It's me Will. Don't talk. Just listen."

Will whispered his plan to Lindsay, making sure to move quickly but quietly. On the other side of the basement Simeon heard the pager beeping. Simeon went over to where he left Lindsay.

"Will! Will! I'm done chasing you. You're hiding like a child and I'll draw you out. I'm going to cut the girl's throat if you don't come out in the next five seconds. One. Two. Thr—"

The flashlight again shone right in Simeon's eyes. Simeon raised his hand to shield his eyes from the bright light. By the time he realized Will was in the chair, the knife blade was already in his stomach. Simeon's mouth dropped open and then he smiled. "You have to go through a vampire's heart, Will."

Will got up and stared Simeon right in the face. "You're not a vampire, David." Will jabbed the blade further into David's inside, twisting the blade as he went. Will let go of the knife and watched David crumble to the floor. He tried to take the blade from his body, but let out one last breath and lay on the floor, lifeless.

Will stared at him for a moment before spitting on his body. He found Lindsay and the two went up the stairs. Lindsay was shaking. He had his hands on her shoulders. Lindsay screamed when they turned the corner and she saw Mark lying a puddle of blood. Will grabbed her arms. "Lindsay! Lindsay!" He waited for her to look at him. "Here's what I need you to do." Will went into Mark's coat pocket and found his phone. "Take Mark's cell phone and call the police. Tell them to bring an ambulance ASAP! Go, now!"

Lindsay ran outside while Will bent down and tried to wake up Mark. "Hey! Mark! Wake up!" Mark's eyes opened, but he was weak. "Hey, I'm gonna get you outta here."

Mark put his hand on Will's and squeezed it lightly. "Did you get him?"

Will looked at Mark and grinned. "Yeah. I got the son of a bitch."

Mark closed his eyes again and Will waited to hear the sounds of sirens. Will cradled Mark and thought about what just happened. He set out to find his brother's killers and did it. Yet he didn't feel satisfied. He was shaking. Even though Angela and David were dead, he still felt as though someone was watching him.

He set Mark on the floor and walked over to Angela's body. Will couldn't believe he killed such a young girl. It was in self-defense, but she had her whole life in front of her. He knelt down and closed her eyelids. He walked to the door and looked outside. Aside from Lindsay talking to the police, all was quiet. All Will wanted to do was sleep for days, but he knew he still had a long night ahead of him. The police would have questions, and he would have to call Mira and his mother.

A few moments later, Will heard the faint sound of sirens and walked back over to Mark. "They're almost here, buddy. Hang in there another couple minutes."

Chapter *Fifty-Nine*

One year later—

Will was back. It took a little over a year for him to come back to his roots, but here he was. As he drove along Route 33 and into the township of Alden, he noticed a few changes. In the old business district, the property where the Janzforth factory stood had been completely cleared away. Some of the other old buildings had been removed as well. There was a new view of the horizon from the road and it was about time, Will thought.

It was a little after noon when Will passed through downtown Alden. He passed by town hall where his mother used to work. The cafe was still there, and was doing quite well at the moment. There was a new veterinary clinic thrown into the mix of businesses and town offices. But Will had just one stop to make today, the cemetery where his brother had been laid to rest.

Will followed the road to the cemetery and went along the winding dirt road. He finally came to the site and parked the car. He got out and walked over to the stone. He knelt down and touched it. He thought about all of the good times he and Eric had had. But the memories of last summer were still fresh in his mind. Will closed his eyes and could see David. He could see Angela coming at him, screaming.

He shook his head and looked at the stone. "I miss you, bro," was the only thing Will could get out. He stood up and made the sign of the cross. He walked away and got back into the car. He sat in the car for a minute and thought about that night. He had replayed it over in his mind every day for a year, but being back in town, being so close to the danger, so close to the actual site, made it even clearer. He had heard the Raineses were buried in the same cemetery, but Will had no desire to find those graves.

Will put his sunglasses on and headed back into town. He made straight for the police station. He hadn't talked to Mark since that night. Will talked to the police when they showed up, but left that very night for Boston. The thought of saying goodbye to Mark, helpless in a hospital bed, was tough to bear. Mark called Will in Boston a few times, but Will always found an excuse not to return the call. He told his father he loved him, picked up his mother from Syracuse, and went right back to Mira.

Will parked the car and went into the station. "Excuse me?" Will said to the receptionist. "Is Mark Thornton in today?"

"Sure, one moment. Who should I tell him is looking for him?"

"Tell him Will is back."

Will sat down on the bench and watched as the woman made a call to the back of the station. A minute later, the buzzer sounded and the security door opened. There was Mark, smiling and on the verge of tears. Will stood up to greet him, but Mark embraced him before Will could say anything.

"Holy shit, am I glad to see you," Mark said with his voice cracking at the end.

"Same here, man."

Mark let Will go and took a step back, taking all of him in. "You look good, man. How have you been?"

"Good, good. It's been a good year."

"I was about to go get some lunch. Wanna take a ride?"

"Yeah, I was hoping you had some time."

The two walked down the street and went to the cafe in town. They sat down, ordered their food and sipped on their drinks. It was a beautiful August day, although there were a few rain clouds off in the east. "So what's new?" Mark asked. "How's your job at the paper?"

"I actually don't work there anymore. I, uh, I went back and couldn't handle it. I got a sick feeling to my stomach every time I had to do obituaries. And when I had to cover a shooting or a robbery, I don't know, it just hit too close to home."

"I understand. You saw the worst of it. So what are you doing now?"

"I'm driving for a beer company. It's quiet, easy and uneventful. I make more there than I did before. But, what about you? How's the job?"

"Well, things are pretty quiet around here now. We have a few more officers on the payroll, so we have a better grasp on things."

"And what about the chief?"

Mark paused for a moment. "Let's just say, he's in the capable hands of the state of New York. Hell, he might even have David's old room in Watertown. I will be having a change of scenery soon, though."

"Oh, yeah?"

"Do you remember me telling you about that FBI guy who was in town looking for Max?"

"Yeah."

"Well, when he heard about how we tracked down the killers, he asked me if I would be interested in joining the FBI. I agreed to go to their academy."

"When does that start?"

"When I finish my rehab."

"That's excellent, man."

"So how is your mother and Mira?"

"Mom's good. She found a civil service job in Boston and has her own place. As for Mira, well, that's part of the reason I came back. We're getting married next year and I was hoping you'd be the best man?"

"Holy shit! Yeah, of course I will!"

"Great. And what about you? Found somebody yet?"

"Damnest thing. I went for rehab on my arm and met a physical therapist there. Her name's Debbie. She's great. I'll probably bring her to your wedding."

"How is your arm by the way?"

"It'll never be as strong as it was before, but it won't keep me from police work of any kind."

Will nodded and a brief silence followed. "Have you been by the Raineses place since you've been back?" Mark asked.

Will shrugged. "Not yet. Wasn't sure if I was even going to go over there."

"Tell you what. After lunch, we'll head over there. There's something I want you to see."

They finished their lunches and headed off to the house. Will had knots in his stomach the whole ride over. As they pulled onto the street, Will searched for the house but couldn't find it.

In the middle of this suburban neighborhood was a hole. A vacant lot. Where the Raines house used to be was an open field with a small garden and a bench at the center. Mark parked the car and the two walked over towards the field. In the middle of the garden was a brass plate in the ground. It read:

"To those who lost their lives, and to those who showed the courage to root out evil, we remember ..."

"They put up this memorial earlier this spring. I tried calling you a few months back, but you never got back to me," Mark said.

Will sat down on the bench with his head in his hands. Mark sat down next to him. He was staring off into the distance. Will leaned back and cupped his hands on his knees. "Do have any trouble sleeping?"

"Do you?"

"I wake up every night, at least three or four times. I wake up and see him standing there, looking over me. I can't get him or her out of my head."

"I hear ya'. I haven't had a good night's sleep since."

"I mean, it's been a year. Shouldn't I have gotten over this by now?"

"Well, it could take years to forget about that night."

"I never really kept up with the news. What was the final body count?"

"Oh, man. You should be glad you left when you did. It only got worse. Let's see. There were the bodies in the factory. You know about Max. There was Angela and David and Hilda. Oh, I almost forgot about the little boy they kept in the refrigerator. They were apparently draining his blood slowly."

"Jesus Christ," Will said, still shaking his head.

"Yeah. David was taking his medication, depressants, and giving them to their victims, turning them into vegetables. They would put fake nails on the kids as well as contact lenses, yellow ones that you can by at a Halloween store. A pretty fucked up plan."

Will sat in silence. What could he say to that. Mark got up and walked over to the sign. "It's funny. This sign, in a way, is thanking us for our courage. Yet we're both gonna be out of this town as soon as I leave for the academy."

Will looked at the sky which had turned almost completely gray. Rain clouds were moving in quickly. "And no matter how far away we get, this town will follow us. Angela and David will always be there."

Printed in the United States
95687LV00002BA/259-264/A